WHAT THE TIDE LEAVES BEHIND

A Novel of County Donegal

MALCOLM MCDOWELL WOODS

Dunnybegs Press

Copyright © 2024 by Malcolm McDowell Woods

All rights reserved. No part of this book may be reproduced in any manner whatsoever without written permission except in the case of brief quotations embodied in critical articles and reviews.

This book is a work of fiction. Any names, characters, companies, organizations, places, events, locales, and incidents are either used in a fictitious manner or are fictional. Any resemblance to actual persons, living or dead, actual companies or organizations, or actual events is purely coincidental.

For rights and permissions, please contact:
Malcolm McDowell Woods
malcolmmcdw58@gmail.com

Cover image: Inch Island from Lisfannon Beach, Malcolm McDowell Woods (image reversed).

First Printing, 2024

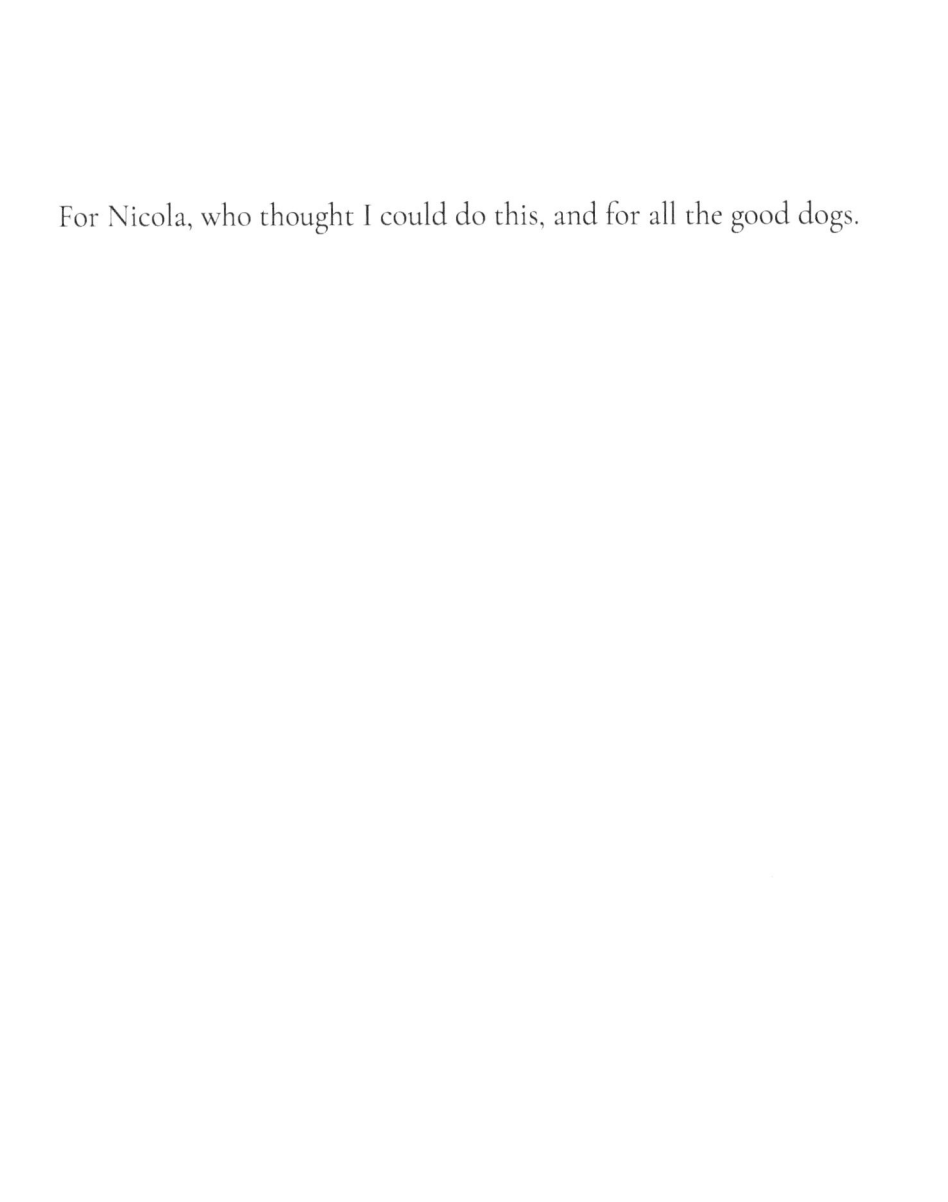

For Nicola, who thought I could do this, and for all the good dogs.

WHAT THE TIDE LEAVES BEHIND

Contents

Dedication   iii

1. An Unexpected Death   1
2. A New Start   6
3. A Dog's Life   11
4. Orphans   16
5. A New Assignment   19
6. A Dream of Flight   22
7. The People's Weekly   24
8. To the Grocer's   27
9. An Urgent Matter   31
10. Lost Dogs of Donegal   34
11. Fintan's Journey Begins   38
12. To the Beetle   40
13. Sausage Rolls and a View   47
14. A Dog's Heartache   52
15. Getting his Feet Wet   55
16. Curiosities and Antiquities   58
17. Fintan Feels Confident   64

18	A Familiar Sight	68
19	Fishing for Good News	72
20	Weathering a Storm	76
21	Fintan is Appreciated	82
22	The Storm Passes	85
23	The Trail Runs Cold	88
24	Hashtag Shamrock	91
25	The Post Arrives	97
26	A Home to Return to	100
27	A Sort of Messenger	104
28	Fintan Goes Factfinding	109
29	An Official Meeting	114
30	A Rose with Thorns	119
31	For Lost Souls	123
32	Molly's American Admirers	127
33	Fintan Has a Vision	132
34	Thomas Becomes a Tour Guide	136
35	The Alpha Dog	138
36	A Signal of Change	146
37	Failing French	149
38	A Mystery Revealed	153
39	No Objections	159
40	The Press Arrives	162
41	A Buyer Appears	166

42	Donegal's Top Dog	169
43	Bad News	172
44	A Summer Walk	174
45	Oslo Might Need to Wait	179
46	The Buyer Arrives	181
47	The Mayor Has a Plan	185
48	A Sudden Storm	188
49	The Veterinarian	194
50	A Trek to the Holy Well	197
51	Cara's Surprise	204
52	A Surprise from America	208
53	Everyone Likes Free Stuff	211
54	Ginny Arrives	213
55	A Town Hall Meeting	216
56	Thomas Speaks	220
57	Ginny's Surprise	227
58	Fintan Breaks a Tie	231
59	At Killfish Bay	238
60	Left Behind	242
61	A Home for Memories	245
62	Epilogue	248
63	Author's note	251

About The Author   253

I

An Unexpected Death

Thomas wriggled in the passenger seat, all the time keeping his eyes on the long, black estate car in front of them and, in front of that, the wee, black-suited man standing straight and proper, with a bowler hat on his head and a golden staff held aloft with his left hand.

Beside him, his sister snorted. "Christ, a lot of bother, init? Can't imagine mum up for all this fuss."

She was probably right, but that was beside the point. This was Ginny poking at him, expressing her own dissatisfaction with the arrangements Thomas had made.

The sleek, tall station wagon in front of them held their mother's body. She had passed a little more than a week ago, Thomas getting the call from the hospice on a Sunday morning that she was gone, that the most essential of her failing organs had finally succumbed and stopped beating.

"It's awful news, sure, but her end was peaceful, passing in her sleep like that," the nurse from the hospice had said. Aye, Thomas had replied, because that felt like the thing you'd say in that situation, but how could she know? Did she go quietly into the night? How could anyone know?

The death was unexpected – a shock. Helen was just 65. A stroke. Out at her cottage in Donegal.

The first responders rushed her fading body to a small hospital in Letterkenny but immediately decided that the regional one in Derry offered better care for her. It didn't matter. The stroke had been major, catastrophic and his mother never regained consciousness. After a week, Thomas made the decision to move her to the hospice. They were better suited to tend to the needs of a body as it completed its time on Earth.

"Here we go. About time!" Her sister started the rental car and Thomas looked up to see the man with the staff slowly walk down the center of the street, leading the funeral procession. Thomas was a bit puzzled. The crematorium was more than an hour's drive away, surely they weren't going to do the drive at a walking pace? But while he mulled that, the procession reached the end of the street and the man stepped aside, gesturing to the small train of cars to turn right, beginning their drive to Belfast.

The journey took them over high hills where the houses, trees and shrubbery gave way to gorse, heather and sheep. Thomas gazed out as though he was in a foreign land, and he was, to an extent. The few times he had ventured to Belfast it was mostly by train, which hugged the north coast and avoided the highlands.

The drive was mostly quiet. Ginny, normally a loquacious type, had fallen silent once they'd reached the main road, and Thomas let her be. She had arrived just yesterday, from Australia, had driven this very route in reverse just last night, and was likely exhausted.

Perhaps she was feeling remorse, he wondered. Remorse at having left Derry – and their mother – years earlier to move with her husband to Scotland, which was bad enough but still just a ferry away – and then to Australia four years ago. Australia, the other end of the world, their mother had said. Perhaps you'll both come visit someday, Ginny had said then, before she and her husband William climbed into the taxi and drove off.

They all knew it would never happen. Their mother was more than happy to spend her remaining days at her home overlooking the flinty Atlantic, watching the storms blow in and the ships pass by.

As for Thomas? Well, apparently, there had only been so much ambition to pass on to the children and it went to Ginny. Or perhaps growing up in the Troubles had affected Thomas more than Ginny somehow. His only ambition was to be left alone. When their mother had declared, five years ago, that she was moving out of the family home in Derry to a new house in the Republic, Thomas had his job at the bookstore bumped from part time to full time and found a tiny furnished apartment in the city proper.

He shelved books, mostly, occasionally ringing up sales when Mrs. Caldwell took her lunch. But the job let him be. He could spend hours alone with the books, carefully filing them and restocking when needed. His memory was encyclopedic, he knew where every volume could be found. That wee paperback on the historic ruins of Donegal? He knew. That science fiction novel about the alien vampires? He could put his finger on it within seconds.

Meanwhile, his sister had gotten divorced ("A privileged feck. I'm glad to be free of him.") and quickly announced that no, she would not be coming home to Derry with her tail between her legs. No, she was staying on in Sydney, where she had become a quite successful real estate broker. ("I'll have to have ye's out here soon.")

Thomas saw his mother infrequently. While the drive to her new home was little more than an hour away by car, Thomas had never learned to drive, and the two-bus ride made for a several hour trip each way.

Hellen purchased a former holiday cottage, a small single-level, whitewashed structure on the side of a long, gradual slope that tumbled down to a short, gently curved bay that resembled the letter C slowly uncurled. The move had been a surprise. Neither Thomas nor his sister had any idea she had been setting money aside for years after Thomas's father had died. Her getaway had been a private plan.

Charlie McKay's life was unremarkable until its very end. He inherited the family newsagents shop on Strand Road, Derry's main street.

He married the shy young woman he rescued from a drunk on the train to Portrush one holiday weekend and fathered two children, one an intense, fire-brand girl who strained to escape her home, her school and eventually, her country, and the other a quiet, timid boy who saw the conflict and hid rather than run.

If Thomas had been shy and withdrawn as a young child, his introspection was cemented in 1996, when his father became infamous as a last official victim of the Troubles. A small incendiary device blew up in his hands as he was attempting to carry it from the cramped store. Packed as it always was with newspapers and magazines, the shop took up the fire with great alacrity. Charlie was dead. Helen was a widow. Thomas was six.

He missed it! A flash of light caught his eye, likely a reflection from a car driving through the crematorium parking lot just outside the non-denominational stained-glass windows of the – what – the hall? He turned to look at it and became distracted by the pattern in the windows, of a bucolic, spiritually safe scene of rolling green fields under a brilliant blue sky, and when he looked back, the Reverend Mary was walking away from the pulpit and the coffin of his late mother had descended along with its raised platform and disappeared from view. She was gone. When he'd leave the crematorium, after the wee set up of tea and biscuits with family and friends and the endless condolences and small talk, when Ginny would jet back to Australia, he'd move into his mother's empty house.

It only made sense, his sister told him, and he had to agree. The empty house was empty and would need looking after until they could sell it, which could take a year or more in this economy. Ginny would pay him, forwarding him money for food and other basic living expenses until the house sold and then deducting that from his share of the proceeds. "You can't keep the job. Even if you could drive, it's too much to do every fucking day, and let's be honest, the job's a dead-end. Bookstores are dinosaurs. Catch yerself on, Tommy, you're nearly 30. You know, in a way, this is a gift. You get maybe a year to decide what the hell you'll do."

They planned a tea and biscuit reception, as anyone attending the service had likely driven considerable distance. The Belfast crematorium was the only one in Northern Ireland, an hour or more drive for most everyone here. Thomas was happy for the food, indeed would have devoured more formidable offerings if they'd have been available. He hadn't eaten yet and was anticipating that they'd stop on the drive back for a proper lunch.

There were sausage rolls, small sandwiches, pats on the back and firm handshakes. "It's a terrible thing, Thomas." "Aye, 'tis. You'll miss her, sure."

Well, not that much. Not really. He was a loner, much like her.

2

A New Start

The next morning, he arose early, had his first cuppa and waited for his sister as she drove from the hotel. "I'll need my latte for the drive," she said, and so, before crossing over into the Republic and heading out for their mother's house, she swung across the bridge over the Foyle to the city's only drive-through Starbucks.

"You take a week and get settled in. We'll stop on the way and get some groceries for you. Shit, Tommy, you need to learn how to drive."

The rental car was a small Renault and Thomas, 6'2", could already feel his legs cramp. He folded his hands on his lap, not really sure what to do with his arms. He looked all elbows and knees, a body of sharp angles topped by his jet black hair, trimmed short but gathered into a short peak that ran front to back along the top of his skull.

Ginny shot a look at him as he fidgeted beside her. "Jaysus, you're a footer!" A long pause. "Tommy, could I ask you something? Are you gay?" She sipped her latte.

He wasn't expecting that, but she was never easy to predict. "Um, no, no, I'm not."

"Mum always said she hoped you'd meet someone and maybe make some plans with your life. You've never dated?"

He shook his head. Not really. There had been one young woman.

Emma worked as an extra clerk one summer at the bookstore when she was home from college. She was studying photography in London and was, like him, quiet and mostly content with her own thoughts and company. They had spent a morning moving the poetry collection to a new bookcase and she had declared, "I like you, you don't run your mouth." They went for coffee following the workday. Emma talked a bit about her love for photography and asked him about his life. His last name sounded familiar, she said.

Of course, the McKay name was destined for the history books. He told her about his father – the final godforsaken victim of the Troubles. One last sorry death.

"It's all about how you look at it," she responded. "Maybe he was the tipping point, the last straw. The peace now, maybe it's because of him, in a way. Very heroic."

He liked her. She was easy to talk to. On her urging, they spent several Sundays together on lazy walks up into the country as she took photographs. It was all a matter of perspective, she told him. All how you framed things. Muddy fields. Cows. Anemic, mid-summer streams. Grubby, whitewashed outbuildings. She saw something different in each.

They were friends, he supposed. She let him take some photographs with her camera – including one of her that he kept still. But fall came and with it the start of school and her leaving. There were postcards the first few weeks but they dwindled and then stopped before Christmas. If she came back the following summer, she hadn't stopped in at the bookstore. He never saw her again.

"I guess I never met the right person," he eventually said, glancing at Ginny.

"You don't trust people, Tommy. Always so withdrawn. Remember that summer after dad died? You didn't speak at all. Wouldn't even come out of your room. I had to bring meals to you."

You get some choices in your life, Thomas thought. You can choose where you live. What you do. How you dress in the morning. But so much of life just happened. Wear a blue shirt or a brown jumper but neither will stop the headmaster from quietly knocking on the door of your classroom and asking for you and then walking you all the way down to his office before telling you the news, that god awful news that sucks the air from your lungs and maybe the will from your soul.

The store was a newsagent that had been his uncle's before his passing. Then Thomas's father took it over. A small place with leaning shelves and everything rubbed sooty gray from decades of newspaper ink. It looked older and sadder than it was. In actuality, it had a steady clientele. Bankers who stopped in for the oddly peach-colored Financial Times; housekeepers who picked up that week's TV News; the unemployed men looking for the Racing Journal; the kids – all the kids – who would tumble in and consider all the sweets and chocolates before finally selecting a Flake bar or bag of Maltesers. And the police officers.

The shop was on the far northern end of Strand Road, which placed it just two blocks removed from the heavily fortified police station, itself the target of numerous bombing attempts in the '70s and early '80s, at the height of the Troubles. Numerous times, bombs had shaken the shop and sent papers and magazines scattering; twice they had shattered the windows facing the street. For nearly three decades, it was routine. The sirens. The alarms. The chaos.

Charlie McKay was not partisan. Protestant or Catholic, Loyalist or Nationalist, he sold to anyone who came through the door with honest money. Even members of the constabulary. Which is why, in one of the last gasps of the die-hard paramilitaries sensing their era slipping away, Charlie McKay's newsagents shop was itself targeted.

Several thousand people died over the course of the Troubles and the survivors were left forever altered. Many fell into depression, or turned to drink or drugs to cope. Post-traumatic stress disorder, a school counselor once suggested to Thomas. But sure, he had been but a wain, born at the tail end of it all. To be honest, the notion of him claiming PTSD for himself left him feeling guilty. He never met with the counselor again.

"We're here."

He looked up and saw the small cottage ahead on their left. Another car sat in the drive. "Grand, Mrs. Doherty is here."

Mrs. Doherty was at the front door and waved at them when they turned into the drive. A small, gray woman with severe features and a pinched smile, she was puffing by the time she reached the side of the car.

"Aye, ye's had a safe drive, then? Terrible what happened."

"Yeah," Ginny answered. "Bit of rain on the way, but we made good time. Thank you so much for looking after the place the past few weeks."

"Ach, it's no bother, love. Your mother was a quiet woman, but that makes the best neighbor, right? I'm sure you miss her terrible. Was it a good service?"

"Small, but nice," Thomas answered, trying to make small talk. He still wasn't fully on board with this whole plan, but had to concede it made the most sense. His sister had her career in Sydney and he wasn't exactly irreplaceable at the bookstore. He'd stay until the weekend and then bus back to Derry to pack up his belongings and have them sent along to the house.

"Tommy, grab your suitcases," shouted Ginny. "Mrs. Doherty and I will get the groceries."

He glanced around. It was indeed remote. His mother's desire had been to get as far away from people as she could and she had been quite successful. Before them, the long sweep of the hill down to the strand. Behind them, perhaps a quarter mile off, Mrs. Doherty's house and then, another quarter mile past that, the small town of Dunnybegs, which would be his lifeline now without a car. Dunnybegs, with its single grocer, its countertop post office, part-time bakery, single chip shop, butcher, and two pubs.

He sighed. He was a loner, sure enough, but he also found it calming living in Derry to be in the company of strangers. The murmur of conversations around him, the steady buzz and hum of life that carried on regardless of his involvement, had always been a comfort to him. Out here, how in the hell would he even know other life was happening?

He was still brooding over that when a small shape moving along the hill distracted him. As it came closer, he realized it was a dog, one of those black and white border collies that seemed to populate every beach in Ireland. It kept on, running towards them, its mouth open. Thomas, who had never spent much time around dogs, felt a bit anxious about this animal charging at them.

"Mrs. Doherty, is this your dog?" he yelled.

The short woman turned back to face him and the dog. "No, dear, that's Molly. Sure, your mother's dog. I've taken her in the past few weeks, but she'll be glad to be back in her house with ye now."

3

A Dog's Life

Ginny stayed with him in the cottage the first night, taking their mother's room and leaving Thomas the couch. "Where does the dog sleep?" he had asked. There was no cage to be seen (kennel, Ginny had corrected him). The dog, once in the cottage, paced from room to room restlessly before finally collapsing onto a rug before the fireplace once it had been lit and remained there for the night, seemingly oblivious to Thomas's frequent nervous glances.

He was not at all familiar – or comfortable – with dogs. There had been a couple of cats in his childhood, one part of a litter from a neighbor's cat, the other a stray that had found its way to his family's back door when Thomas was five. He felt comfortable enough with cats. They were small and predictable and mostly slept and you really didn't have to commit to doing much in order to care for them. Dogs, though, well, they were altogether alien. They smelled – of wet socks and mud – and moved in a menacing manner, all explosions and leaps. They had no worries looking you in the eye. Their shit was as big as a human's.

All things to give one pause, indeed, but most of all was their size. Cats you could lift up and move out of your favorite chair, or shoo them from the room. When they weren't seeming indifferent to one's existence, cats exhibited a healthy fear of humans. There had always been a clear hierarchy with the cats. Even an individual as unassuming as Thomas had been the dominant one in his relationships with cats.

But this one, with Molly, had started off on the wrong foot, with the dog charging at him from across the hill, causing Thomas to take a few steps back toward his car door and reach for the handle, in case he needed an escape from the attack. Who lets dogs run free, anyway, he thought that night, as he squirmed on the sofa.

It was a small couch, but then, so was the house. Its front door opened onto the living room, with a fireplace on the exterior wall to the left. A door in the right rear of the living room opened into a small hallway. To the back, a kitchen, and along the short hall to the right, first a small lavatory and then the one bedroom. It was probably the ideal place for his mother, as it didn't offer much in the way of overnight accommodations for visitors.

Thomas always felt his father's death had changed his mother. No longer would Thomas catch her humming as she worked in the kitchen, shelling peas, ironing or washing dishes. And the television, which had remained on all her waking hours, went dark. She no longer wanted to hear news or be entertained.

She wanted to be alone, it seemed. She would wait it out, first another 12 years until her youngest was an adult, and then several more after that, as she searched for the right property. But she would eventually find her solitude, on this exposed bank facing the Atlantic. No television needed. No radio. Not even a telephone at first, though Ginny signed her up for mobile service and sent a phone after the first several months came and went without so much as a card from her mother. Ginny called her weekly; Thomas often remembered by the end of each month and gave her a ring, but the conversations were short and clipped. She was alone, companion to none but the changing light and the steady work of the waves.

And, at some point, to a dog.

Thomas glanced at it, curled in a tight circle before the fire, nose tucked under her tail. A border collie, though most probably not a purebred. Black and white mostly, with coppery red fur on her chest, as though iron stains had run down her mouth. She was sound asleep. His own fidgeting on the couch didn't seem to bother her.

It was Molly's bark which had caught Mrs. Doherty's attention the morning of the stroke. As Mrs. Doherty told the story, she heard the bark when she stepped outside to hang some wash to dry and immediately sensed that something was wrong. In truth, she had cursed and sputtered about the endless barking for more than an hour before finally setting off to see what all the feckin' racket was about. Her knocks on the door brought more barking but when she slowly swung the door open, Molly fell silent and darted into the hallway.

It would be another half hour before emergency responders arrived, but speed seemed moot by then, in any case. The damage had been done in the first 30 minutes or so in the middle of the night. Hearing that had given Mrs. Doherty some relief and led her to whitewash her own story a wee bit, as there was no harm in it. Had she raced over first thing, Helen McKay would still be a tin of ashes today.

After the ambulance departed, Mrs. Doherty had closed the windows, watered the few potted plants on the doorstep, used the key Mrs. McKay had long ago given her (it was Helen's idea that they swap keys – it took some convincing), to lock the door and then gone off home.

It wasn't until several days later, after she had let a policeman into the house to look for the mobile phone in an attempt to reach the woman's relatives, that she again saw, or even thought of, the dog. Mrs. Doherty was trudging back up the lane to her own house when she saw it, about 50 feet away, walking parallel to her. The rain was slight but wind-driven into near-horizontal needles. The dog looked miserable, cold and wet.

She called out to it and the poor, bedraggled thing followed her home, where she gave it a plate of chicken scraps and let it warm itself by the fire. And for the next several days, that became their routine. In the morning, the dog would bark at the door to be let out and run off down the hill, presumably to wait by its home for the owner to return; as dusk set, she'd return to Mrs. Doherty's for a warm bed and a meal.

And now the dog was back in its own home, content by the fire, but surrounded by a pair of strangers.

It was a sign of how perfunctory Thomas's telephone conversations with his mother had become, how devoid of anything truly personal or revealing, that the subject of the dog had never once come up. Thomas had no idea how old the dog was, or how long it had lived with his mother. Or what he'd ever do with it.

He woke to the clatter of his sister in the kitchen and the whistle of the kettle. She'll absolutely die out here without her lattes, he thought, and allowed himself a small smile.

He righted himself on the couch and was rubbing his eyes when Ginny blew into the room like a bird released from a cage. "Christ, no coffee in the house at all! You didn't bring any yourself, did you?" Her short blonde hair, already perfectly styled, curled towards her face and her makeup seemed heavy for the time of day. She wore dark leggings and a colorful, long jacket that put Thomas in mind of an embroidered rug.

She moved to the window and pulled open the drapes. "It's beautiful here, Tommy. I almost envy you for this." The front of the house faced the sea and the ocean was where it always was, a slightly darker gray than the sky and the line between them a distant blur.

It's a prison sentence. Bloody solitary confinement, he thought, but kept to himself.

He sighed and looked up at her, silhouetted before the window. "Maybe we can drive into Dunnybegs later and pick some up," he suggested. "I've a few more things I need myself."

"Ach, well, I can drop you off on my way out, Tommy. But I'm away today. I'm staying in Belfast tonight and fly out tomorrow."

He shouldn't have been surprised by her eagerness to get the hell out of there – after all, he was just as keen to leave – but he thought she'd hang around a few days, let him get settled in and such before abandoning him. Nope. A three-day visit. Here to eulogize their mother and then gone again to the other side of the world.

As Ginny darted back to the kitchen for a second cup of tea, he stood, stretched, and walked towards the window. There was a writing desk against the wall next to the window with a globe on it. He spun it so Ireland was front and center, bright green in the light from the window. Australia was out of sight, hidden on the other side, in darkness.

4

Orphans

They had a last hug outside the grocer in Dunnybegs, after they had finished their morning tea, after breakfast, after Ginny wrote out a list of tasks he would have to do in the next several months in regards to their mother's estate, and the ashes once they arrived, after a discussion about whether they should let the dog in the house when they left or leave it outside (they decided inside was safer), after he lifted his sister's suitcase into the boot of the car and they drove the short way up to the town and after she followed him into the store and asked after a hot cup of coffee.

She left the car running – she was not wasting any more time here than necessary. "Now you have mum's mobile and you should carry it with you always. I'll text you before my plane takes off tomorrow." She reached out and rubbed his shoulder and he thought for a moment she was going to pat his head. She would always be the big sister and he the little brother, never mind he stood a good eight inches taller. Her nine years seniority were irrefutable. "Shit, Tommy, it's going to be good for you, being out here, the fresh air and all. Figure out what you'll do with your life. Who knows, maybe the place will sell right away. It is a great location."

He mumbled a noncommittal response and she stepped forward

and embraced him. "You and Molly are orphans now. Take care of each other."

He watched her drive off and then ambled back into the store to gather up some dog food, a newspaper and biscuits.

Orphans. The word echoed in his thoughts as he walked the road back to the cottage. His father's death had been crushing. Such a shock, such a gaping hole in the home. It had left him feeling completely untethered, like he might just float away in any breeze. His sister slid further down into her sullen teen self. Six-year-old Thomas turned to his mother for comfort, for anchorage, but her hugs became loose, her arms lightly wrapped around his back, hands no longer clasping. His father's hugs were bear hugs, with Thomas feigning a struggle to escape. They left him breathless from fits of giggles.

His mother's death felt almost anticlimactic, perhaps because it was years in the works. Her move to this far corner of the world (might as well have been) effectively removed her from his life. When her death finally came, he hadn't felt much emotion at all and even at the memorial ceremony was unmoved. How could you measure a loss for someone who had retreated from your life years earlier?

There had been an arrow of sunlight as they drove to the store. The quick slice of gold pierced the clouds and set the gorse on the hillsides afire and left the whitecaps in the bay sparkling, but it had clouded over again when he emerged for the walk back to the cottage and soon, a rain shower blew in from the sea. He unfurled the coat's hood, which draped over his forehead and left his face dark. Matching his mood.

He'd never been the sort for parties, or for wild drinking. But he was not a feckin' recluse! And while he entertained no great career ambitions, he had enjoyed the book trade and imagined he might create a good life for himself in the store. Figure out your life, his sister had said. He thought he already had. Shit, she was the one running across the planet to an empty home. Why do you always need a destination?

Molly stirred when he opened the door, sleepily rising, shaking her head and then ambling towards him, only to slide past his legs and out the still open door. "Ah, duty calls, eh?" he muttered after her. He left the door slightly ajar and went into the kitchen to unload his groceries. The kitchen was small as well, with a counter height refrigerator, washer and dryer. A small dining table and two chairs hugged the long interior wall, snug up against the room's radiator. A pair of clothes hangers hung over the radiator held a housecoat and a folded pair of his mother's trousers.

He glanced around the room. A calendar hung on one wall. A framed painting of a bird on another. Over the sink was a small window that faced up towards the town and beside that, a small mirror had been poorly jerry-rigged. Poorly, he thought, because the person standing at the sink couldn't see themselves in it. He moved to stand front and center before the sink and peered at the mirror. It held the reflection of the windowsill and desk in the front room. He stooped, matching his mother's height, and looked again. Now the mirror captured the view from the front window – the long sweep down to the beach, and Molly sniffing along the shoreline. He straightened and adjusted the hang of the mirror so he could see out the window himself and for a long moment, stood still, watching the waves, entranced.

Suddenly, a strong gust carried up the hill and threw the door open, breaking his trance. He hurried over to close it and stepped through the doorway to look for the dog. On a small bench to the right of the door was an old handbell. He picked it up and swung it, letting it clang a few times. Down on the strand, Molly looked up and began a swift run up the hill towards him. She stopped before the doorway, gave a couple good shakes, and hurried in.

"Well, you're a pretty smart dog, huh?"

She paused as she passed him and looked up at him, before settling in front of the fire, now just glowing embers. He closed the door and walked back into the kitchen to put the kettle on. A cup of tea would take the chill of the walk off.

5

A New Assignment

Fintan O'Dowd sat his diminutive frame in the hard plastic chair and peered at the receptionist at her desk, absent-mindedly clicking the top of his retractable ballpoint pen over and over. He was wearing his one suit, with white shirt and tie, but the shirt had already wriggled free of his trousers' waistband and fell over his lap. He fumbled at his tie, straightening it, not really noticing that the wide end stopped a good five inches above the narrow. His hair was still thick and red, with sprays tumbling about haphazardly, though he had indeed spent time before the mirror that morning attempting to tame it. The hair and clothes, combined with the perpetual red patches on his cheeks, left him looking forever flustered and hurried.

"She will see you now."

He stood quickly and stepped towards the office door, casting a quick glance back to see that, yes, the seat was damp from his sweat. He had been summoned to the fifth-floor office of the Undersecretary of Economic Development - his supervisor's boss. He was nervous.

The undersecretary looked up and smiled as he walked in. She was in her mid-40s, wearing a navy-blue trousers suit and a perfume that poked at his nostrils, leading him to sneer involuntarily. She nodded towards a chair and he sat.

"You've been with us thirty-nine years, is that correct?"

"Yes, I have. Right out of university." He immediately wondered if he was being made redundant. He'd been counting the years until he'd turn 63, at which point he planned to retire and never, ever, write an economic harm/benefit analysis again. This was coming two years ahead of plan, but he could probably manage.

The undersecretary lowered her gaze to the folder in front of her. "You've been in the economic reporting department most of that time. Nothing remarkable here," she added, paging through the folder's paperwork. "I can't really find anything much here about your performance. No great accomplishments, but no major complaints, either."

He swallowed hard. Ran a hand through the mop of hair.

"Did you know Willie Gaines?"

He knew of him. The lucky bugger had long ago scored what Fintan considered a dream job in the agency. Deputy Regional Administrator for County Donegal. Gaines had hated the job. Constantly complained about the stifling boredom.

County Donegal was in the far northwest corner of Ireland, as remote from Dublin as one could get, literally and figuratively. Due to the awkward geopolitics of the island, the county was almost surrounded by Northern Ireland, a part of the United Kingdom, which had no real interest in the area.

In large part due to this, the economic explosion that had transformed Dublin into a bustling, modern, European capital at the turn of the century had not extended to the most distant, northern reaches of the island. As modern roadways and railways snaked out across the land, bringing the 21st Century to most of Ireland, Donegal remained forgotten. It was why the 80-mile-as-the-crow-flies journey from Derry could take up to four hours by bus, depending on the wait between buses. Donegal had been left to its own, a forlorn patch of land of near-unmatched beauty and a dwindling, aging population. Economic development was a misnomer in Donegal, and Gaines' job was marked by long stretches of inactivity, broken by the occasional business closing. To Fintan, however, that boredom sounded blissful.

"It turns out he passed away five months ago. We, um, only recently became aware of that, I'm afraid." She looked up at him.

"I'm terribly sorry."

"Yes, well. You see, we are nearing our annual reporting deadline. We need someone who can easily move into that position and produce the needed reports, documenting the past twelve months of economic activity. Normally, this might be a considerable challenge, given the amount of economic activity in most of our districts. A lot can happen in five months."

"Indeed."

"Fortunately, it's Donegal," she half laughed. "We don't anticipate it will be too difficult to get up to speed. Make a few visits. Document the latest retired fishermen, the deceased farmers and of course, any changes in the riveting roof thatching industry." She stopped, as though waiting for him to laugh or at least smile at her attempted humor, but he was silent.

She sighed. "We'd like you to take over the position on an acting basis. You'll move to the third floor. Have your own office. And you'll need to make a few trips to the area."

"Of course," Fintan blurted out. "I'm, um, very honored and I want you to know I won't let you down."

She looked him up and down. "Yes, well, it shouldn't be too difficult. If you have a pulse, you'll be a step up. Back to your desk now and you can start on the new job Monday."

He stood up and thought of offering his hand for a handshake but she'd already turned her attention to another folder on her desk.

As he reached the door, she called after him. "Mr. Dowd, do get a good road map."

6

A Dream of Flight

Thomas spent the end of Saturday back in his Derry flat, packing up the rest of his clothes and boxing up the few belongings that he'd need or want at the cottage. His pots and dishes went into boxes, too, to be picked up by one of the city's many charity resale shops. He hadn't really thought about what to do with it all until he walked into the kitchen. Most of his own stuff had been his mother's castoffs, but he'd hardly have room for them at the cottage. No need to lug them all that way.

He moved on to his collection of books, which was considerable, but it occurred to him that he had not ever re-read any one of them and was honestly unlikely ever to, so many of them were boxed up for the charity shop as well.

The furnished flat meant he didn't have to figure out what to do with furniture. When he finished that night, he had four overstuffed trash bags, a suitcase and an even dozen boxes ready for the move. He arranged them in the center of the room and sat back to contemplate the pile.

It was a bit sobering to realize that all of his life could fit on a small rug. In fairness, he was shedding an even greater boxed collection of kitchenware, books and other detritus. Still, the small size of what he'd determined to be his most vital belongings cast a pall on his evening and he soon opted to try to sleep, curling up fully clothed on the now naked bed.

That night he had a dream. He was at an airport. In a security line. With someone. A woman. His sister? No. Emma? Maybe. She was several people ahead of him in line and, while he could not see her face, he could hear her laugh. Yes, it was Emma. Finally, he made it to the security officer, who demanded his passport, but when he tried to fish it from his pocket, he realized that he held a collection of dog leashes in both hands. There were 6 or 8 or more dogs at his feet, pulling at him, snarling, barking and yapping.

"Sorry, but we can't let you through, not with those," said the officer. "You don't have the paperwork. What were you thinking?"

He was flustered and speechless and the dogs were tugging him from different directions, almost causing him to fall. The people behind him began yelling at him, telling him to go home, to get out of the way. And then they started pushing him back away from the gate and he was forced to turn away. As he did, he caught one last glance of her, far down the long aisle now, not looking back. He didn't even know where she was going.

He had other dreams that night – bits and pieces of imperfect memories and furtive hopes, but they vanished with the morning light. Only the airport dream stayed with him as he made a pot of tea and readied himself for the move.

# 7

The People's Weekly

Fintan walked a bit taller on Monday, as he stepped off the elevator and onto the third floor of the Economic Authority and Agricultural Ministry building in central Dublin. He stopped before a wide, angular desk and announced his name to the young woman behind the counter.

He was met by a blank expression. "Are ye here to see someone then?"

No, he thought, I am here to accept my new posting and be delivered to my very own office, but before he could speak, a tall, lanky man with round glasses and a bushy brown beard walked up. "Mr. Dowd? I'm Cooper, I'll show you to your spot."

They began a trek that wound through a maze of cubicles in an assortment of beige, manilla and light cream colors. One whole side of the third floor, Fintan knew full well, was a solid glass wall overlooking the River Liffey. He had spent the weekend picturing himself at his new desk, watching the life of the city pass by below him. But their full path was made under pale green fluorescent light, no windows to be seen. They stopped at a doorway labeled 382 A-K and passed through into a long, dingy corridor interrupted by a series of open doorways. At F, Cooper halted and gestured Fintan into the room. The dwarf space held – barely – a desk facing back towards the doorway and a file cabinet. The single overhead light fixture buzzed loudly and flashed every few seconds.

"We'll get someone around for that," said Cooper. Fintan still wasn't sure if it was the man's surname or not.

After a bit of fumbling at a keyboard, Cooper successfully logged him into the agency-wide email and meeting notification system, expressed his condolences about Willie Gaines, and explained that the staggering tower of papers on the desk represented the past five months of unopened mail, official notices and other business that had languished following Gaines' expiration. Cooper, who had started just three months ago and thus had never met Gaines, explained that folks just figured Gaines had been using his vacation time.

"Guess he's on permanent holiday now, eh?" he sniggered.

Fintan managed a weak smile as Cooper disappeared down the hall. The stack of paperwork on his desk was formidable, but it was easily surpassed by the leaning, ragged tower of yellowing newspapers on the floor beside his chair. Fintan slowly pulled his reading glasses from their case, huffed on the lenses, rubbed them with the tail of his dress shirt, which had again escaped his trousers' waistband, gently slipped the specs on and then dropped his head, peering over the glasses to scrutinize the paperwork. The items on the top, of course, would be the most recent and perhaps most pressing. On the other hand, the papers on the very bottom of the pile would be the oldest and, thus, the most neglected. After much consideration, he still hadn't concluded on the proper course of action, so he unscrewed the top of this vacuum bottle, poured himself a hot cuppa, and pulled the top newspaper from the stack at his side.

Fintan's job the previous decade or so involved analyzing the reports written and submitted by regional administrators like Gaines, so he well understood what he was to do. The newspapers were scanned for any stories that related to local businesses in the region, or for other articles that might otherwise relate to the region's economy.

Up first was the most recent issue of the Donegal People's Weekly. It carried a front-page article about the local primary school's production of the musical "Cats" illustrated by a large photo of a ragtag group of children with cat ears and painted-on whiskers. They were sprawled out, crawling and mid-jump, a collection of pantomimed cat-like behaviors. Beneath that story ran a report of a single vehicle accident, of a motorist that had run off the road and injured one sheep. The motorist, according to the report, "appeared under the influence of the previous several hours spent at The End of Nowhere Pub."

Fintan scanned the first few pages, where the most pressing news might appear, and then skipped to the business section, which carried a single story profiling a local woman who made knitwear. Fintan sighed and tossed the copy aside. Had he spent another few minutes and paged through the whole edition, he might have read the sole obituary, for one Helen McKay of Dunnybegs, who had died after a short illness, or the three letters to the editor, arguing the merits of a proposal to rename one of the countless small bays that scalloped the northwest Atlantic coast.

Bays come in all shapes and sizes. Many along the coast were half-moons or shallow bowls, lined with bright golden sand and dotted with jellyfish. The bay in question was shaped more like a letter C than a crescent, with the two sides curling towards one another, and marked by a trailing line of rocks that lay mostly submerged. It was a well-protected bay. Once in a great while, however, during very low tides, entire shoals of fish were left stranded on the sands, rotting in the daylight and drawing flocks of seagulls and other shorebirds, who furiously battled over the remains. As long as locals could remember, it had been known as Killfish Bay. It had served the place well since before their grandparents' grandparents. There was no need at all for a change.

8

To the Grocer's

That same Monday, Thomas had woken in his mother's cottage, put on a kettle, and opened the door to let Molly out. His mood hadn't lightened. This was still a sentence he was serving and it was beginning to dawn on him just how remote his current place in the world was and just how much free time he would have to find ways to fill. He had brought his laptop along with him but realized the previous evening that the cottage had no internet service. No television. No internet. No fucking clue what he was going to do.

The spoon clattered as he scraped at the sugar in the bottom of the cup. Actually, his Monday was planned. After some toast, he'd walk up to the store to get milk, a newspaper, some eggs, a few cans of beans, sausages, digestive biscuits, some fish, perhaps, and toilet paper. Then, after coming back to the cottage and making himself a proper fry-up, he'd begin sorting through his mother's belongings.

He picked up the mobile and typed out a quick message to Ginny.

Hi sis. Back in cottage. Moved everything here yesterday. Will get to work shortly on mother's stuff. T

He started to set the phone back down, but stopped himself.

May look into getting television and/or internet if possible. Short term, of course.

He had no idea what time it was in Sydney, but glanced over at the globe and reckoned she was probably asleep. He looked back at his mother's phone, still in his hand. It was a fancier model than he'd expected and light years from the basic flip phone he'd been able to afford. He swiped at the screen and a row of applications appeared. Birders World. Weather. Daily Crossword. He set it back down and looked out the window.

It was a gray morning, with the clouds layered out over the sea in a series of silver and gray ribbons stretching from left to right. A brisk wind carried up the slope, bending the dune grasses towards the cottage. The sea was the color of his teaspoon and it broke in waves that scrambled across the sand before falling back. The tide was high, he noted. Thomas hadn't been here long enough to intuitively know the comings and goings of the ocean, or of the rare deadly low tides that gave Killfish Bay its name.

It was mid-March. The days were beginning to lengthen. Over the bay, the sun lingered above the water a minute or more each day. Mornings remained dark and cold, however. There was little heat in the sun when it did break through the gray, nothing to cut the damp chill that swelled up from the bay.

He discovered a small pair of binoculars when he was putting some of his things away the night before and he reached for them now, walking towards the window. He peered out over the bay. It was still there. The beige crescent of sand, the undulating steel-blue sea fading off into the horizon, the sky a series of folded soft gray flannel sheets. He set the binoculars down. There was nothing particularly in need of a closer view. Monotony, upon closer inspection, was no less monotonous.

Molly had returned by now, so he let her in and set about getting ready for the walk to the store. Raincoat. Umbrella. Boots. He wondered if he'd ever feel safe venturing out here without toting rain gear along. He'd been a resident now for the better part of four days and had witnessed a good two dozen rain showers in that time.

It was as he reached for the umbrella that he noticed the leash, the end of it appearing out from under a sweater on the coat rack by the door. He took it from the rack. "Fancy a walk, Molly?"

The dog had already made a tour of the small house, first onto the kitchen for a gulp of water and a few bites of food, then back into the living room, where it settled before the dying fire. She looked up at him upon hearing her name and tilted her head to the side as though she were really considering the idea of the walk. But she quickly stood and padded over to him, sitting at his feet and waiting as he attached the leash. And then they set off up the road, with her smartly walking alongside him.

The wee grocery store in Dunnybegs was standard issue: a lit-up, three-foot-tall, plastic ice cream cone stood beside the door; a wide front window adorned with signs promoting newspapers, the lottery, sweets, beer and cigarettes, and bundles of firewood and a rack of propane tanks settled along the outside wall.

He looped Molly's leash around a leg of the firewood rack and entered the store. The older stout woman who had rung him up on his previous visits was absent, replaced by a young woman with short blond hair. "Ock, is that our wee Molly? Sure, she can come in," she called out. Thomas hesitated, but he was already well into the store and Molly seemed fine waiting outside.

"You know the dog?" he asked.

The young woman extended her hand. "Sure, she's a regular. I'm guessing you're Helen's son. I'm sorry for your loss."

"Thanks," he replied, immediately regretting how flippant and upbeat he sounded. "I'm Thomas. Are, ah, are you new here?"

"Cara. Home for a few days. Rose, Roisin, is my aunt. I help out here when I'm home. How are ye gettin' on?"

Thomas glanced back at Molly, who was sitting obediently outside, before turning back to Cara. The young woman's stare was intense and made him feel even more awkward. "Ah, you know, it's wild quiet here. Not used to that."

She laughed. "It wasn't until I started at school in Galway that I realized how quiet it is here. When you grow up around here, you just accept it."

Thomas nodded, but he couldn't imagine ever getting used to this remoteness.

"Have you been to the Shamrock yet, or the Beetle?" They were the two closest pubs, one just at the end of the several block-long main street and the other a mile or two away. He hadn't.

"Well, Thomas, we should change that," she said. "I'm here all week. If you'd ever care for some company on your daily walks, just call up here. We can introduce you to some of the locals after. How about Saturday?"

Thomas had planned to bus back to Derry that day, to stop in at the bookshop to pick up a few books and then visit some of his old haunts.

"I'd love that."

They arranged to meet at the store at noon and then Cara left him to do his shopping. The sun had broken through the cloud cover by the time he untied Molly's leash and started the walk back to the cottage. Ahead of them stood the house, its white-washed walls bright in the sunlight, and past that, arcs of random flashes as whitecaps broke in the bay. The air felt fresh, the sun warmed his face, and Thomas hummed. He walked briskly, and Molly trotted alongside. Thomas was looking forward to lunch. And to Saturday.

9

An Urgent Matter

Fintan ate his lunch at his desk, sweeping several manilla folders aside to clear space for his sandwich and tea. The sandwich was two slices of dry, brown bread around several thin wafers of ham. Monday and Wednesday were ham. Tuesday was egg salad. Thursday was cheese. Fridays were left to his own desire and were almost always ham again. An apple and three milk chocolate digestives filled out each day's lunch.

As he ate, one of the folders slipped from his desk, scattering its contents across the floor. URGENT. The word was writ large in red, capital letters atop each page.

Aw, shite, he thought. He decided to leave the folder and papers on the floor as he finished the sandwich and then two of the biscuits, reasoning that something potentially that urgent might interfere with his digestion, but by the time he took a final sip of his tea, his stomach was already rumbling. He reached for the top page and began reading.

URGENT

Dear sirs:

I have perhaps mistakenly operated under the assumption that government behaved in Ireland in much the same manner it did throughout the rest of the developed world. This is apparently not so. My company is an international leader in aqua farming and our proposal would drastically transform a desolate, forgotten place into a thriving economic center.

Unfortunately, while local reception to our proposal has been incredibly welcoming, the silence we have endured from the Irish government itself has been abhorrent. I thereby declare that International Fisheries will abandon this effort by the 31st of March if no action has been undertaken by your ministry to allow us to move forwards. There are plenty other fish in the sea.

* Actually, there aren't. Which is the leading reason International Fisheries aqua farms are such successful operations around the world. Ignore us at your own financial peril.

Sincerely,

Clyde Van der Vaart

Fintan read the cover letter without exhaling. "Oh feck." It was already April 16.

Fintan scrambled to gather the rest of the pages and read through them. And then he flipped through the various other folders and envelopes on the pile, identifying a half dozen or more with the International Fisheries logo, some as much as four months old. He felt chill. His lower abdomen had stepped up efforts to process the sandwich in record time. His heart was racing. And then he looked to the phone on his desk and noticed for the first time the blinking message light. Aw, shite.

He remained steadfast at his desk that afternoon, save for several trips to the loo, commencing immediately after listening to the first of what were in fact 17 voice messages left by various personnel at International Fisheries, up to and including Clyde Van der Vaart himself, who made abundantly clear his growing anger. In a first for him, when Fintan left for the day, he actually carried work home with him – the full collection of correspondence from International Fisheries.

That evening, he read through them. The proposal was for a fish farm. It would be constructed within the confines of a small, protected bay in a sparsely populated area in the northwest. Some dredging of the bay and reconfiguring of a natural rock breakwater would be required at first, but then farming operations would begin in several phases and eventually a processing plant would be constructed, bringing the potential for dozens of jobs to the area surrounding the bay. Fintan had never been there. But he chuckled at the somewhat ironic name of the place. Killfish Bay wasn't exactly where you'd imagine a fish farm.

By bedtime, Fintan had settled his nerves by reminding himself that the lack of formal response to the proposal was entirely his predecessor's fault, and that the situation might actually represent a terrific opportunity. If he were able to salvage this proposal and bring economic development to the area in question, he'd be treated as a hero in the office. He was keenly aware from a lifetime of report writing that such matters rarely moved swiftly, and that timelines were nothing more than fantasies drawn up to excite investors and local politicians. The lapsed deadline was unfortunate, but the search for another site wouldn't have gotten very far in two weeks. He set out his clothes for the morning and, as the milk for his hot chocolate warmed on the stovetop, pulled an old road atlas from the odds and ends drawer in the kitchen.

In the morning, he'd send an official correspondence to Mr. Van der Vaart, apologizing for the delay, explaining the unfortunate circumstances behind it and asking for more information about the proposal. This last was a delaying measure. In truth, he had all he needed to begin action on the proposal, which would require first an economic impact report and then a separate environmental evaluation from the Ministry of the Environment before a final approval could be given.

First, though, Fintan was headed to Dunnybegs.

10

Lost Dogs of Donegal

The first few days of Thomas's week passed unremarkably. He settled into a rhythm, slowly and methodically sorting through his mother's belongings. He boxed up most of her clothes so they could be passed on to a charity shop. His sister had advised that any financial documents should be saved, but he grew tired of trying to determine which ones were important and which weren't, so he ended up throwing most of her old paperwork in the fire, where they flared brightly, briefly lighting up the room.

He made steady progress, emptying cluttered drawers from the living room desk and then a few from the kitchen, saving for now her silverware and cooking utensils. The pantry was well-stocked with canned goods and breakfast cereals, as well as flour and sugar. He briefly entertained the idea of learning to bake during his exile, dismissed it, and then opted to keep the food items, just in case.

Her bedroom dresser was more trying. Several drawers held additional blouses, sweaters and trousers, which he roughly folded and stuffed into boxes. Two smaller drawers held a variety of undergarments, which he was reluctant to handle. Instead, he carried those drawers to the living room, and emptied the contents into a large plastic rubbish bag. Finally, he set upon a small bookcase next to her bed, which held a few brightly colored glass figurines and a shelf of books and magazines. He set aside the glass knickknacks to be wrapped in newspaper later and began gently tossing the books and magazines into a box when a slip of paper fell to the floor.

It was a snapshot. Old. Black and white. He reached in and retrieved it.

It was very old. But he recognized the young woman in the photo immediately – it was his mother. She was sitting side-saddle on a low stone wall or fence, looking at a young woman to her left. Thomas squinted at the photo. He did not recognize the other woman. She had dark, wavy hair, held a cigarette in her hand, and rested her free hand on his mother's shoulder. They looked carefree. His mother's expression seemed warm and open, content.

He stepped backward, to the sofa, and sat, still staring at the photo. It had been so very long since he had witnessed anything resembling happiness emanating from her. He realized he had been holding his breath and he gulped but the air caught in this throat and gurgled in a quiet wail. And suddenly he was crying, years' worth of tears running down his cheeks and spreading across the stubble on his chin. He didn't bother trying to contain it, he couldn't, really. The sobs just came and came.

He was lost in grief and then in loneliness. For how long he cried, he didn't know. But when he was finally able to draw in a deep breath and look up, the day was dying and the sunlight out over the bay was receding. He set the photo on the side table and made a move to stand up, but realized there was a weight on his legs. Molly was on the couch next to him and her head resting on his lap, her eyes upturned towards him.

He hadn't noticed her jump up, indeed had never seen her on the couch at all. And his first instinct was to shoo her off, but he stopped himself, and instead rested his left hand on her head. The fur was softer than he'd imagined, and he ran his hand from front to back, feeling the bony ridges under the warm, smooth coat. The fur was longer around her neck, and hung over her collar. He absent-mindedly grabbed at that fur and scratched at her neck. Her tail wagged.

He looked down at her face, staring back up at him. "Ah, shit, girl. Orphans, huh? We're just a couple of lost dogs in Donegal."

For another hour or so, they both remained on the couch, Thomas lost in memories, and Molly curled in a ball tight against him, the warmth of her body somehow reassuring. When he finally rose, Thomas carried the photo of his mother over to a short bookcase and leaned it against a row of paperback mysteries.

After a dinner of beans on toast and more tea, he caught sight of the full moon over the water through the living room window. It was a clear night and the wind had calmed. He was about to let Molly out when he decided that a bit of fresh air would be nice. He pulled on his coat and walked out with her, aiming for the road down to the beach.

The bay wasn't far off, but the narrow road leading to it snaked down the low, sloping hillside. There were more direct footpaths through the field, but Thomas hadn't memorized them and, while the full moon provided some illumination, he found the roadway safer. Besides, he was in no rush. Molly, off leash, generally accompanied him, darting off every now and then to rush through the dune grasses and heather before ambling back to his side.

The road emptied into a wee car park that held at best five or six cars but was now deserted. This was not one of the more popular beaches along the coast that drew hundreds during the summer months. Those beaches had toilet facilities, caravan sites and one or more ice cream trucks on the weekends. This one contained a single sign, announcing the name of the bay, noting that no lifeguards were present, and warning against rip currents. A stone wall ran the length of the lot and at each end a footpath wound through the dune grasses down to the sand.

The tide was in.

Molly had run ahead and was lying still a few yards back from the water's edge. Thomas walked down to join her, looking out at the moon hanging low above its own reflection in the sea. The waves were mild and unhurried and, though it was still brisk enough that he could see his own breath, Thomas found himself thinking how lovely it would be on a summer night.

He tilted his head back, moving the moon out of sight and staring up at the empty sky overhead, which slowly filled with stars as his eyes adjusted to the dark. He held his breath and searched for familiar constellations but found it challenging due to the sheer number of stars. The sky seemed alive with them. So many other suns, so many other planets circling them. And he wondered if somewhere out there in the interstellar dark, someone, or something, was also standing silently, peering up at the night sky, at millions of stars, of which the sun was but one small light in the heavens.

He shivered, both at the cold and at the feeling he was being watched, as silly as it seemed. He looked down at Molly, who was peering ahead intently. And when he followed her gaze out to the water, he saw what had captured her attention. Maybe fifty feet out, the head of a seal had broken the surface of the water.

Though it had the moon at its back and thus was mostly a silhouette, Thomas thought he could see the seal's eyes – black, unblinking circles against the dark grey of its fur. He let out a quiet gasp and lowered himself to squat next to the dog, reaching out his right arm to steady himself on Molly's back. The seal seemed unbothered by their presence, and Molly, surprisingly, made no move to chase out after it. For five, maybe ten minutes, it remained motionless, its gaze directed towards the two of them as the tide shifted course, serenading them with rhythmic soft shushes as each wave withdrew into the sea. And then, quietly and suddenly, it slipped back under the surface and disappeared.

After a few minutes with the seal still gone and the moon about to follow, Thomas began the trek back up to the cottage, with Molly rushing off from his side and then hurrying back as though on an elastic rope. Thomas remained quiet, lost in thought about his mother, about the stars overhead and about the seal in the sea. He felt alone, and was glad each time Molly scampered back to his side.

11

Fintan's Journey Begins

The drive up from Dublin took Fintan longer than expected. Most of his other overnight travels had taken him around the central and southeastern regions of Ireland, areas served by modern carriageways that moved traffic along swiftly and that bent around the countless small villages that appeared every few miles.

The route to Donegal offered up a different experience, with main roads that unexpectedly devolved into farm lanes more than once and that unfailingly delivered him straight into the crowded center of each and every small village along the way. These towns were mostly interchangeable. In each, the road Fintan was driving became the main thoroughfare, a two-lane street lined with small stores, beauty salons, pubs, bakeries and cafes, often brightly painted. Some towns had squares, though most of those had been turned into seas of gray asphalt limited with substandard fences and the odd bench. These small urban centers were uniformly congested, with a lane of the road often blocked by a delivery truck or farmer's tractor.

It was slow going and Fintan was glad he had brought a Thermos of tea with him. Twice he pulled into parking lots in town squares and enjoyed a drink with a few digestives. It was at his second such repast that he took stock of his surroundings and noticed that a considerable number of the businesses lining the square were in fact vacant. About half, in fact.

The realization reminded him why he was on this journey. Economic development. It had been easy to get approval for the trip, as the region was long overdue for a fact-finding visit, dying for it, you might say. Fintan hadn't mentioned anything about the fish farm proposal to his superiors yet. No use getting folk needlessly upset. Not if his plans worked out.

He clambered back into the small royal blue sedan and drove on. More villages, more vacant businesses, more smoke from peat fires in the air and even an occasional thatched-roof cottage. And then, every now and then, as the road surmounted a hill or cleared a sweeping turn, the Atlantic, steel blue in the distance. He was getting close. He was tired.

The route to the bed and breakfast he had arranged for two nights was more complicated than he had anticipated. Some of the roads his map depicted were missing or unmarked and he must have spent the final hour of his drive circling the property before finally seeing the familiar B and B sign.

It was dark by the time he had been greeted by his hostess, shown the commode room, given instructions for the television set in his bedroom and brought in his overnight bag. He extracted and unwrapped a ham sandwich, sat on the edge of his bed, and took a bite. He'd explore in the morning, after breakfast.

12

To the Beetle

The days following Thomas's encounter with the seal saw a change in weather, bringing steady rains that lashed at the front windows of the house. Molly's trips outside were short and infrequent. Thomas remained indoors, pretending an interest in the continued sorting of his mother's belongings but mostly passing the time reading two of her paperbacks. He was happy to see the forecast for Saturday calling for high pressure moving in, bringing brisk winds and sunshine.

That morning, he was up early to be ready when the charity van stopped for the boxes of clothes. The driver was a sullen young man who engaged in little pleasantries but managed to fit the load of boxes into the back of the vehicle. At eleven, he had a change of heart about his choice of clothes for the day, and went back into the pile beside his bed, pulling out a pair of jeans and discarding the pair of khaki trousers he had put on earlier. He washed his face again – his skin oiled up quickly – and ran a comb through his thick black hair. Then, he announced to Molly that it was time for their date and attached the leash to her collar.

On the walk up to the village, he argued with himself over whether or not this actually constituted a date. Cara herself had suggested they spend the afternoon together, had she not? It had been a long time since he had been on a true date with a woman. Sure, he and Emma had spent time together, but it never felt in any way romantic. That thought sent him off a journey of self-doubt and recrimination. What if Emma had been interested and he just hadn't realized? Had he been interested in her? It was true he still thought about her and wondered how she was and what she was doing, but the friendship – the relationship, such as it was – had just slowly slipped away, like an outgoing tide.

He was still deep into these thoughts when he and Molly stepped through the door of the shop, setting a small bell ringing and drawing Cara's attention.

She was in the produce aisle, stacking bananas when they entered, but glanced over at them. "There you are! I'll be finished in a moment."

He wandered over to look at the row of daily newspapers by the check-out area and was passed by a smallish, slightly disheveled man, who hurried past and out the door, clutching a stack of newspapers and struggling to shove his wallet into his coat pocket.

When Cara made her way to the front of the store, Thomas attempted a smile and a weak "hello." She was shapeless, attired in a baggy black fisherman's knit sweater and grey sweatpants. She pulled a navy wool cap over her head, brushed a few stray hairs from her forehead and smiled back.

"Rose, I'm away, then," she shouted at her aunt, who was in the rear of the store, rearranging a display of sausage rolls under a heat lamp. "Come on, I'm free until three. We should be able to get a few miles in by then."

Thomas followed her out the door, somewhat alarmed by the realization she really intended to walk several miles. Outside of his trips to and from the village center, he'd been pretty inactive since the move.

"How is it going with Molly, then? How's are you getting on?"

"Well, I'm not really used to dogs, you know. I'd never had one before," Thomas answered. "Felt a bit strange at first having this other, ah, animal, in the house. But I'm getting used to her. It's actually nice to have the company. She spends most of the day in front of the fire."

She stopped. "Get on with ye," she said. "Sure, you're not turning her into a layabout, are you? This is a working dog. Border collies like Molly are meant to be herding all day long, up chasing sheep all over, not laying by a fire."

"Well, she goes out several times a day, but I'm not much myself for long walks," he answered.

She gave him a look of disappointment. "I imagined as much, which is why I suggested the walk. You need to be getting out with her like this every day, you know. Your mother did."

"Really?" He couldn't help but sound incredulous.

"Aye, saw her regularly last summer. Up to the village and along the coast road and back. They'd be out for hours. I'm sorry about her passing. Such a shock. She seemed so healthy."

Their walk from the store took them back toward the bay, but they turned southward along the coast road upon reaching the intersection, with Thomas resigning himself that they were in for a long walk.

"We can take the road south a few miles and then double back along the pathway that runs along the coast. Have you walked it?" she asked. He hadn't. "There's a cluster of houses a couple miles along, still technically Dunnybegs, but they call it Drumford. There's a wee pub there, the Beetle. Has a nice fireplace to warm up for the walk back."

They walked along the side of the road, letting Molly off leash so she could dart up into the fields as she wanted. He learned a bit about Cara. That she went to school in Galway and was studying animal behavior and veterinary science and was a year out from becoming a real veterinarian. That her family lived a few miles north of Dunnybegs and that she bicycled into the shop to help out whenever she was home from school. That she was gay.

This last bit of information had been dropped casually in comments about her school life, about the friends she had made in Galway. Her family knew. Seemed okay with it, though it was probably just as well that her granny was no longer alive, as the thought of her granddaughter being a lesbian would likely have killed her. Cara laughed as she said it. "I mean, what difference does it make? I'm the same person. We're all just alone and looking for company, right?"

Her question made him think of the night he saw the seal in the bay and of how lonely he had felt that night. There was a part of him a bit disappointed to hear of her sexual orientation, but it was overcome by a gratitude at the company. He hadn't realized how lonely he'd been since the move.

The Beetle was a small stone building set by itself on the ocean side of the road. By the time Thomas and Cara rounded a bend and saw it opposite a small gathering of white-washed houses, they were ready for a drink and the warmth of a fire.

It took a moment for Thomas's eyes to adjust to the dark inside, but when they did he saw a large room, with the bar running along the wall to their left and a fireplace at the far end, opposite them. A few tables were haphazardly arranged across the room. It was empty, save for an elderly man sitting at the bar and the bartender behind it.

He shifted to face them and smiled at Cara. "Allo, love, are you minding Molly now?"

"Donal, hello," she answered. "I've brought Thomas here to meet you. He's Helen's son and is staying at the cottage with Molly."

"Hello son." The bartender reached a hand out to shake Thomas's. A massive hand that engulfed Thomas's. "Terrible what happened."

"Ta," said Thomas. "You knew my mother?"

The man pulled two pint glasses of Guinness which he placed on the bar before them and then poured a bit more into a teacup, before bringing the cup around to the front of the bar and setting it on the floor, for Molly, who lapped it up. "There you go, Moll. Sure, she was a regular. Always stopped in on their walks. She'd have a pint and sit at the bar, chatting and reading her phone."

"They have great wi-fi here," interjected Cara. "Wild fast."

Thomas paid for the drinks and they carried them to a table by the fire, Thomas trying to imagine his mother as a regular at a pub. Facing Cara across the table, he noticed a small button on her sweater. "What's that about?" he asked.

**KEEP IT
KILLFISH**

"Oh," she looked down at it. "Forgot I still had it. Some folks this winter wanted to change the name of the bay. Said Killfish Bay was depressing. They were trying to get the local government to change it to Salmon Cove or some bullshit like that."

Thomas took a gulp of the beer. "I don't know. What does it matter what the place is called? I mean, Killfish Bay doesn't exactly sound idyllic, does it?"

"It's heritage, though. It's our history here. And no outsiders should change that."

"I knew it used to be more populated and prosperous years ago, right? Was this a fishing village?"

Cara shot a look at the bartender, who had been quietly studying them as he wiped glasses dry. "Ask Donal."

He walked out from behind the bar. He was a big, sturdy man, maybe in his late fifties. A growing belly. Again, huge hands and a thick face with grey hair slicked back. He walked towards them and pulled a chair along with him, sitting down at the side of their table.

"Son, it's a big feckin' sea next door. It was all fishing here. Me Da was a fisherman, as was his father and his father's father. As long as we can remember folks fished."

"So that's why it's called Killfish Bay?" Thomas asked. "It was a fishing village?"

The bartender shook his head. "Too shallow. The fishing harbor was down in Killybegs. Still a few boats left, but they don't catch anything these days. When I was a lad you could go out just a mile or two offshore and run into huge shoals. They swam along in the gulf current. Pollock. Cod. Mackerel. Even John Dories. There were times the water would be so thick with them that you could see their shadow from the pilothouse on the boat.

"And there are stories about Killfish Bay - Bá an tSlaid Éisc. About how, every once in a great while if the current was just right, the tide would suddenly draw out and nearly empty the bay, and whole schools would be trapped. Folk would run out into the water with baskets and scoop up as many as they could carry – more than they needed or could store."

"Not anymore?" asked Thomas.

Donal shook his head. "Sea's fished out. Fish are gone. So are the fishermen. And most of the others. Gone. Hell, most left the country altogether, like my own brother." He raised himself up and walked to the fireplace, where he set more peat on the fire. For a moment, the smoke curled back into the dark room and hung about the air like an old memory.

After finishing their drinks, Thomas and Cara left and began the walk back home, walking first towards the sea cliffs that loomed before them until they located the footpath which ran along the coast. As they spoke less on the way back, Thomas was free to notice how much scenery he had missed on the walk down. The geography here was an unending series of promontories and bays, of low, wide strands and then massive, tumbled rock formations that climbed from the sea, some leading to cliffs more than a hundred feet high. To their left worked the Atlantic, an endless roiling parade of whitecaps. The sea was turquoise in the bright sun.

The road they had followed on the way down was to their right. Beyond that, lay rolling hills covered in a patchwork of greens, divided by dark hedges and stone walls and dotted with bright yellow splashes of wild gorse in early bloom. And ruins. Thomas hadn't even noticed them before. Homes. Some nearly intact, others just foundational walls or lonely chimneys.

As they neared home, the western sky transformed, with huge cumulus clouds erupting over the sea and reaching for the sun. Rain was coming, and along with it an earlier end to the bright daylight they'd enjoyed. They hastened their pace and, as they reached Killfish Bay, they turned up one of the worn pathways through the dunes, avoiding the car park altogether.

For once, the parking lot was not vacant. A small royal blue car was stopped before the sign in the lot. The driver, the same man Thomas had passed in the store earlier that day, was out of the car, intently reading the sign, and then peering back at a large unfolded map on the hood of the car. He was a short man, with rumpled clothes. A Thermos sat on one corner of the map, holding it flat.

13

Sausage Rolls and a View

Fintan began the day with a good fry up at the bed and breakfast – hearty brown bread, eggs, sausages and a few rashers of bacon. His hostess even offered to make a pot of tea for his Thermos, after hearing his plans to sightsee for most of the day.

He departed, endeavoring to pay attention to the roads leading away from the house so that he may more easily find it upon returning that evening. He aimed toward the sea again, and finding it, angled his car north, following the coastal road as it zig-zagged along the meandering coast. When a bend in the road opened to reveal a small village with several fishing boats bobbing in the harbor, he thought he may have found the place he was seeking, but a glance at his map proved otherwise. Still, he slowed and turned into a parking lot overlooking the harbor.

It looked ancient, the dock and pier, all brutal, crumbling concrete with rusting iron bollards. Near the end sat a massive anchor, thick with untold layers of glossy paint and spotted with gull droppings. Three boats were moored along the pier. At the northern end of the dock, a lone man sat on a wrought iron bench, fussing over a cigarette. For the briefest of moments, Fintan considered leaving the car and walking down to the man, but decided instead to pour himself tea. The fellow looked not entirely agreeable.

The day had become bright with sun, but a dampness hovered in the air and his breath steamed as he exhaled after a sip. He turned and scanned the roadside ahead of him across from the dock. A chippy. A charity resale store. Pub. Empty space. Another resale shop. It was a solid stretch of buildings, several blocks of multi-story structures, some topping out at three or four levels. He guessed at least one had once been a hotel, with grand bay windows that opened out onto sea views. Once.

He wiped the dregs in his cup with a paper towel and screwed it back onto the Thermos, placing it on the floor of the passenger's seat. His road atlas was on the seat next to him and he casually glanced at it, though he had lost faith in its accuracy and at this point felt more confident simply following the coastal road north.

Which he did, passing through several more small towns, some no more than a loose huddle of ramshackle cottages, others fairly bustling with pubs, chippies and thrift shops. In each, Fintan made a mental note of the empty storefronts and "To Let" signs, as well as the numerous abandoned dwellings that lay scattered amidst the hillsides along the way.

By late morning, feeling quite peckish, Fintan determined that he would stop for lunch at the very next town, but was disappointed to discover that it offered no cafes whatsoever, just a pub and small convenience store. Sighing audibly, he pulled in to park in front of the store.

Inside the well-lit space, the smell of old food drew him to the rear of the store, where a handful of sausage rolls and a small mountain of chips bathed under heat lamps. The potato chips had lost their will, and were drooped over each other like layers of seaweed on a shore rock. But the sausage rolls looked fine and the smell of the buttery pastry and pork proved irresistible. Fintan fetched two from under their heat source and dropped them together into a waxed bag.

"Grand day, innit?"

The greeting startled him, and he nearly dropped the sack. The speaker was a stout woman wearing a dark green shop apron. "You visiting, then?" she asked.

"Um, just doing a bit of sightseeing," Fintan managed.

"Lovely day for it. Hint of summer in that sky. No chips, then?"

Fintan shook his head. "Say, do you have maps?"

"Aye. Up here." She guided him over to a shelf crowded with newspapers and magazines. He trailed behind, noticing the pleasant aroma of her perfume and the shape of her as she walked. There were several maps of varying scale and scope and he gathered one of each, along with the most recent copy of the Donegal Peoples Weekly, after which he followed the woman to the register. There, he added a chocolate bar and a roll of peppermints to his purchase. "They're a gift," he offered. It wasn't true at all, of course, and he regretted saying it immediately.

The woman smiled back at him as she rang up the sale. She wore her pale grey hair pulled back from her face. Her eyes were the color of the Atlantic and her cheeks ruddy. Something about her manner at once calmed Fintan and made him jittery.

"I'm Fintan," he stammered. "Up from Dublin."

"Welcome to Dunnybegs, Fintan," she replied. "Enjoy your sightseeing now, and come again."

He smiled at her and then gathered up his purchase, declining a plastic bag and chastising himself for not bringing his own. He was still in this state – slightly agitated, somewhat distracted and a bit giddy – as he headed towards the door, pocketing the sweets and fumbling with the newspaper and maps, when he hurried past a young man and a dog in the entryway. It was odd to see a dog in a store, he thought to himself, but he was, after all, in a very rural area.

He drove northward a while, passing through several more villages of various sizes, all of which displayed similar stages of economic distress and which would melt together in his memory of the journey. There were no large housing developments, no improved roadways, no McDonalds, no train stations, no big box retailers.

But there were sheep. Lord, there were sheep! Spread across the hillsides, scattered throughout the roughly shaped fields and lining the streams that crisscrossed the land, were untold thousands of sheep, in a rainbow of hues – their coats a mishmash of purples, greens, reds and blues, their fur long and scraggly, their movements slow and sleepy. Every now and then he'd spot a small one snug up close to what he guessed was its mother and at one point spent several minutes wondering what a young sheep was called before it finally dawned on him. "Jesus," he said. "Lambs!"

He already knew that the region lacked much heavy industry, having scanned previous profile reports before leaving work, but he was taken aback by the absence of much of any other businesses, save for the stores and pubs in the small towns. And the sheep. The fish farm could have a big impact in revitalizing the area, he thought. If he could pull this off, re-engaging with the developers and then letting his supervisors know how close they had come to losing this, well, Fintan O'Dowd would be a hero.

He followed the coast north another twenty-odd miles, then curved inland, slowly turning to head south to return to Dunnybegs for a final stop at the bay itself before heading back to the bed and breakfast. By the time he drove into the small parking lot at Killfish Bay, the sun was being swallowed up by dark clouds that bloomed out over the Atlantic. The sea itself had darkened from the brilliant turquoise of earlier that day into a muddled gray-green and even in the protected bay, waves were building.

He exited his car and spread a map over the bonnet, using his Thermos to keep it from flying up in the wind. This was indeed the bay in question. He gazed out over the bay. Much larger than he had imagined. He could see, in the distance, waves crashing over a line of nearly submerged rocks that acted as a natural breakwater. He turned in a slow circle, looking first to the north and then up the slow, gentle sloping hills that led to tiny Dunnybegs. A handful of houses occupied the hillside surrounding the bay. And then the road to Dunnybegs, itself a pitiful wee clump of businesses that would be dwarfed by any single block in Dublin.

14

A Dog's Heartache

As the trio walked up from the bay, Thomas wondered to himself whether it would be appropriate to invite Cara in for some tea, but before he could settle on a course of action, she abruptly turned towards the road and away from the trail leading up to his house.

"I'm off now," she said. "Have to work at the store for the rest of the day." She glanced back at him and smiled. "Now, Thomas, for the good of that wee dote, you should be doing a walk like that five times a week, if not daily." He stopped to watch her walk off, as Molly scrambled back through the brush and sat a good fifteen feet back of him.

He looked back at the dog, which was sitting up stiffly and examining him, her head tilted to the side. "I heard her," he said. Behind Molly, the sky had erupted into a brooding and violent collection of storm clouds rimmed in gold and sliced with glowing rays of sunlight. Absent-mindedly, Thomas lifted his mother's phone from his chest pocket, aimed it at Molly, and snapped a photo.

It might have been the first time he had really noticed the beauty in the sky since moving into his mother's house. He shot several more photos of the sky itself and then of the bay, wishing that the man in the wee car wasn't in the parking lot, muddying up the scenery. Then he turned and began the hike back up the rest of the trail to the cottage, stopping frequently to stare at the drama of the sky. Ahead of him, Molly jumped up onto the low stone wall that separated the walk from the roadway and he snapped a photo of her standing atop the wall, the still-bright hills behind her.

From there, he quickened his pace to the cottage, needing to pee and beginning to feel a chill as the breeze strengthened and the sky further darkened.

That evening, the lashing rains came, driving against the windows in the living room and bedroom. Before bed, Thomas let Molly out the back door, as it offered a bit of protection from the wind. She shot out and was back within moments, making straight for her spot in front of the fire.

This was where she slept each night since Thomas had moved in. While there was a dog bed in a corner of the bedroom, Thomas slept with the door closed, partly out of habit and partly out of feeling a bit uncomfortable with the dog being so close by at night. But, after getting ready for bed and making sure the door was bolted, he stopped by the sleeping dog. "You want back into your bed, Molly?" he asked. "Come on."

She rose sleepily, stretched, arched her back, shook her head and then followed him into the bedroom. Which is when Thomas noticed that the dog bed was occupied by one of his mother's slippers and the pair of trousers that had hung in the kitchen. The dog must have brought the objects to the bed when Thomas was out. Molly circled several times before dropping herself down in the center of the pile and letting out a deep sigh.

It hadn't occurred to him, but the dog was clearly missing Helen. "Shite, Molly. I'm sorry, girl." He still had no idea where Molly had come from or how long she had been with his mother, but the sight of the two of them out walking was familiar enough to the locals. He slid down to sit beside her and ran his hand along her back. "You probably miss her more than me."

He sighed and looked around the darkened bedroom, bare, save for the furniture and his own still-unpacked boxes of belongings. A realization had been growing since his walk that day, and the sight of so many empty houses and "for sale" signs along the way: this place wasn't going to sell quickly. He – and Molly – might be here awhile. He scratched Molly's head and she turned and gave his hand a quick lick.

"We've got work to do, Molly. We have stuff to unpack and put away and another walk to that pub. But for now, we'll sleep." He raised himself up, lumbered to the bed and climbed in, pulling the sheets up to his chin. It was dark, and the sound of the driven rain came in waves. Each time the pelting rain fell away, he could make out the sound of Molly's breathing. It was a calming sound.

He woke up feeling well rested. The morning was cloudy but bright – with high, thin clouds obscuring the sun. As he waited for his tea, he stood at the living room window and watched Molly weave through the dune grasses down to the sand. The sight of her with his mother's belongings the night before had remained with him and he felt some guilt that he hadn't really thought about how she might be doing before this.

In part, he reasoned, that was due to his lack of familiarity with dogs. But spending a few weeks now with Molly had changed him. Hell, he'd even found himself talking to the dog. Whether that was due to a growing level of compassion or the madness of the daily loneliness was up for debate. But in the last few days, he found himself beginning to believe that the dog understood much of what he said, or felt.

Cara had reminded him that Molly was a working dog, bred to herd sheep. She needed exercise and tasks to keep her occupied. Her morning run on the beach wasn't enough. He would have to commit to daily walks with her. This, he told himself, was for the dog's benefit.

15

Getting his Feet Wet

The previous afternoon, Fintan, having convinced himself that he had indeed found the bay in question and then having his hunch confirmed by the sign at the edge of the tiny parking lot, wandered down to the strand and stood, facing the waves, for some time, though he was unsure just what he was looking for.

It was a desolate place. Just cold ocean, hills and a few small houses scattered about. Perhaps if he were to walk the length of it, get a full picture of the place? He started out, but stopped after ten minutes or so and turned back. It was getting windy and gray and, honestly, it all looked pretty much the same everywhere he looked – just sweeps of ruddy brown, steel gray and olive. You wouldn't be making postcards of this, he thought.

Truth be told, Fintan had no idea what a fish farm might look like or what made a good spot in which to locate one. Water? Check. Empty space to build any sort of factory or warehouse that might be needed? Check. Roads or railways to move the product back to civilization? Well. The coast road would have to do, for now. But surely once the farm was up and successful, there would be support to widen and improve the road to Letterkenny.

He closed his eyes. The vision of the day came to him: the ribbon cutting for the new roadway to Letterkenny and he, himself, invited to wield a pair of oversized scissors. This was all due to his dogged determination to resurrect the project. The jobs, the factory, the new houses, all his doing.

Just then, a rogue wave rushed in and washed over his feet, startling him. He scampered back a few steps but lost his balance and tumbled onto the sand, thankfully just out of the wave's reach. "Bloody hell," he uttered, first struggling to his knees and then rising up, sweeping the sand from his pants.

He shot a look up the hill and was relieved that the young couple walking the dog was nowhere to be seen. His clumsiness had gone unseen. This was enough for the day, he thought to himself. He had done a thorough exploration of the region, crisscrossing the area surrounding the proposed fish farm. He had inspected towns and villages from behind the wheel of his car and had seen enough to conclude that the area was economically depressed and in need of critical business developments such as the fish farm. Sure, the proposal called for just eight jobs to begin with, but one had to take the long view of such matters.

The car awaited, as did a last small cup of now lukewarm tea. He carefully folded the selection of maps on the passenger seat, took the final square of his chocolate bar and righted himself for the drive back to the bed and breakfast before the rain came on. As he was about to turn south onto the coast road, however, he saw the wee shop he had called into earlier in the day. Perhaps a roll of mints, he decided.

He pulled up in front of the store and set the parking brake. The short main street of Dunnybegs was practically bustling, with upwards of a dozen people walking along either side of the road and several parked cars lining the block. The store itself was busy with customers, which was to say three of four folk were shuffling about the aisles.

Fintan selected a roll of peppermints and walked to the register, frowning when he realized the woman he had spoken with earlier had been replaced by a young woman. "Is something wrong?" she asked.

"Oh, no," Fintan mumbled. "I, ah, just, I was in earlier today to buy some maps and spoke with an older woman. Is she here?"

"That's Roisin. Aye, she's away home for the night. Can I do anything for you?"

He could feel himself blush. "No, no, no. I just wanted to tell her the maps, um, the maps worked fine."

"Aye, grand," she replied, handing him his change. "Will you need a bag?"

Fintan shook his head no and hurried to the door. Jesus, what had come over him? He made a U-turn in the road as the first few raindrops fell and started south.

Back in his room at the B&B and after a filling meal, Fintan took out the oversized envelope containing the correspondence about the fish farm. It all seemed pretty simple. The proposal called for repositioning and supplementing the natural breakwater, which meant it would also require approval of the environmental engineering folks, but Fintan's own recommendation would weigh heavily. And then there was something about renaming the bay itself, which made Fintan smile at the incongruity of locating a fish farm in a place named Killfish Bay. He had no idea what changing the name would entail or even what agencies might be involved, but one of the letters from Mr. Van der Vaart mentioned that the company had already begun a campaign to gauge local support for the name change. Again, Fintan smiled. He may not have had much experience doing actual fieldwork (well, none actually), but he had heard enough to know it probably meant some local politicians were getting a bit of extra cash.

He carefully folded and placed the documents back in the envelope. He would drive back to Dublin in the morning and, upon his return to the office, would send the company another letter, announcing that he would very much support the proposal. With any luck, that would be enough to resurrect the proposal.

16

Curiosities and Antiquities

After a breakfast of toast, eggs and beans and several hours of cleaning, Thomas headed out to the store with Molly alongside – a short walk to start their new daily habit. He tied Molly's leash to the plastic ice cream cone out front and went in for the paper. When he emerged, he caught sight of the dog, sitting stiffly next to and facing the cone, the two of them reflected in a large puddle. The pose seemed majestic, the scene a bit ridiculous. He took out his mother's phone and snapped a photo.

Then, for some reason, he thought of Emma, and the odd positions she'd get into to take a photo. All in how you frame it. He bent down, resting his right knee on the pavement, and raised the phone again. Now the image of Molly and her reflection filled the whole right side of the frame, mirrored by the ice cream cone and its reflection on the left and then the warm glow of the shop in the background.

After that, they strolled the length of the block and back again, him lost in thought, remembering his photo walkabouts with Emma. As they walked, a woman passing by with a basket of flowers smiled and gave Molly a pat on the head. Then the butcher out at the front of his shop ran in and fetched her a small piece of meat, which she hastily downed. The dog was definitely well known, he thought. It was so hard to fathom, this idea of his stoic, sour mother rambling about the countryside with a dog by her side, chatting with strangers and barmen. Christ, she was as much of a stranger to him as the dog was.

They went home, but instead of preparing lunch, he stuffed his laptop in his backpack and headed out, with Molly, for the Beetle. Drab, low clouds had settled in for the day, but the air was dry and held no threat of rain. They followed the path along the coast, which offered more scenic views than the roadway, though there were also more hills to climb. The air smelled of salt, heather and seaweed. Molly, full of energy, occasionally darted off through the grasses to scamper down onto the sand and chase shorebirds. Thomas watched her, and noticed that after a few minutes, she'd routinely glance up to ensure he was nearby.

There was a small crowd in the Beetle, and Donal himself behind the bar. Unbidden, he poured a stout for Thomas and placed a saucer on the floor for Molly. Thomas selected a table near the hearth, shed his jacket and had a first mouthful of the beer. "Do you serve food?" he asked, wiping the foam from his upper lip.

"Beans on toast, tomato soup or a ham sarnie," answered the barman. "This ain't a feckin' carvery." Before Thomas could answer, he shuffled off, fetching plates from a table near the door, occupied by a single diner, a short, older man with unruly red hair.

"The soup would be great," Thomas shouted as Donal walked past on the way to the small kitchen. Molly had settled on the rug before the fire and was already asleep.

Thomas opened and powered up his laptop and logged on to check his emails. He considered messaging his sister, but knowing it was the middle of the night there, decided there wasn't enough pressing news to risk waking her.

He hadn't been on email for several weeks, and there was a long slog through various offers of worthless things for sale, fundraising schemes, prize drawings and a few urgent inquiries from solicitors in Nigeria, offering untold riches. And then, an email from Emma!

She was in Derry, or had been the other day, and had stopped in at the bookstore, where she had learned of his news.

"So excited for you! This is like an all-expenses paid vacation!"

Her writing was like her speech, full of exclamations and unrelentingly positive. He felt himself smiling just reading her words. Where he saw a prison sentence, she saw a holiday. What will you do, she asked? Write? Hike? "Whatever you do, you must take a lot of photos. Do you have an account on photolife? If not, get one and let me know your account name. I'll follow you. Search for Emma801. That's me. You can see my exploits at school."

And that was it. He searched for PhotoLife and discovered that it was primarily an application intended for smartphones. He picked up and looked at his mother's phone. He had begun taking some photos with it, he thought. And an account might allow him to keep in touch with Emma while she was back at school. He turned on the phone's wifi and clicked to download the app.

Then he turned back to his computer, and started an email to his sister. No doubt she'd be back into her work and social obligations by now. He looked it up and verified the 11-hour time difference. She'd probably be off to bed by now. No urgent need to send a message, which might wake her. The email he wrote told about his first few weeks in the house. He briefly recounted the cleaning and sorting. She'd be glad to know he was following through with that, so the place would be neat and tidy in case any potential buyers appeared. He didn't tell her his thoughts, that the real estate market out here seemed pretty dead on arrival and their mother's home was far from being the only house on the market - or the cream of the crop. On his very walk to the pub, he had passed several vacant homes that appeared truly massive in size.

He did tell her about Molly. Seemed to be a curious and intelligent dog. Empathetic, too. He wished he knew a bit more about the dog's past and history with his mother. He told her about meeting Cara and their walk and his new habit of daily hikes with Molly, never mind that this had been the first. He was discovering a part of the country he hadn't known much about. Remote. Windswept. No, windscrubbed.

Treeless. Even the low shrubs permanently bent and twisted by the winds that rushed up from the Atlantic, hell-bent for the hills. And the light. The amazing light. How even the grayest clouds or deepest blue skies appeared to hold a golden light within. It was probably the ocean, he thought. The light reflecting from the sea, the water molecules scattered in the air, refracting it in all different directions, helter-skelter-like.

Perhaps it was the approach of spring, carrying along brighter colors and longer days; the place had seemed all grays and browns the day they'd arrived. Now he was noticing nuance. The different shades of green woven together up the hillsides. The bonfires of gorse in full bloom. The violets and scarlets of the heather in thin ribbons along the fields leading down to the shore. The slate grays and silvers of the shore rock.

And the sea. The sea was a living thing, morphing daily, hourly even, some days. Blinding turquoise. Pale green. Pewter gray. Ink. Even the hue of a milky coffee at times, following sharp storms. A living thing.

Which reminded him to tell her about the seal. And about the Beetle. And the shore walk. And the two small islands, far off in the southwest. And he would have gone on if Donal hadn't delivered his soup. Instead, he signed off, told his sister he'd write again later in the week and turned to his lunch.

Donal was lingering nearby, poking and footering with the fire.

"So, you've lived here all your life, then," he asked.

"Hereabout."

"I've only been a couple of times before this, for short visits to my mother. Never really got to look around much before. There are so many abandoned houses."

Donal hung up the fire poker and straightened. "Aye, full of ghosts."

"You said people left when the fish ran out."

"Most of those houses stood empty longer than that," he said, wiping his hands on his apron. "You do know some feckin' Irish history, lad? Famine homes."

"I guess I figured with the fishing it wasn't so much of an issue here."

"Famine wasn't just a lack of food. Was a lack of food left for the Irish. Sure, start up through Muckish there and you'll find the Trail of Tears, the road to Derry and the boats to America. A wee bit on is the Bridge of Sorrows. The ones leaving said their last goodbyes there, all of them knowing they'd never see each other again." He looked down at Molly and sighed. "Lots of ghosts here. The dead won't ever leave. They'll wait forever for those to come back over the mountain." He walked away, back to the bar, and Thomas returned to his soup.

He was about to close up his laptop but noticed a reply from his sister. She was up late.

I'm glad you're settling in, Tommy. Molly sounds like a good companion. I'm sure mom was happy to have her company. It is hard to imagine the two of them hitting up bars, though! I guess there was a lot we didn't know about her. Anyway, I've got to get to bed. Take pictures! Love, Gin.

He smiled. Twice now he'd been told to take pictures. He looked down at Molly, in a tight circle before the bright fire. He knelt down on the floor before her and took a photo with his phone: Molly, her nose buried in her black and white tail, the warm peat embers glowing behind her. He hated to wake her, but it was time for the walk home.

He set an alarm for the next morning. He was up to get the early bus into Letterkenny and then the transfer to Derry. By catching the early bus, he'd be able to run his errands and be back before dark.

The bus route was circuitous, snaking up into the hills and angling down through valleys. At higher elevations, the plant life was low and close to the ground - subdued lichens and heathers in the early dawn light. The ground here was thick with peat and the streams that cut through the land ran the color of stout. Sheep were everywhere, having been moved up into the highlands for spring now that the land was coming back to life.

In the valleys, the land was crisscrossed by hedges and low stone walls and the roadsides were banked by thick tangles of wild fuchsia and rhododendron that blocked the view of the fields beyond. Farther inland from the coast and protected from the harsh Atlantic by the hills, human life seemed more prosperous here, though that was relative. Many of the cottages still had thatched roofs and most of the cars and tractors he saw were antiques. And the road itself, a main route, was often no wider than the bus.

The Letterkenny to Derry route leveled out onto rolling farmland and eventually located the River Foyle, following it into Derry. Thomas was bound for the bookstore, and a book.

Mrs. Caldwell was working, alongside a young woman with purple hair and a nose ring, who appeared to be in training on the intricacies of the ancient cash register. His replacement, no doubt. He was drawn into a short inquisition about his new surroundings and long-term plans, reminded that he had missed a visit from Emma, and brought up to speed on the latest gossip. This being Mrs. Caldwell, who was not the most loquacious sort, said gossip consisted entirely of her displeasure over the manner in which the window displays had been configured. "No idea what he was thinking, no one needs that many cookbooks!"

He nodded, and made his way back to the local history shelf. Anyone doubting the stereotypes about the Irish and their way with words would quickly be set straight by the amazing number of books written by the Irish about the Irish. The local history bookcase reached seven feet tall and three feet wide, more than half of the shelves filled by books on the Troubles. But he was seeking older history.

Thomas scanned the bottom shelf, where he knew the book he was looking for had sat, undisturbed, for decades. It was a thin paperback, a good fifty years old. "Curiosities and Antiquities of Western Donegal." If he was going to spend the next several months walking about the damn county, better to have some idea what he was looking at.

17

Fintan Feels Confident

The following week found Fintan back in Dublin. He had changed his mind about reaching back out to International Fisheries, deciding instead to wait for the company to respond to his first communication the week prior. He also decided to hold off on discussing anything about the fish farm with his supervisors and, as luck would have it, the first several days back in the office were sidetracked by two, day-long, impromptu sexual harassment training sessions announced following the finding of a semi-pornographic magazine in the newly-labeled unisex toilet on his floor. Fintan had nothing to do with it, of course. He guessed it belonged to the fellow three doors down who wore auto-darkening eyeglasses and always smelled of fish.

Still, though he loathed the training sessions and the awful role-playing games they involved, Fintan was happy for the distraction and for the delay it afforded him.

On Thursday, he received an email from International Fisheries. Not from Mr. Van der Vaart himself, but an assistant by the name of Ove.

Dear Mr. O'Dowd:
Our deepest sympathies for the passing of your comrade. We remain deeply distressed and angered by the lack of follow up displayed by your agency,

however. It is simply inconceivable that an important project of this nature could be so ignored by bureaucrats loitering in their office tower hundreds of miles away.

Indeed, our representatives personally visited the region and began cementing positive working relationships with local governments many months ago. They reported strong enthusiasm for this project from those government officials and from locals they engaged. It's important to note that our 20-year projections had indicated a potential for the creation of more than 200 jobs - and that does not include any infrastructure projects needed to support a venture of this size and importance.

Please be advised that a sector-leading firm such as ours does not sit still for long. In fact, we have already begun to more closely examine several other potential sites – all of which are located outside of your country. Frankly, financial losses due to your agency's delay are considerable. While we remain open to discussions as to how the Irish government may provide the necessary support to refloat this site, we simply must keep moving forward.

Sincerely,

Ove Knutson

Fintan smiled as he read the final paragraph. He slid the keyboard forward and unpacked his lunch: two ham sandwiches, two foil-wrapped triangles of soft cheese and a single-use container of chocolate yogurt. He set aside the three chocolate digestives for the mid-afternoon snack. Of course, International Fisheries was taking a hard line. This was a negotiation. They likely felt as though the situation provided the company with some leverage to demand greater government support.

He chomped at the sandwich, biting off almost half of it, leaving a small curl of crust. The yogurt was a concession to his health - his doctor had suggested probiotics for his nervous stomach. And so was his new routine of leaving the hearty crust on his sandwiches - though he still didn't eat them.

It wasn't likely that International Fisheries hadn't gotten far in selecting a new location. If he was right, people there were probably elated that their proposal hadn't been discarded outright. If they'd gone so far as greasing the pockets of local politicians, they'd already invested a considerable amount to develop this location. Starting over somewhere else was expensive. They didn't critically need money, they needed a face saving. They needed some poor bureaucrat to grovel.

And Fintan - well this Fintan, on the cusp of securing a huge economic development proposal for a Donegal backwater in the twilight of his long service to the agency – he could grovel.

He quickly typed out a reply to Ove. He expressed gratitude and relief that the company had not entirely abandoned the Dunnybegs site. He explained that he was the point person going forward on this proposal. And then he played the ace up his sleeve, disclosing that he had personally traveled to the region this past week on a fact-finding mission. The bay in question, he wrote, seemed perfectly suited to such an operation, in his opinion (which was entirely uninformed, though Ove did not need to know that). He would begin his work in earnest this week, he wrote, compiling the necessary research to prepare an economic impact statement - gathering unemployment data, average household income figures, business openings and closings (all fed into an arcane formula to determine an economic vigor rating for the region) and housing vacancies.

The data was critical, he wrote, but his own observations led him to believe the proposal would have full agency support. Then there was the issue of environmental impact. Fintan suggested again that his own findings would weigh heavily here. What he understood to be true but opted not to write was that no one in Dublin really gave a rat's ass about something in the far northwestern, god-forsaken corner of the island. Move some rocks? Dredge the harbor? Feck sake, only a few seagulls would ever notice.

He added that the locals he had spoken to all voiced excitement about the potential for new jobs coming to the region, though in truth it had only been the large, brutish bartender where he ate lunch who suggested business would be better off if folks drank more. Finally, he wrote, he agreed that time was of the essence, and he promised to move on this matter without further delay, if the company was prepared to resubmit its proposal. He was, he wrote, their humble servant.

That email sent, he composed another, this one to his supervisor, requesting a meeting on a matter of some urgency. Finished with that, he tossed his uneaten crusts into the garbage pail and set upon the cheese wedges, his wee fingers peeling back the foil covering.

18

A Familiar Sight

It was late afternoon when Thomas's bus disgorged him before the Dunnybegs butcher shop. The sky was preternaturally dark and the air damp. A storm was offshore some miles, bearing down on the coast.

He headed into the shop, carved into the ground level of the second townhouse on the main street. Fergal, the butcher, was chopping at a slab of beef behind the counter. He gave Thomas a nod when he entered. Fergal was a round man of average height, with a red face and dirty gray mustache. Thomas had never seen him in anything other than his white smock and tweed cap. He fastidiously kept a clean shop, and it never ceased to amaze Thomas that his smocks were spotless, given that he spent a good half of each day hacking and sawing apart blocks of meat.

The other surprise had been discovering that Fergal was the town's mayor. Thomas had come across him one day walking down the street, with the ceremonial chain of office draped over his chest. He did not meet Thomas's idea of a politician. The man wore a constant look of displeasure, as though he had encountered spoilt meat. It made him appear most unpleasant, though in person he was quite amiable.

As Thomas surveyed the cuts of meat in the case, Fergal stopped his work and fetched a bone from a small bucket behind the counter. "For herself. And what can I get you?"

Fergal did this every time Thomas stopped at the shop. Seemed Molly was a favorite here as well. Thomas picked out some bacon and minced meat and was waiting for his change when he noticed a small flier on the wall behind the counter. It was a letter-sized sheet of paper with the words GET OFF across the top in large print in two lines. The OFF spelled out Our Fish Farm.

"What's that about?" he asked, nodding at the sheet.

"Jobs," answered Fergal. "Folk wanting to bring fishing back to Dunnybegs. Plans for a big fish farm offshore there. Be grand to see some investment here."

"In our bay out here?" Thomas asked. "Wouldn't it ruin the view?" His reaction surprised himself. He hadn't spent much time thinking about the view before, or considering it 'his.'

"That view doesn't bring jobs." Fergal looked out the window, shook his head and sighed. "Not that it matters, most likely. The folks who were thinking about it have gone radio silent. They've probably forgotten about us. Everyone does."

Thomas stuffed the purchase into his backpack and set a brisk pace walking home. The western clouds over the sea were the color of coal smoke and charging across the sky. Rain soon. He wanted to get Molly out before the storm hit.

When he opened the door, the dog was already up by the door, her tail doing a slow wave back and forth. He let her out while he put away his purchases. He left the bone on the kitchen counter; she could occupy herself with that later, when the storm would keep them indoors. She returned quickly, pushing through the partially closed door and coming to sit by his feet as he washed a few dishes in the sink. He looked down at her and then at the reflection of the front window in the mirror. The western sky almost looked like night.

He'd spent most of his day on a bus and Molly had been indoors. It would be good for them both to get a short walk in, before the rain. "C'mon Molly, let's take a wee stroll." When he started towards the door, the dog jumped and darted through the doorway before him, then quickly turned to see that he was following.

The fresh air was not the only reason he wanted to head down to the strand. Armed with the news about a potential fish farm in the bay, he wanted to take a good look at the area. The butcher Fergal had seemed excited about the idea. No doubt a big development like that would be welcome in this depressed area. More jobs would mean more house buyers, most likely. But then he thought of Cara's button, Keep it Killfish. Surely that was related? She had sounded pretty adamant in her opposition to the name change. Was she against the fish farm itself?

And then he thought about the cottage, and the several others dropped across the slow slope of the land as it drew down to the sea. Would building a farm in the bay make them less valuable?

He honestly had no idea. He knew nothing about real estate or about fish farms, for that matter.

He looked out over the sea. Waves were crashing over the row of rocks that protected the bay and wide sweeps of whitecaps were rolling towards the shore. The tide was in. The sound of the surf was a constant low roar. Molly had wandered down near the water's edge and sat still for a moment, in profile to him. The wind was tugging at her fur and pulling her left ear horizontal. He took a couple of quick photos, changing exposure between them to capture more detail in the blackening sky, and then called her to head home.

The dark was settling in over the land now as well. The distant hills were dark green shadows huddled beneath the dull gray eastern sky. Lights from the few homes scattered about appeared as bright stars spread across the land. Before him, Molly scrambled up and over the stone wall and darted up the hill towards the road. Thomas stared after her and then his gaze returned to the stone wall. He had photographed Molly on the wall a week or so previously, but something else about the wall called out to him. He had seen it before.

Back in the cottage, he shrugged off his coat and hat, kicked off his shoes and slumped onto the couch. He grabbed the photo of his mother he had set aside. There she was, with the mystery woman, sitting on a wall, with low hills rising behind her. He started at the wall. Then he picked up his phone and scrolled through his several dozen photos, stopping when he found the one he had taken of Molly. Of Molly, sitting on the wall. He held it up next to the print.

Both he and Molly were damp by the time they had reached the house, from sea spray being picked up and carried aloft by the strong winds. Still, he considered heading back out until the sound of big drops rattled the window. He wanted to see the wall for himself, to stand there again and look back up towards the land.

It was the same wall. He was sure of it.

His mother had lived here these past several years - her final years. She had searched for a place on the coast and finally found this one. Both Thomas and his sister believed she had been running away, escaping the cruelty of her life in Derry and seeking solitude in this unknown, remote place.

Except it wasn't unknown. She had been here before. Some forty-odd years earlier, a smiling, happy Helen had walked down to the bay and stopped to sit on a wall and pose for a photo. What was she doing here? And who was the woman beside her?

19

Fishing for Good News

The president of International Fisheries Inc. was back from his golfing vacation. Two weeks in Hawaii had left him bronzed and relaxed. He was a large man, a former football player in high school who now endeavored to stay in shape but whose body reflected his 60 years of physical activity – sturdy, yes, but with a spreading midsection and a slightly bent over stride, due to years of knee and hip issues. His white hair was short cropped and his jaw square. He dressed casually, with khaki slacks and a teal polo shirt.

From his office, on the fourth and top floor of the wide building stretched along one of the less attractive piers on the Seattle waterfront, far from the Public Market and tourists, he could see the looming Olympic Mountains and noticed that the snow cover was diminishing. Summer was on its way.

International Fisheries was, contrary to Van der Vaart's constant claims, quite removed from the top ranks of companies in the fishing industry. There were numerous Russian and European Union companies who operated gargantuan fishing fleets and constructed farming operations the size of small states. International Fisheries instead specialized in smaller farms, mostly operating in third world countries, where regulations were more relaxed and politicians more easily persuaded. It was the key to the company's success - lax regulatory oversight meant less monitoring and that meant fewer employees. And the people he did employ earned miniscule wages. Overhead was low; profits robust. And now the company was on the verge of implementing a whole new operational breakthrough that guaranteed, Van der Vaart believed, incredible success.

Truth was, consumer awareness of food safety issues was catching up with companies such as International Fisheries. There were organizations now that graded fish based on such issues as sustainability, humane processes and regulatory oversight and the fish from International Fisheries had received more than a few failing grades. The easy profitability of erecting huge farming pens in sewage-ridden waters had likely reached its zenith.

Fortunately, Van der Vaart had experienced an epiphany.

Commercial fishing had already undergone great changes before the notion of farming fish had appeared. Fishing was a multi-part operation. Ships went out to sea and, using a variety of methods, caught fish. When enough had been caught, the ships returned to port, where the fish were transferred to a facility to be processed. Over time, that system saw the establishment of true fishing ports, protected harbors where whole fleets of fishing vessels docked, and then the building of processing plants. But it also meant that more and more people – and companies – were financially dependent on the catch. More and more fish had to be caught to remain profitable.

If the ships could be made larger, if they could hold more fish, if they could remain at sea longer, well, that helped. Eventually, someone hit upon the idea of processing the catch onboard the ship. The fish could be flash-frozen and held onboard while the ship continued fishing, remaining at sea longer and reducing the unproductive time spent docked in port. Commercial open-sea fishing vessels were huge, now, and could process and store vast amounts of fish.

Fish farming, of course, removed the need for the ship altogether. You built a farm and hired laborers to harvest the fish and then move them to a processing facility. You could get by with relatively few employees at the farm, but you still needed a processing plant onsite.

Van der Vaart's brainstorm, his spark of genius, his baby that would transform International Fisheries into a top tier operation, was this: build a series of farms located close together and utilize a ship to travel from farm to farm, harvesting and processing the fish. No on-shore processing plant would be required, just the one ship. Each farm would require no more than a handful of employees to provide routine maintenance and push some buttons – hell, if you had several farms located closely together, it could be the same crew, scuttling back and forth. By reducing the number of employees needed, Van der Vaart could slash overhead costs and build farms pretty much anywhere.

This idea literally opened up the world to International Fisheries. No longer would he be limited to third world cesspools. His idea would work anywhere he could establish a minimum of three farms within a 100-or-so-mile stretch of coast. His team had eyed up several locations along the Black Sea, but Van der Vaart was more enthusiastic about the northwest coast of Ireland. Hell, he could grow the fish anywhere for about the same cost, but the premium he could get from selling fish caught off the coast of Ireland? Priceless!

His team had located a prime spot and had already spent time on the ground, first assessing potential local reaction and then undertaking a support-building operation. There were concerns over the place name, but efforts to change it to something more palatable seemed promising. The locals had been won over, his team reported.

But there was a problem: Dublin. He hadn't anticipated the complete lack of response he'd gotten from government officials. For six months now, his team sent letters, emails, even boxes of apple wood smoked salmon, along with detailed descriptions of the proposal for the first farm. All of it disappeared into a bureaucratic black hole in dreary Dublin.

He'd resorted to bluster. Nothing. A personal trip to Dublin with envelopes of cash was next. But that morning, on his way into the office, Ove had sent him a text. "Good news," it said.

20

Weathering a Storm

The storm arrived that evening in Dunnybegs, shortly after Thomas finished his dinner. The whole of the island would feel it, but the stretch of coast from Sligo up to the far northern tip of the Inishowen peninsula would bear its brunt. A monster. The sea curled and rose up in 40-foot waves that slashed at beaches and picked up and heaved boulders. The wind intensified to a steady, unrelenting howl that bowed and uprooted trees miles inland and drove the spray from the surf up and over 100-foot-tall sea cliffs. It was a spectacular storm, formed far out in the middle of the Atlantic and then exploding up in a long northeastern arc along the Gulf current, gathering strength hourly. Its gravity sucked the bottom out of barometric pressure readings and violently swallowed the remaining daylight. At Killfish Bay, the swells easily surmounted the natural breakwater, and the surf surged across the dunes and into the small parking lot.

Thomas wisely stayed in. He watched his new television at first, but the noise - the howl of the wind, the thundering crash of the surf and the angry drumbeat of rain strafing the windows – was overwhelming, a ceaseless screaming that circled the house in its fury.

A short while later, the power cut out. He wasn't terribly worried about his safety, the house had stood here for more than a century, after all, but the energy of the storm, combined with the revelation about his mother, had left him anxious. He found himself longing for company - the first time since moving here that he really felt keenly aware of his solitude. Hell, his mother had pretty much died here, lying alone for who knew how long before help arrived, too late.

He got up and paced into the kitchen, found a torch and then his mother's old bottle of sherry and poured himself a wee dram. He stopped and peered into the bedroom. Molly was curled in her bed. He walked over to reach down and rub her neck. When she raised her head, he noticed one of his T-shirts rumpled underneath her and one of his slippers on its side by her hip.

"Ah Molly, are you a bit anxious, too? Come on, girl." He turned and walked back into the living room, Molly following. He dropped back down on the couch, set his glass on the table, tucked the torch on his left shoulder and picked up the book he had bought earlier that day. Then he patted the seat beside him and Molly took his direction, jumping up and circling twice before plopping down next to him, resting her head on his left thigh. He looked down at her deep brown eyes and scratched beside her ear before settling his left hand on her side, which was smooth and warm. She closed her eyes and let out a deep sigh. Unawares, he sighed too.

The book was a revelation. Written first in the 1950s, it painted a picture of a place even less spoiled by modern life. Donegal, the author maintained, was a magical place, ignored by most of the world, but revered by the folk who lived here. They knew its treasures – the sacred wells, the fairy rings, the standing stones, the ancient crosses erected by St. Columba himself. By the author's description, every bend in every road stood ready to reveal another of the region's riches, either historic relic or geographic beauty.

It was a sparse book, 78 pages of mechanical prose. The author was an English civil engineer who had vacationed in Donegal since his own childhood in the early '30s and his aim was to succinctly document the relics and ruins of the region. His writing, devoid of flourish or fluff, was a balm for Thomas, who devoured the text, adding notes in the margins and dog-earing particularly interesting pages.

In this realm, on the particular topic of preserving these treasures, Donegal's remoteness had served it well. Abandoned famine cottages stood next to pastures where cows moseyed and munched at the tall grasses surrounding the base of each standing stone of an ancient ring. And the bushes that had grown for centuries from the fertile soil of a sacred spring still received new tokens and wishes daily, neatly tied to their branches.

Outside, the sky beat at the earth. The sea hurled itself upon the shore over and over. The heavens howled and shrieked. The windows rattled. The fire smoldered on. The sherry evaporated, warming Thomas's throat and steadying his nerves. Molly remained coiled in a tight circle at his side, her breathing slow and hypnotic.

He finished the book and then started in on it again, scrutinizing the hand-drawn map and noting the curiosities and antiquities near him. The hills and fields were strewn with them.

Even as nature itself seemed determined to wipe the land from the earth, as desolate and empty the place had until now appeared to him, he was struck by how much history – and how much life – the place held.

At some point in the evening, the crescendo of white noise lulled him to sleep, and he woke at first light, curled awkwardly on the couch, Molly still at his side. The house was cold, and he was stiff. He stood, straightened himself, listened for the rain still slapping the front window, and shuffled to his bedroom. Molly followed, and as he settled into his bed, he looked down to see Molly making a small circle in her bed.

"Hey Molly," he called, patting the bed beside him. She didn't hesitate a moment, leaping up and dramatically dropping alongside him. The bed itself was cold but Thomas could already feel Molly's warmth pressing against his leg. They both quickly lapsed back into their slumber.

It was Molly, eager to get outside to relieve herself, that finally woke him, mid-morning. The rain had stopped and the sky was brightening, with brilliant white and dark gray clouds racing overhead, revealing a deep azure sky beyond. It would be a grand day for a walk.

Later that morning, he packed his laptop and new book in his backpack, corralled Molly and headed out. He'd start south, stopping at the Beetle for a light lunch and cup of tea, before turning inland, away from the coast.

He had intended to walk the coastal walk the entire way, but sections of it were lost in deep mud after the storm. The first such pool he encountered was both deeper and more viscous than he had anticipated and he almost lost a shoe. After that, he angled for the road and followed it south. It meant some of the most dramatic views of the sea cliffs were obscured by the land and vegetation, but today he was more interested in some of the sights mentioned in his book anyway.

It was quiet in the Beetle. Donal was behind the bar, fussing with the taplines. He nodded at the man and dog as they entered. "I've no stout for ye's," he shouted.

"Actually a cup of tea would be grand. And a sandwich, when you get the chance."

Thomas chose a table near the fire and Molly quickly spun twice and lowered herself into a ball before the fireplace. The fire was bright and warm; Donal must have recently gifted it with a fresh brick of peat.

Sitting facing the fire, Thomas imagined what the place must have been like in better days. It was always dark, regardless of the time of day. A string of colored Christmas lights were hung along the wall behind the bar and their jewel tones warmed the clear and brown liquor bottles gathered haphazardly below them on the back counter. The two neon-like signs were from more modern times, but the fire and candles on each table supplied much of the light. It made the place feel like a sanctuary of sorts, which, come to think of it, it was. After a back-breaking day in the fields or days away at sea, the warm, cozy Beetle must have felt like heaven. Even on a sparkling bright, crisp day, the Beetle felt like a prelude to a nap.

Molly had the right idea. Thomas got out the phone, got down on his knees and took a photo of her curled before the golden flames.

Then he sat back at the table and opened his laptop, signing on to the wifi signal. He had figured out how to access his email account with the phone, but he found typing on it tedious.

An email, from Ginny. She had no news to report on the house. No interested buyers, though of course he'd probably know of any before her. Some money from their mother's estate was freed up and she'd deposit it in his bank account. Would cover his basic expenses through the summer, which was her way of breaking it to him that he'd most likely be here at least through fall. She hinted at a possible visit at the end of summer. It would be nice to see her, he thought.

Next, he logged onto PhotoLife. The first photo he had posted, of the bay at sunset, had two likes, from Cara and Emma. He had no other followers. And then he checked their pages. Both full of university life, of selfies and lattes and busy streets and books.

College wasn't for him. He did try, attending Magee College in Derry for a year, but nothing really interested him. Stay at it, people told him. The first year is all general ed classes and you'll find something that sparks you, that ignites a passion. It wasn't math. It wasn't science. Wasn't writing or business. He stuck it out for a year but was relieved when the spring semester ended.

Passion. Such an awkward subject. Did people really just suddenly discover it? What, did they read something in a book or hear something in a lecture and think, Oh my god, this! This is what my life has been missing!

He had encountered no such epiphany. Ever. Actually, he hadn't thought much about it. But now, sitting in this wee pub on a remote corner of the world, he felt a little envious of Emma and Cara, of their cluttered, intense lives and their passions.

He clicked "like" on their photos, one by one, and then uploaded a couple of his. Molly at Killfish Bay, the setting sun casting daffodil-colored rays across the dark sky; Molly, at the shop, her and the plastic ice cream cone mirrored in the puddle in the foreground; Molly, on the stone wall at dusk, the lights from houses scattered across the hillside behind her like so many small bonfires; Molly in the Beetle, a picture of serenity before the cozy fire.

She was such a photogenic dog, the proto-typical Irish farm and beach dog. He wondered how many other people had come across her on the beach at Killfish and snapped a photo of her and then reminded himself that Killfish was far off the beaten tourist path.

Now, spending time here, he found that difficult to understand. It was breathtakingly beautiful, this corner of the island, with its coast scalloped by the never-ending tug of war between earth and sea. Even on the gloomiest of days, with the sky so low that it collects on the heather and moss and the horizon itself disappears, even then the colors were radiant. The purple of the heather. The striations of green up the hillside. The tannin-dyed waters of the small creeks. The olives, slates, reds and khakis of the pebbles on some of the beaches. And the sky! The sky that never looked the same twice. Was the sky like this in Derry? Had it been this luminous? He hadn't noticed.

His reverie was interrupted by the clank of Donal dropping the plate with his sandwich on the table. Brown bread, butter, ham and cheese. He took a bite and the simple flavors settled on his tongue. Bliss! The saltiness of the ham, the sweetness of the butter, the tang of the cheese and the nuttiness of the bread. The flavors danced together. The ingredients were nothing special - he had seen Donal in the grocery store stocking up for the bar - but on this day at this moment, they were delightful in their straightforwardness.

He ate slowly, washing each bite down with a sip of still-hot tea. He was no less lonely than he had been the night before. If anything, he'd been reminded of how remote and still his life was. Yet he felt surrounded by life, by warmth. Such was the power of the Beetle.

21

Fintan is Appreciated

Hamid Bakari smiled slightly as Fintan entered his office. Hamid was the assistant to the undersecretary of economic development and, while his office paled in comparison to the undersecretary's, it was clearly superior to Fintan's closet of an office. Like Fintan's, it had a smallish window, but this one would not require one to mount the desk to peer out.

"Fintan! Good to see you. Tell me, how is your family?" Hamid leaned back in his chair and clasped his hands on his chest.

"Well," stammered Fintan, "it's just my parents."

"Of course. And how are they?"

Fintan looked down at the desk. "They are, ah, well, they are both passed away. I meant they were my only family." He didn't really blame Hamid for being unfamiliar with his personal life, they had only met a few times since Hamid arrived a decade or so prior.

"Ah, well..." Hamid looked away, out the window for a moment, as if a distraction might appear, but then sat forward and stared right at Fintan. "Your email said you had some potentially big news."

Fintan was relieved to move on to business. "Well, sir..."

"Hamid. Call me Hamid." His mouth remained in a slight, wry smile.

His eyes were slightly obscured by wire-framed glasses that had a faint tint to the lenses.

Fintan managed a smile. "Well, on my very first day at this assignment, I discovered that an important piece of business had fallen through the cracks."

"Go on."

"A major international fishing concern had submitted a proposal to construct a fish farming operation in County Donegal."

"A fish farm? I hadn't heard anything about that."

"No, of course not. You wouldn't," said Fintan. "You see, the proposal arrived sometime immediately following Mr. Gaines'... well..."

"After he passed away? Ah, I see."

"I think the company figured the initial lack of response was, umm, just the usual pace of governmental affairs so thought nothing of it. They continued their planning, even sending representatives to the area in question to lobby local citizens and politicians. It seems they were met with a welcoming response, so they continued with their plans."

Hamid nodded.

"But eventually, the complete lack of communication from us impacted their planning, as it would. And just the week before I started in this position, they sent us a very angry communication declaring that they were abandoning the project and giving up on any future plans to do business in Ireland."

"Oh dear." Hamid frowned and turned his gaze back to the window. He took a deep breath.

"Well Fintan, thank you for bringing this to my attention. Of course, you are in no way responsible for this, you needn't worry. I think perhaps if we just put this matter behind us and never mention it again, no one will be the wiser."

"Oh, no, that isn't the end of it. You see, I responded to the company right away and explained the unfortunate situation in our office and asked them to reconsider."

"Oh." Hamid looked a bit puzzled, as he tried to sort out in his mind whether or not this represented a positive development.

"I think, well, I think I have them convinced to go ahead with the proposal, sir."

Hamid's face brightened, ever so slightly. "Well, there would need to be an economic assessment performed, and then they'd require environmental approval. It's all a lot..."

"With all that in mind, sir, I took a vacation day and personally visited the area in question. I toured the region, conducted an informal economic review, and even visited the aforementioned bay itself."

"On your own time?" Hamid grinned. "Now, that is initiative!"

Fintan felt himself blush, but pressed on. "The region appears quite depressed. Many empty storefronts, abandoned houses, etc. The small bay being considered for the farm is unremarkable and the residents and business people I spoke with were in favor of any sort of business development that could bring jobs." He leaned back and smiled.

"Remarkable! And the company has agreed to reconsider?"

"I believe they will," said Fintan. Hamid's response was even more positive than he had dared hope. Still, he was soaked in sweat.

Hamid stood, and quickly walked around the desk, his right arm extended to shake Fintan's hand.

"Fintan, this is the sort of work that gets noticed, you know. Next, you should conduct an economic assessment."

"I already have, sir."

"Hamid."

"Yes, sorry."

Hamid now had his other hand on Fintan's shoulder and was leading him toward the door. "Wonderful. Now, you will need to schedule an official fact-finding mission yourself."

"Yes sir, I will."

"And Fintan, do it on work time this time." Hamid laughed and Fintan smiled and then he was out the door and Hamid had closed it.

22

The Storm Passes

The sky over Donegal cleared in the afternoon. Steady winds helped dry the roads. About a mile or so south of the Beetle, Thomas and Molly followed a road angling up into the hills, away from the coast. Occasionally, the view opened to reveal the ragged coast, its cliffs and bays dark against the brilliance of the blue sea and undulating whitecaps. He glimpsed at one point the next town south along the coast, with its built harbor and forsaken fishing vessels. And all along the walk, houses, some occupied, with dark smoke pulled from their chimneys at sharp angles by the breeze, but many empty and some just the barest of foundations. Fossils, hinting at the lives once lived here.

Stone walls in various stages of disrepair crisscrossed the land, partitioning the fields into irregular shapes. Thomas thought of the men, women and children who had built those walls. Backbreaking work, digging and hauling rocks big and small from the surrounding fields. Thinking about the walls reminded him of the photo of his mother and the mystery woman. Next time he headed out to the pub, he'd bring it along. Perhaps someone there would be able to identify the woman?

Just then, a flash of starlings broke from the hedgerow along the roadside, ascending en masse overhead before curling back towards them. Molly barked at them, crouching, her tail swishing, but the flock disappeared over a hill.

Shaken from his thoughts, Thomas realized that they were likely close to the turn-off he was seeking, and as they walked on a short distance, he saw it – a small unmarked lane slicing through a stand of trees.

The lane was dirt - mud actually - and he was forced to circumnavigate large, boggy puddles along the pathway. Molly bounded forward, unbothered. She would need a bath, he thought.

Their path emerged from the trees and curved leftward up a small ascent. At its crest, Thomas saw their destination. Arranged in the field before him lay a circle of upright rectangular stones, some 150 feet or so in diameter. Dozens of stones, many as large as himself.

His book told him this stone circle was four to five thousand years old, perhaps older than Stonehenge or the pyramids.

He slowly walked the full circle, reaching out his hand to touch each stone. The millennia had worn and eroded the surface of each, but some bore faint designs carved into them, still apparent to the touch, though their meaning had been lost to the ages.

The circle may have had associations with the calendar and the passage of seasons, with the location of the sun in relation to the stones measuring the days of the year and marking the four ancient Celtic feast days. In fact, the feast of Beltane, May 1, was just days away. In some places, it was still celebrated, the triumph of the sun over the darkness marked by the lighting of bonfires

He took some pictures of the stones, but the size of the construction and the bright sunlight left the photos washed out and unremarkable. "Hey, Molly! C'mere girl."

The dog, which had wandered off to sniff at a hedgerow, galloped up and sat before him, her head stiffly erect and her eyes sharp. She was enjoying the walk.

He took several photos of her - she lent scale to the monumental stones behind and around her. As he did so, he looked around them. The stone circle sat on high ground, with commanding views of the surrounding land, to the coast on the west and the higher hills of Donegal to their northeast. Sparse white clouds sped overhead on the jet stream, the sky thatched with several jet contrails.

It was breathtaking.

He thought of the storm the previous day, of how the sea and sky punished the earth and of the darkness that held the day in its grip. Winter could be brutal in a place like this, a steady broadside of gales that chomped at the coast and drove the near-frozen rain horizontally. Yet folk lived here, surviving for 5,000 years at least. They huddled by fires and each spring they lifted the rocks that the earth pushed to the surface of their fields and then scraped at the thin topsoil to farm or they took to that very monster sea in hand-hewn boats and fished for their dinner.

And on this day, as Thomas slowly turned to take in the view – of the patchwork greens on the distant hills, the far-off sapphire sea and the flames of bright yellow gorse blooming in the countryside like so many Beltane bonfires – he understood why they stayed.

23

The Trail Runs Cold

Fergal arrived home from his day at work to find a shepherd pie in the oven and a stack of mail on the kitchen table. His wife, Bridie, was at the sink, washing up a few pots and utensils from the meal preparation. She glanced over her shoulder at him and nodded toward the table.

"Plenty of mail today. And I opened a pint for ye."

"Ta, love." He nudged beside her and dipped his hands in the soapy water, shook them over the sink and grabbed a dish towel to dry them. Then he took the first big drink of the stout and held it in his mouth a moment before swallowing. Then he grabbed the full stack of letters and looked through them, examining the return address quickly before tossing each one back on the table.

"Anything today?" Bridie asked.

He sighed. "No. Not a thing."

Another disappointment.

As a mayor and business owner, Fergal was used to a deluge of mail. Most of it was trash. Usually, the official mail, from Letterkenny or Dublin, got sorted out first. He'd save those for opening on Tuesday or Thursday evenings. The mayoral position was a very part time post and he preferred it that way. A time and place for everything, he always thought.

But lately, he was almost frantic as he rifled through the mail each day, looking for something, anything, from International Fisheries. Six months previously, he'd never heard of the company. But then the first letter arrived, followed by a handful more and finally, by the appearance of several representatives of the company. They had visited him in an official capacity, seeking his informal backing for the proposed fish farm. Fergal, being a careful and deliberate person, had been lukewarm in his response though privately he was excited about the potential development.

It was the follow up visit, by a higher up at International Fisheries, when things got a bit more interesting.

To begin with, the fellow had turned up at his butcher shop and spent most of the time talking about his business. "You don't have many seafood offerings, do you?"

Fergal had conceded that he hadn't, but that it was not for lack of desire. Just not enough customers and, with the disappearance of any local fishing concerns, the stock he could obtain was pricey. His dream, he had told the man, had always been to expand into the empty space next door, to become a fishmonger, but with his current sales, no bank would underwrite the loans needed.

Which was when the man, Ove, he was called, had leaned toward Fergal and said, "Perhaps we could help."

A successful fish farming operation would mean a good supply of locally-raised and caught fish, of course, which is what Fergal had assumed Ove was suggesting. Later, when he ran the conversation back in his mind, he realized that the farm would probably specialize in just one species of fish and obviously wouldn't be able to supply an entire store.

No, Ove had been suggesting something else entirely. Financial backing.

International Fisheries was a huge operation, with farms across the globe. They were eager to break into the European market. Very eager. "Would 30,000 euros help?"

Was it a loan? Fergal could call it that, if he wanted, Ove had said. "It would be in the company's interest to have a local retailer selling our product." Maybe a partnership would be a better description, though considering Fergal's role as mayor it would perhaps be better if he didn't really talk much about the 'investment,' as Ove called it.

That had been four months ago. For several weeks, communication from Ove continued. Fergal obtained access to the space next door and visited it several times, walking through the space and imagining how he'd transform it. The project would have to be fully approved before any money could be freed up, or course, Ove had told him. That made sense. But Ove had also assured him that the company was in fast-moving mode. "This is how we stay on top of the game," he told Fergal. "We move fast."

And then, all communication stopped. The letters stopped. The emails and texts ceased. Nothing had yet been signed. Fergal sent several emails, which had gone unanswered.

Each day, he hurried home. Each day, Bridie set the day's post on the kitchen table, next to his stout. Each day, he shuffled through the stack. Nothing.

"Maybe send them another email?" Bridie suggested as she lifted the pie from the oven. The smell was heavenly. Good mincemeat. Fergal sighed. "Aye, I'll try again tomorrow."

24

Hashtag Shamrock

The days immediately following Thomas's walk to the standing stone circle were poor. The weather soured. Low clouds settled in over the land and stalled. The Gulf Stream was torpid. He and Molly walked, but only up to the store and back. It felt as though one were striding through a cloudbank and every surface of oneself was soaked within minutes. Each time they returned, he toweled Molly off and she warmed herself by the fire. He did the same, supping a hot cuppa.

His work meant cleaning and sorting his mother's belongings, and he had made as much progress as was possible for now. The furniture and appliances would remain as long as he occupied the house and he was reluctant to remove any of the paintings or other knick knacks decorating the place. The one painting he had removed revealed a white shadow on the wall, unblemished by smoke from the chimney or stove. He replaced that painting and opted to leave the others hanging.

He was still without an internet connection in the cottage. He had been reluctant to commit to it when he was so unsure how long he'd be in the place, but now, as it was beginning to look as though he may be there through the summer, he was reconsidering. His mother's mobile, of course, had access through her cell signal, but Thomas was reluctant to run up its fees.

On the third day, it brightened somewhat, as the pale light of a weak sun worked its way through the cloud cover. It offered no promise of warmth, but the sight of it cheered him and he decided a walk to the Beetle was in order. He stowed his laptop in its backpack, grabbed a rain hat just in case, and headed out with Molly.

He pointed toward the road, as the coastal path was still a muddy mire after the past several days' weather. When he got to it, though, he was struck by a blast of wind. The gusts were barreling straight from the south, meaning the whole way to the Beetle would be into the face of the gales. He stood stock still a moment, and then wheeled to face in the opposite direction. He still hadn't visited the Shamrock.

It was a much shorter walk. They passed the mart, Fergal's store, the post office, a hairdresser, a resale shop, the empty, boarded-up entrance to what had been a substantial hotel, several more empty storefronts and the brightly painted front doors of the few people living along the main road. Molly, of course, was greeted warmly by everyone they passed, with shouts of "hey girl!" and pats on the head, but by now Thomas was recognized and greeted as well. The classic greeting from the men was a slight dip of the head and a mumbled "hiya." Women were generally more willing to make eye contact and ask about his day or health or express condolences about his mother. He was slowly becoming a member of the community himself.

The Shamrock was at the end of the block, its exterior walls a deep green hue and the name over the door in a bright yellow, celtic-inspired font.

Thomas wasn't generally inclined to spend much time in bars. They were often too noisy to concentrate or converse and he wasn't much of a drinker. He was also a creature of habit, which helped explain why he hadn't ventured into the Shamrock yet - the Beetle was now familiar.

But the Beetle had also changed his perception of pubs. It was not a chaotic collection of rowdy twenty-somethings like the ones in Derry. It was cozy, quiet and warm - a gathering place for the community, likely helped along by the relative lack of young people in the area.

He opened the door, holding Molly's leash in his hand.

"Are ye going to let the whole Atlantic in? C'mon. Get yous in here."

Molly hurried in and Thomas followed, letting the door close behind him.

"Molly girl, it's been a while!" The man behind the bar appeared genuinely pleased to see the dog.

The bar was a long L shape running the length of the room to Thomas's right. A scattering of small round tables lay before him. Along the left side were a series of booths separated by four-foot-tall walls. There was a couple in one of the booths, their heads barely visible over the riser. An ancient looking fellow sat midway along the bar. And behind it stood the bartender.

Eamonn was his name. A small, wiry man with a crooked nose, wisps of dark brown hair and a perpetual look of anxiety on his face. A former merchant marine from Sligo, he spent most of his adult life at sea, coming up to Donegal for short visits just long enough to get his land legs under him again.

One of those visits, an evening visit to the Shamrock for a pint or two, brought him face to face with Isabella, the stout and robust widow who ran the place. Eamonn came back the following night, and the one after that, until work called and he left for several months at sea. But when he returned following that trip, after sailing to South Africa and then India, he purchased a small cottage just up the hill, wooed Isabella, whom he had determined while at sea was the love of his life, eventually married her, and never left land again.

That was fifteen years ago, the best years of Eamonn's life. Years of warmth and comfort and safe harbor and laughter and of losing himself in her hugs. She changed him. The quiet, introspective loner became an attentive barman and good conversationalist. On Sundays, they walked, strolling the lanes and pathways of Donegal, and Eamonn, the lifelong sailor, grew enamored of the hills and bays that held little Dunnybegs snug. He could no longer imagine what it was he had seen in the wide-open sea, in the endless roiling waves of muddy blue and gray, the horizon empty.

They still walked, Eamonn and Izzy, but the boisterous woman who pointed out landmarks and shared personal histories had disappeared into her own fog bank.

Alzheimer's, the doctors called it. Dementia. She was losing her mind. She had come unmoored from her past and now spoke mostly gibberish. And now the positions were reversed, and Eamonn was her safe harbor, her comfort, as much as was possible.

They had years earlier moved into the flat above the pub for convenience and Eamonn manned the bar and Izzy remained upstairs, watching her collection of beloved Westerns on the television and drifting. The townspeople all knew, of course, and no one raised an eyebrow when Eamonn and Izzy passed them on the street, with Izzy raging about Indians or bandits.

Eamonn was not one for regrets. His time at sea was what it was. He had a good twelve years with Izzy, before she began to slip from him. But his eyes were those of a sailor watching water fill the boat.

"You're Helen's, are ye?" he asked Thomas, who had settled onto a stool at the end of the bar nearest the door. Thomas wasn't sure about the place, and the seat was the most non-committal in the place.

"Aye. Thomas." Molly circled and dropped down at his feet. She seemed comfortable enough in the place.

Then the other man at the bar stood and walked towards them, before sitting down again next to Thomas. He looked ancient. A tweed coat and cap. Muddy dungarees and wellingtons. A face of lines and creases. Grey, rheumy eyes. He made a wet, growling sound, spit into his empty glass and looked over Thomas. "You taking care of our girl?"

"Molly, oh yes," Thomas answered. "She's taking care of me."

"I'm Eamonn," said the bartender, setting a pint of Guinness before Thomas and then nodding towards the old man. "This is Billy. He's harmless."

"The feck," said the old man. "I could still toss ye over the bar!"

Eamonn laughed. "You settling in okay, lad?"

Thomas told him he was, recounting the walks he and Molly had been taking, and the long process of cleaning out his mother's belongings. He told them about the book he'd bought and his growing interest in the history of the place.

"He's your man for that," said Billy, pointing at Eamonn. "He and his missus have walked every path for miles around."

Green, red and white Christmas lights ran along the wall over the booths and a free-standing fireplace warming the place by the back door. Thomas's initial wariness was fading. The beer may have helped. The three chatted a bit. Billy was a farmer. Had lived here all his life. Looked to be in his 80s, but who knew?

After some conversation, Thomas pulled his phone from his pocket. "Do you have wi-fi here?" he asked.

"I do. Give me a few minutes and I'll turn it on," answered Eamonn.

Billy saw Thomas's puzzled look and grinned. "He's afraid to waste it, lad. Doesn't like to leave it running."

After a few minutes waiting for the router to boot up, Thomas logged on with this laptop, entered the password Shamrock and opened his PhotoLife account.

He scrolled through the photos he had posted. Emma and Cara had both "liked" several of the images and Emma had commented on one, complementing its composition. But that was it. No other likes or comments.

Beside him, Billy was eyeing the screen. "You's on PhotoLife?" he asked.

"Um, yeah. Just started the other week. Not much of a response, though."

Billy spat again in the empty cup. "Ye need to use feckin' hashtags!" he growled.

"What?"

"The hashtags! It's how other folk find you. You know, the wee tic-tac-toe thing, followed by some shite like landscape, or Donegal, or bordercollie. All one word, like."

Thomas maneuvered to Emma's account and scrolled through her posts. Indeed, each one of her images was followed by a long list of hashtags, and her images had dozens of likes and several comments. Cara's, too.

"Here, go back to your photos and we'll add some," Billy said. Thomas was dumbfounded. Billy's hands were stained dark and his fingers gnarled and twisted. He couldn't picture him using a computer at all.

Eamonn smiled at Thomas. "Billy has a granddaughter away at school in America, don't you Billy?"

"Aye, my wee Saoirse. I have a tablet so I can video chat with her. And follow her on PhotoLife. If you tell me your account, I'll follow you, too."

"It's um, Mollybegs," Thomas answered. Jesus, Billy looked like an image from an old Irish history book, but he was more technologically advanced than himself.

The three of them scrolled through each of Thomas' photos and added what they thought were appropriate hashtags. Then they watched as Thomas uploaded several new photos from his walk to the stone circle. Next, they briefly searched within the application, discovering that certain hashtags, such as #donegal, #bordercollies and #Irishtourism, were very popular. "People love dogs," said Billy.

"Aye, as common as sheep, like," added Eamonn. "People love them, and Molly's a beautiful wee dog."

Thomas glanced down at her, still curled into a tight ball, snoring lightly.

"She is beautiful," he agreed. Then he slid off his stool and knelt down several feet away from her, before taking a photo of the sleeping dog.

"Hashtag sleeping dog," said Billy, flashing a toothless grin.

"Hashtag Shamrock," added Eamonn.

25

The Post Arrives

At half past five, Fergal began the closing-up process in his shop, draping plastic covers over the cuts of meat in the display cases, washing down the work surfaces and ensuring each day that the refrigeration units were set to the correct temperature. They always were – once programmed, they ran continuously. He checked each day anyway.

The cash drawer was emptied, its contents counted and then deposited into a bank courier bag, minus 50 Euros to be left for the following day. When the shop was clean and the knives slotted away and the money sorted, Fergal double checked that the back door was bolted, donned his coat, tucked the bank bag under his arm, turned off the main overhead lights and walked out the front door. He shuffled to the end of the block, tipping his head to several passers-by, turned down a side street and climbed into his car.

The route home was a short five-minute commute, but the drive to and from the bank to deposit the day's earnings added ten minutes. He joked the car could drive itself, after so many years, and Bridie knew to time the dinner so that it was ready by ten to six.

When he opened the door of his home, he could hear the radio in the kitchen and smell the sausages frying. Donegal pork. When his doctor had advised him several years ago to cut down on his consumption of red meat and pork, Fergal's response was a quiet shake of his head. "Catch yourself on! You can't ask a butcher that," he answered. He knew all the farmers who raised the pigs and cattle and he made the sausages himself. He vouched for the food he sold. And he wasn't about to give up eating it. May as well ask a priest not to pray!

Bridie was in the kitchen and a hot cuppa was on the table, milk and sugar already added. And there, atop a stack of post next to his mug, was a slim white envelope from International Fisheries. Bridie turned in time to catch his gaze settle on the letter and she smiled, knowing that the customary peck on the cheek with which he greeted her each and every day would wait until the letter was read.

"Well, about time!"

Fergal pulled out a chair and sat down briskly. "I never doubted..." he said.

"No, of course not," added Bridie, as she set plates on the table for the two of them.

With his butter knife, he slit open the top of the envelope and retrieved the letter.

It was from Ove. Good old Ove! It began with platitudes and pleasantries, so much that Fergal grew a bit anxious that it may be a lead up to a let down, but then Ove wrote that the project – this wonderful development that would put Dunnybegs on the map – was indeed moving ahead. Ove himself would be returning to the area within a few weeks, followed by other company officials and assorted employees.

And then, Ove added, perhaps he and Fergal could sit down and begin the paperwork for the partnership arrangement that would fund his shop's expansion.

Fergal held the letter up to the light and turned to Bridie, his eyes wide with excitement. Then he jumped from his chair, nearly toppling it with his zeal, before grasping Bridie around her hips and twirling the two of them. Bridie, who was preparing to serve up their dinner and held the frying pan of sausages in her left hand, squealed.

Fergal turned up the volume dial of the radio and hummed along with the music.

"Silly man, it's just an advert for a petrol station!" she said.

"Then it'll be a short dance," he answered, laughing, before leaning in and giving her a kiss on the cheek.

26

A Home to Return to

Over the next several weeks, Thomas's life settled into a routine. With no trips to Derry scheduled and the clearing out of the cottage more or less complete, his days were open. He awoke each morning with Molly warm by his side; she had abandoned her dog bed entirely. He was growing accustomed to the sound of her faint snoring and found it actually helped him sleep, though the first time she had a dream and made a muffled bark, he jumped awake startled, which woke Molly, who had a unique ability to switch from deep sleep to peak alertness in an instant. Perhaps it was a border collie trait, this hyper-vigilance always close to the surface.

Upon rising, he let her out the door and then went to the toilet himself, returning to let her back in, at which point they both wandered to the kitchen. He'd fuss there awhile, as the kettle heated and the tea steeped and Molly ate, and then carried the first cup back into the living room, to sit and gaze out the front window.

He no longer trusted that first glimpse of the sea and sky to forecast the day, the weather here was just too changeable, the weather rushed along by the usually swift Gulf currents. Unless there was a monster storm approaching, like the husk of an old Caribbean hurricane charging across the Atlantic, or the odd high-pressure system stalled over the coast, the forecast remained consistently inconsistent: periods of showers giving way to sun. Breezy. Always breezy.

They set off for their daily walks by mid-morning, with Thomas stowing a thermos, some biscuits, a packable raincoat and the Donegal antiquities book wrapped in a plastic bag in his backpack. Some days they'd meander north or south along the coast, where Thomas discovered new-to-him beaches and craggy cliffs with breathtaking views out over the Atlantic.

Occasionally he'd pack himself lunch and he'd find a picturesque spot and spread the raincoat on the ground, where he'd sit and eat, contentedly. Molly, after thoroughly inspecting the surrounding area and exhausting her sense of smell, would amble back to his side, resting her warm chin on his legs.

In between bites, he'd refer to the book, re-reading the author's laconic accounting of the surroundings, or paging ahead to see what sites may be nearby. He'd also begun scribbling his own notes and comments in the margins.

And he took photographs. Molly standing on a ridge, looking enormous, the steely Atlantic behind her. Molly, in the doorway of a ruin, the skeletal remnants of the door frame embracing her silhouette. Molly, sitting peacefully in the middle of a dirt lane that meandered up the hillside, all the way to the horizon. She was a perfect model.

As Thomas had never spent time around a dog before, he took her quiet obedience for granted. As soon as he motioned for her to sit or stay, she complied, holding the pose until he said okay, until he himself moved (for some reason, she seemed to respond better to visual cues than to verbal directions). Then, more often than not, she'd bound toward him, her mouth open, her eyes gazing up at his.

He was falling in love. With this dog. This sweet, gentle soul. Such good company. He found himself talking to her frequently. If he spent too much time in a chair, reading or watching the television, she'd interrupt, bounding over to him with a ball in her mouth as if to say, hey, time to play. So, they'd play. Him throwing the ball, her chasing after it, then darting back to drop it at his feet. And at some point, they'd wrestle for it and he'd grab fists full of the scruff of her neck, running his hands through the thick patch of fur and then bury his nose in the thicket, breathing in the smell of her, of grass and mud and smoke and salt and the hint of his laundry detergent.

And he was falling in love with Donegal. With its sad, desolate beauty, its rainbow of greens, its luminous sky and electric blues, its jagged, jangly coast, its singing ghosts and leaning skeletons. With the smell of peat and the warm embrace of the Beetle. With the people, the stubborn holdouts, and their endless reservoir of perseverance.

As spring advanced, the land's charms further revealed themselves. On their hikes, Thomas and Molly walked along lanes hemmed in by the hanging purple and magenta blooms of wild fuchsia, the thick hedges alive with birds flickering and chirping at one another. Sudden bursts of starlings would occasionally flush from the shrubs, tracing a meteoric arc in hushed gray across the dazzling sky before collapsing down and alighting in a stand of trees. On coastal walks, he gazed in wonderment at the gulls hovering effortlessly on the stiff sea breezes.

One walk several miles northeast led them to the ruins of an old church set beside a centuries-old cemetery. He walked carefully among the graves, struggling to read the worn names and dates on the markers, until he came to the one he had been looking for, an ancient stone with a Latin cross carved into the surface. According to his book, the stone was associated with St. Columba, or Colmcille, the patron saint of Derry. That put its origins in the sixth century.

Thomas stood, silent. He reached out with his right hand and gently traced his index finger along the faint channels of the carving still visible in the stone. He wasn't at all a religious person – living through the tail end of the Troubles had starved any spiritual impulse he may once have had. But the age of this relic left him speechless. And then he thought of the craftsperson who had worked that design into the hard granite, before insulated jackets and thermal windows and hot water heaters. Once again, he marveled at the tenacity it must have taken to subsist here.

"They were a sturdy lot," he said aloud, though Molly was a good hundred yards further up the hillside just then. Continuing on in the cemetery, he moved into a section more recently utilized, and saw surnames he recognized from the townsfolk he was getting to know - Gallaghers and Dohertys and O'Neils and others. He felt something – jealousy? Not quite. Excluded, maybe. He looked westward, across the rolling hills and sweeping fields and the lanes that wound through the land. These names belonged to this land. Even Molly belonged here.

But him? Where did he belong? When the house would be bought and his small circle of belongings removed, where would he go? And what would he do? His sister had suggested that this time away might be good for him, that his path might become clear here, but it still felt somewhere off in a fog bank to Thomas.

Departing the cemetery, he struck a westerly path, figuring he'd eventually meet the coastal road and follow that south. He never rushed these walks and any detours they encountered just meant more roads to explore. He and Molly had been doing these hikes for weeks now. The longest had kept them out of the house a full twelve hours. Roisin, at the grocer, had suggested he get one of those watches that counts your steps. "Sure yer puttin' miles on, but getting none of the credit for it," was how she had put it.

The number of steps was insignificant, though. He was coming to know this place like he had no other. And each day, when he and Molly turned to head back to Dunnybegs and the little cottage, they were headed home.

27

A Sort of Messenger

A looming wall of clouds blowing in from the Atlantic had obscured the setting sun by the time Thomas and Molly reached Dunnybegs. Warm, amber lights glowed from the homes and businesses along main street, and Thomas had the idea to pick up a few heated sausage rolls from the store and carry them into the Shamrock to enjoy along with a pint.

"How's yerself?" asked Eamonn when Thomas and Molly clattered through the doorway. "Knackered, hungry and thirsty," he answered, choosing a stool at the far end of the bar, closest to the fireplace. Molly instinctively settled onto the rug before the fire.

"Aye, well, the thirst I can help," said Eamonn, reaching for a pint glass and tilting it under a tap. At four-fifths full, he set the glass down on the bar as the fine bubbles settled before topping up the glass and placing it before Thomas. "Aren't those sausage rolls grand," he said, nodding at the bag Thomas had opened and spread out on the bar. "Meat's from Fergal."

"Really? Huh, I always figured they were from some big company that turned out everything from sausage rolls to pizza."

"They were, back in the day. But Fergal just couldn't stand for that.

Started making his own and giving them away, said there were too many good farmers here to be gettin' meat from the north."

"And Roisin O'Malley at the grocer, what did she make of that?"

"Ah, Rose, she's a sharp one. She and Fergal put their heads together and found a government scheme that paid you to promote Donegal products. Meant they could sell those at the same price as the mass-produced shite she'd been selling before. Now, if only someone of ye's started making good beer around here and I could get paid to sell it!" He chuckled.

There were a few other patrons in a booth along the wall and, while Eamonn went off to see if they needed refills, Thomas tucked into the rolls, breaking one in half and tossing it down at Molly, who downed it in a single chomp.

Suddenly, the door flew open, revealing a light rain falling now, and the silhouette of Billy Gallagher, who ambled in and, recognizing Thomas, sat on a stool next to him.

"Helen's boy – Tommy was it? How are ye gettin' on?"

"Och, I'm doing grand," Thomas replied, not bothering to correct the man.

"And how is your social media life?" Billy asked, tipping his head at Eamonn as the barman set a full pint before him. "Ta."

"I haven't really checked since."

Billy slowly savored a swallow of stout and then shook his head.

"What? What's wrong?" Thomas asked.

Billy hacked a loud, wet cough into a handkerchief that, by the looks of it, he had owned since childhood. "Well, fer feck's sake, if you're going to have a social media presence, you need to be active and post every day or so, at the least. Otherwise, they'll forget about you in a blink."

He blew his nose into the cloth and took a quick gulp of the beer. "Chrissake, ye'll never be an influenza like this."

"I'll... what?"

"Ack, you know, like those American sisters with the huge bums. They post several times a day and, sure, don't they get paid millions for it."

"Oh, an influencer." Thomas smiled. "I'm not really trying to match them. I mean, I don't have the bum for it." This was his attempt at bar humor. Eamonn smiled. Billy, though, seemed lost in a coughing fit.

"Got your phone with ye?" Billy asked. "Let's have a look. Eamonn, turn on the wi-fi!"

They waited a few minutes for the wi-fi to "warm up," in Eamonn's words, and then Thomas launched the PhotoLife app on his phone.

There were notifications. A lot.

He scrolled down his feed. His first photo had acquired 46 likes. But his most recent post already had 123. And the one before that, an image of Molly atop a dune, with a robust orange sun setting into the dark blue Atlantic behind her, had been shared by an account operated by the Irish Tourism folks. It had a staggering 1,293 likes!

"Wow."

"That's how it works," said Billy. "Ye don't need a huge bum, just a wee dog. And the right hashtags!"

"I guess," said Thomas. He was shocked. Thirteen hundred people had liked the photo. Most of the rest of his images had between 50 and 300 likes. And he had 438 followers!

He hadn't uploaded any from the past week or so - which meant he had a good twenty or so from their hikes all ready to go. He could, as Billy had urged, maintain a presence.

The door blew open again, revealing a gloomy, wet night, sending another, stronger, gust chasing through the pub, and finally, introducing the figure of a small man, struggling to draw down his umbrella and shaking the rain from his unruly, red hair. He moved no further than the first stool at the very end of the bar nearest the front door and sneezed.

The barman walked down to greet his newest customer. Billy spit into his empty glass and turned to Thomas. "You'll be making us all famous, lad!"

Eamonn shuffled back over to take their empty glasses and nodded towards the man at the end of the pub. He leaned towards them. "Mind what ye say," he whispered. "Government official. Up from Dublin."

'Ack, what'll he be on about," grunted Billy. "They only show up when they want more money."

"I tink it's that fish farm scheme," said Eamonn.

"The feck we need that for?" hissed Billy. "Tell him if he needs to see a farm…"

"Is that the farm in the bay here?" interrupted Thomas. "I'd heard about it but wasn't sure it was happening."

Eamonn set another full pint glass before Billy. "Dey come and go, these plans. It'd be nice to have the jobs, though. Get some life back into that bay. And see all these empty seats filled with thirsty fishermen."

"I guess," said Thomas. "But there's plenty of life in the bay, isn't there?"

"If yer talking jellyfish, sure," said Billy.

For some reason, Thomas's thoughts drifted back to the night a month or so prior when he and Molly watched the seal. "Say," he looked up at Eamonn. "You were a sailor, can I ask you something? A while back, one night, I walked down to the beach in the bay. It was a quiet night, a gorgeous sky overhead. And then a seal appeared, just a bit out in the water. Just stared at me, silently, for, I don't know, ten or twenty minutes. Are seals an omen of some sort? I just, I felt like it was trying to tell me something…" his voice tapered off as he realized how silly he must have sounded.

But Eamonn looked deep in thought as he wiped out a glass and set it on the counter.

"Well," he began. "A seal is a sort of a messenger, it's said. You know, moving between the realms."

Thomas nodded.

"They're of both the land and the water. In between." He turned to Thomas. "Tell me, were you thinking of your mother at the time?"

"Um, I guess, I mean I had just walked down from the cottage, taking a break from going through her belongings."

Eamonn raised his eyebrows. "Ah, well, the people who deal in such things might say it was the spirit of your mother, or a messenger, sent by your mother, you know, to let you know everything would be ok."

Thomas swallowed hard. "A messenger, huh?" He fell quiet, then began fumbling in his pants pocket and pulled out some bills to pay, which he set on the counter to pay for his drink. "Well, something to think about. Now Molly and I best be getting along home." As he stood, Molly sleepily rose to stand next to him.

"Ay, before you go, would ye take a photo of Molly?" Eamonn asked. "And can you mention the Shamrock in the photo?" As he spoke, he pushed the money Thomas had left on the bar back towards him.

Afterwards, once Thomas posed Molly before the fire and Eamonn rearranged the tables and chairs next to Molly and replaced a lightbulb in a table lamp, and after Thomas collected his money, thanked Eamonn and bid goodnight to Billy and left, Billy motioned Eamonn over.

"What the feck was that all about?" he chuckled. "Are ye's dealing with the fairy folk yourself? What do you know about myths and omens?"

Eamonn leaned against the bar and looked towards the front door.

"Ach, I don't know shite about it. But I know every lad misses his ma. What's the harm in a wee white lie if it stops him feeling sad, like? Sure, he's a good man."

28

Fintan Goes Factfinding

Fintan's drive up from Dublin followed the route he had driven previously, save for a short detour when the map he'd carefully unfolded and refolded to highlight the section of the country in which he was driving fell off the passenger seat and he mistakenly made a right hand turn and actually drove southward, back towards Dublin, for half an hour.

Outside of that, and a short stop at a particularly bright looking little bakery found during his detour for a sweet bun, washed down by some of his own tea, the drive was uneventful. He had arranged two nights' accommodations at the same bed and breakfast he had stayed at before and his room was ready for him when he arrived.

This, unlike the previous visit, was official. He was here on state business. He had made that clear on the call to make the reservation and used a government purchase order to arrange payment.

It was late afternoon by the time he checked in and unloaded his small suitcase. His hostess had recalled his predilection for sausage rolls and tea and prepared both for a light supper. The evening was young, he decided to venture out for a wee look around before it grew too dark.

There had been some changes since his last visit. The greens of the hills were more vivid, the fuchsia along the roadside in bloom and the light dallied a bit longer. The land had grown more colorful and inviting, even with what looked to be rain dragging in from the Atlantic soon.

He had brought a small digital camera along and he used that to take several photos of streets, empty storefronts and To Let signs. He even spotted a few hand-painted signs declaring Keep It Killfish. He imagined there may have been a small group of people opposed to the fish farm project and made a note to ask the local mayor about that when they were to meet the next day.

After a few hours of roaming and taking pictures, he found himself driving along the main street in Dunnybegs and noticed the bright colors of the Shamrock Bar, looking warm and inviting now that the rain and dark had moved in. May as well pop in and have a shandy, he thought to himself.

It was a smallish space, but warm, with a handful of folk inside. Fintan eyed up a seat nearest the door and sidled up to the bar. The smell inside was of stale beer, peat and a hint of pig manure, likely from the elderly man at the other end of the bar, next to a young fellow and a dog. Regulars, he thought. The farmer's ancient, hulking tractor was parked along the road.

He thought, briefly, of moving down to their end of the counter, of engaging the two of them in conversation about the region, the economy and, ultimately, the fish farm. He was, after all, on an official fact-finding mission, a representative of the state. But the hour hand had lapsed past 6 – the workday was done – and the truth was he always found it a bit difficult to talk to strangers. He ordered a shandy and kept to himself while he nursed it.

It had always been that way. He was the boy who held himself back from the neighborhood games, the one who sat by himself at lunch, who missed the college dances, the good employee who made no waves nor attracted much notice. In college, a young woman had told him his aura was beige. Some observers may have pitied him, but he was comfortable in his routines and in the quiet rhythm of his life. Or was.

In fact, as he reached his sixties, his attitudes about life – his complacency with solitude and uniformity – had almost imperceptibly undergone a metamorphosis. He had considered this on the drive up, that even this, his handling of this business proposal up in the far end of creation, was new. The Fintan of old would have shuffled papers, made it go away, and sidestepped any criticism. After all, it was hardly his fault his predecessor died.

Instead, here he was in Dunnybegs, taking the initiative to resurrect this fish farm, visiting a pub, and, truth be told, actually anticipating a return visit to that wee grocer's tomorrow, in hopes of seeing that woman. A woman!

In the bed at his accommodation that night, he thought again about this new self. This was not him being a late bloomer, he decided. It was too late for that. No, this was not him returning to what he should have been. This was him, in his sixties, changing his attention. He had lived his life and was happy with it. But he needed a new view. This was his heart directing his gaze outward, away from his small existence, toward a world full of people, of sunsets and sunrises and small warm pubs. His retirement was approaching, and his choice now was to expand his world, to live. A little.

He arrived at the breakfast table fully dressed for the day, in his one suit, a pale blue shirt and a bright green tie that once again hung on him awkwardly, the fat end several inches above the narrow one. He tucked a napkin into his collar to save the shirt and tie from the runny eggs and the blackcurrant jam slathered onto his toast. When he finished, his hostess brought his thermos, full of tea, so he could milk and sugar it for the day before heading out.

He spent the first hour driving the region, making notes and taking photos. It was a soft day, the clouds close overhead and a light mist filling the air. He drove north, where the coastline became more dramatic and tall cliffs held firm against swirling seafoam, and then followed the curling road down into another small town nestled alongside a small bay. This one held a harbor and pier. A few anchored fishing boats bobbed in the waves, their colors fading, their hulls rusting. Several small pleasure craft lined the pier.

Fintan was still early for his meeting, so he maneuvered his car into a parking stall near the dock and turned off the engine, fixing to have a cup of tea and listen to the radio. Then he noticed a couple approaching, walking along the path that bordered the water. A man and woman, walking a small dog. Fintan took a deep breath. He would need at some point to break the ice and speak to people here. He screwed the top back on his thermos and exited the car, walking in the direction of the couple.

The man was small and thin, wearing a thick black raincoat and a tweed cap. The woman, who walked arm in arm with the man, was considerably larger and several inches taller. She wore a bright red overcoat and a colorful floral scarf. Charging along before them, was a dachshund, muttering and worrying, with a red handkerchief around its neck and a small cowboy hat on its head.

Fintan waited until they were within earshot. "Eh, excuse me, grand day, innit?" He regretted saying it immediately. It was decidedly not a grand day: cool, gray and damp.

The man tipped his head in greeting but kept this pace. "Ach, aye, it'll have to do."

The couple was beside him now and moving swiftly, the dog, still muttering, pulling them along.

"Say, would you, ah, mind if I asked you a question?"

The man stopped. The woman looked over at Fintan, with a worried expression on her face. "Dixie, hold up," the man called to the dog. "What can I do for ye?" he asked Fintan. "Are ye lost?"

When he heard the man's voice, Fintan realized he was speaking to the man behind the bar from the night before. "Oh, no, I'm, my name is Fintan. I'm from Dublin. I, ah, am with the Department of Economic Development and I'm up to gather some information about a business proposal."

"I see." The wee dog was making a warbling sound and making small jumps with its front feet, bouncing in place. "I'm Eamonn, and this is Izzy. Is this about the fish farm?"

"Well, yes, how did you know?"

"You were in our pub last night and mentioned you were here from Dublin, investigating a business proposal. The fish farm's the only new business that's poked around here in years. Beginning to think they lost interest or something, I was." The woman had begun to fidget, her gaze darting back and forth between the men.

"The fish are gone," she blurted. "Can we go?"

Fintan shifted on his feet. "So, you're in favor of it?"

"If it means jobs, aye. Too few around here." The dog pulled at its lead. The woman began walking forward and pulled at Eamonn's arm. "Sorry, have to go."

"No, fine, thank you," said Fintan. He stepped back and the couple charged on. He watched them hurry off, the dog bounding in front, the two of them arm in arm. No one else was around to speak with, so he wandered back to his car and turned the ignition. He was off to his meeting with the mayor of Dunnybegs.

29

An Official Meeting

This was Fintan's first official meeting with anyone in government, outside of his own department. When he first arranged the meeting, he had envisioned a city hall welcoming of some sort, perhaps even a ceremonial meeting, but Mayor Fergal McCart had instead given him directions to a butcher shop, on the main road in little Dunnybegs, a few doors down from the Shamrock.

The shop was a bright, tidy place, with a series of display cases arranged in a wide U facing the door, all stocked with various cuts of meat, sausages and hams. The butcher was behind the central counter with his back to the door when Fintan entered, but he turned at the sound of the small bell that jingled with the door's opening. He wiped his hands on his apron and smiled. "Morning, what can I get for ye?"

Fintan stammered. "No. I mean, I'm, well, I was told to meet with Mayor McCart here." He looked around confused.

"Ah, are you Mr. O'Dowd? I'm yer man, Fergal McCart, purveyor of fine meats and sausages and mayor of Dunnybegs." By now he had strolled out from behind the counter and extended a hand toward Fintan, who glanced at it with some apprehension before weakly offering up his own hand.

There was a small round table and two chairs to his right, set before the window. The mayor took a seat and Fintan followed his lead, lowering into a chair facing him. He was a round man with a thin swatch of black hair and a dark grey mustache. It occurred to Fintan that if only the mustache was darker, the butcher would resemble Oliver Hardy. But his thoughts were interrupted when he noticed the small figure by the butcher's side, next to the door – a small ceramic statue of an Italian chef, wearing a red and white checkered apron and holding a bottle of wine in one hand and a plate of spaghetti in the other. It was a cartoonish figurine, but bore more than a passing resemblance to the butcher himself – down to the mustache.

Fergal must have noticed Fintan's expression. "Ha, you think it looks like me?" he chortled. "A gift from the missus a few years ago. Found it in Sligo, I think. Was herself painted on the mustache."

"It does bear some resemblance," answered Fintan. "It's an Italian version of you."

"Buon appetito," blurted the butcher, startling Finan, who flinched.

"Sorry! I'm quite excited by your visit. This fish farm scheme has been around awhile. I was beginning to think it may not happen."

Fintan gave a thin smile. "Dese things often have a few ups and downs. As you must know yourself, the government can move quite slowly at times. Of course, we do have to dot all our Ts."

Fergal shot him a quizzical look but then nodded in agreement. "There's always red tape, innit?"

"Well, I prefer to think of it as being thorough." In his long career in bureaucracy, Fintan had heard all the jokes, all the insults and all the demeaning comments about his profession. But who would keep order, if not the mid-level government workers? Politicians? There's a laugh. Change direction on a whim. Business leaders? Ego-driven and self serving. No, the backbone of the government – the nation! – was made up of men and women like himself. Unchanging. Steady. Slow? Perhaps. But it was good to be methodical.

Fergal was flushed. He couldn't get a read on this new fellow from Dublin. "Och, I, uh, didn't mean that in a bad way, of course," he stammered. "I'm glad the project's still being considered. And I understand the need to make sure everything is in order."

"Indeed. So you're in favor of the farm?"

Fergal nodded. "Aye, it'll be a boon. Sure, you can see for yourself it's a sleepy wee place. Always been a hard place to make a living, but since the fishing fleets have gone, well, there's nowt left. The wains don't stay. Away to college and never come back."

Fintan leant back in the chair and glanced around the shop. "Do you sell seafood here?"

Fergal shrugged. "I'll order something if a customer asks, but I've no local suppliers. It's all EU fish. Russian trawlers, Lithuanian processors. Pay through the nose."

Fintan had opened a small notepad and was jotting notes as he spoke. "I have seen a few posters voicing opposition to the fishing scheme. Do you think there are many opposed?"

"When the plan was first announced there was some opposition. A few folk put up posters and sent around a petition, but I doubt many folk signed it." He stretched his legs before him and ran his hands along the top of his thighs. "You know, Mr. O'Dowd, this began as a fishmonger's. It was my uncle's. He started out as a fisherman like my Da but injured his leg and had to give up the sea. I grew up in this place. Loved it. Loved the smells. Could gut a fish by the time I was ten. After my uncle passed, it was me in line to take over. Twenty one! Mind you, I had the shock of my life to see how poorly the business was doing. By then, most of the fishing fleet up and down the coast had gone. It was change or die. So, I learned all I could about beef and lamb and pork and the shop became a butcher shop. And it's done OK. There are good farmers in Donegal. I know most all of them by name. Which certainly helped when I first ran for mayor."

"It does look like a profitable business."

"It's quality meat. The finest mincemeat, ground here. And I make all the sausages myself. You won't find better in any of your fancy shops in Dublin!"

Had Fintan known that the delicious sausage rolls he'd been

enjoying were Fergal's he'd certainly have agreed. The two men spoke a while longer, chatting about the economy, housing and the protests (Fergal maintained that he thought most were upset about the idea of the name change more than the fish farm). But in short order, Fintan became aware that his stomach was empty and started thinking about the sausage rolls from the grocer down the street. As he was preparing to leave, Fergal darted back behind the counter and bundled up a half dozen links. "Not a bribe, a sample," he said, handing the package to Fintan. "You know, I am Italian," he said, looking over at the small statue. "My granny Rose was from Sicily. Married an Irishman." He opened the door and followed Fintan out onto the street.

"People are surprised. They think all the Italians in Ireland sell ice cream."

Fintan chuckled. "You could sell that in your shop. Expand."

"Actually," answered Fergal, "my cousin Rory runs an ice cream truck. A Mr. Softee. He stays further up the coast, where the tourists are. I'm hoping to expand, though. If this fish farm starts up, there'll be local fish again. This space next to me is empty. I'm going to knock down the wall and become a fishmonger again. Call it Pietro's, after my father."

"That's a nice way to remember him," said Fintan.

Suddenly, he was pulled to the side, as Fergal wrapped an arm around his shoulder. "It's a lovely view, innit?"

Fintan followed his gaze, down the block and to the bay beyond, a small patch of calm before the open blue sea and the line of bright clouds on the horizon.

"It's beautiful. But then you look up and down this street. And it's mostly empty. God bless, there's always a pub. But there used to be a chemist here, and over there was an electronics store. The first thing I ever bought for myself was a shortwave radio. Had to gut a lot of fish to pay for that. And that, across the street, that was a hotel, believe it or not." His eyes were nearly closed. Fintan suspected he was trying to see his past.

"It's lovely, Mr. O'Dowd. But that's not enough. I understand some folk may be upset that the fish farm will ruin the view. But it might pump a little life back into Dunnybegs. There are decent, hardworking folk here. I hope you keep them in mind when you write your report."

30

A Rose with Thorns

After the meeting, and with a cold bundle of sausage under his arm and a growling stomach, Fintan walked down the short main street to the grocer's. When he entered the store, he was chuffed to see the woman back behind the counter.

"Samplin' all our local delicacies, are ye?" she said, smiling.

"Oh, this?" Fintan asked, gesturing at the package. "I'm just after meeting with the mayor, he sent a few sausages along with me."

"Well, they're the best you'll find, but you know that. You've already had them."

Fintan was a bit puzzled.

"You were up from Dublin a while back, weren't you? Had the sausage rolls, if I remember," she said smiling. "The mayor makes them. I just put out a tray for the afternoon. Would you like a couple, Fintan, was it?"

That she remembered him, let alone his name, was almost more than Fintan could bear. He felt his cheeks flush. "I, ah, well, yes, I would. Two please. And if I could have a cuppa, that'd be grand."

He watched her as she turned and headed for the hot case in the rear of the store. She wore a dark grey skirt, sensible pale cream blouse and a purple store apron. Her hair, near white, was pulled back in thick braids on either side of her face and curled into a bun at the back. The faint breeze caused by her movement carried a wisp of a sweet, fresh scent, and the smell sent Fintan back to his childhood, watching his mom hang the days' laundry outside in the tiny backyard of the family home. She often sang as she did the wash, and Fintan was sifting through old memories trying to recall the tune, when Rose returned and held a cup before him.

"Careful, it's hot," she said, smiling. Her eyes captivated Fintan. They were the color of the sea, a steely blue-grey that shouldn't have held any warmth but in fact filled him with comfort.

"Up on official business then, Fintan? I mean, a sharp dressed man such as yourself up from Dublin twice in a few months, now meeting with our mayor. And then there were all the maps you bought. Are you a planner?"

Still flustered, Fintan took a sip of the tea as a stalling measure, but regretted it the instant the scalding liquid hit his tongue.

"Well," he managed, after holding the tea in his mouth a moment to let it cool, "as a matter of fact, I am here on government business." He glanced around to ensure no one else was within earshot. "In fact, it's very good business for the area."

Back behind the counter, Rose tilted her head back and her smile abruptly vanished. "Och, it's not that bleedin' fish farm, is it?"

Needless to say, it was not the response Fintan was expecting. In his shock, he took a gulp of the tea, fought the urge to spit out the flaming beverage, swallowed and stifled a scream as the beverage scorched its way down to his belly. "No, no, no," he responded. "I mean, yes, the fish farm. But it's a good thing. The economy in this remote region is primitive. I've documented numerous empty buildings in the villages all up and down the coast. Tree or four right on this street! This development could bring jobs, which would bring customers into your store. People who'd want fish and chips, takeaway pizza, curry. It could keep young people here. It's progress. Imagine a motorway to Letterkenny!" He looked at Rose, but her face had lost its warmth.

She sighed. "Lunch is on the house today, Mr. Fintan." She walked out from behind the counter and strode to the door. Fintan was heartbroken, she was seeing him out the door! Jaysus, he thought to himself, what made me say primitive? But Rose had opened the door and stepped outside, gesturing for him to follow. Once he did, she came and stood beside him and pointed in the direction of the bay. It was a small half-moon bay, its southern end was a curl of bleached gray boulders dropping down into the sea like a row of seals, and before it, a sweep of scrubby grassland speckled with gorse and a few whitewashed cottages. The sun was fighting through the clouds, and the sky a mosaic of light and dark clouds racing overhead.

"Fintan," she began, turning to look him in the eyes, "the people who are here are here because of this. The sea, the sky, the air. Some days you fight to remain upright in the gales. Some days the rain is straight sideways and some days it's ice and your ears go numb and your skin, well, it nearly blisters from the sharp needles.

"This store was my parents.' I've worked here more than fifty years, starting as a wee one, sorting the day's newspapers into piles for my Da to deliver, my hands filthy from ink. I was 24 when he passed. It hasn't made me rich, but I have dinner on my table every night and I'm able to help my niece go to university. Never once thought of leaving.

"Do you know why, Mr. Fintan?" He shook his head. His cup of tea and small bag of sausage rolls were in one hand, the package of sausages under his other arm.

"Well, just look." She swept her left arm in a half circle, pointing first to the coast road leading south, then the bay itself, where the sun had suddenly broken through and the whitecaps now sparkled against the sapphire water, then onward north, to the jagged sea cliffs visible in the far distance.

"This is why people stay. Some days, the beauty of it will sting your face and bring tears to your eyes. And your modern fish farm would ruin it. You might add more people, and more money, but you'd lose this. You'd lose the reason to stay." She sighed and looked back at him with sadness in her eyes. She patted his left shoulder with a hand, letting it rest on him a moment. "But that's just me," she said. "An old lady. Primitive. Now, on your way Mr. Fintan. Don't want your sausages to thaw."

Fintan managed a slight nod, but his tongue was tied and his mind full of thoughts. Though his coat was thick, the heat of her touch warmed his shoulder. The woman turned and hurried back through the door. Fintan watched her and then turned his gaze back to the sea.

31

For Lost Souls

That same day, Thomas and Molly had ventured out again to the rolling hills further south. The morning's fog had crept up the hillsides and settled on the land, coating the grasses and trees and leaving the roads slick. Thomas's destination had been an old sacred spring, the Well of the Three Holy Women, and they found it, after a forty-five-minute walk on roads bordered by dripping hedges plump with violet fuchsia.

There were sites like this throughout Ireland. Natural springs had long been associated with ancient legends and steeped in mysticism. The introduction of Christianity had added a new layer. Many were rudimentary, unimproved sites, but this one had received considerable attention. The spring itself had been funneled into a fountain of sorts, surrounded by rough stone walls. A pocked cement platform lay before it, the whole assemblage nestled into a dense thicket.

Thomas stood on the cement and examined the scene. The surrounding hedges were crowded with all sorts of trinkets, scraps of ribbon and fabric, photographs and torn notes. These were the wishes, dreams and prayers of the faithful, who visited the site seeking comfort. To the right of the spring, beside the platform, rose a pile of small stones, perhaps three feet tall at the peak and a good five feet in diameter.

According to the book on Donegal antiquities, each of these wells seemed to have a particular specialty - ailments, maladies or other misfortunes that a visit to the well could help alleviate. This particular well was reputed to cure a wide assortment of illnesses, but was mostly known for helping lost souls find their way home. Visitors seeking help or cures often pocketed one of the stones and took them back to their houses, though it was believed that the stones had to be returned to the well in order for the cure to stick.

Beside him, Molly settled onto the warm surface of the platform and curled into a tight circle. As with many of the sites they visited, Thomas wondered if Molly had been here before with his mother. He glanced back at the bushes and looked over the tokens and knickknacks scattered about. A pair of baby shoes. A dark blue wool knit cap. A small glass bottle containing an old photo. A metal cup. A doll. A ragged shirt. Rosaries. A cane.

He stepped toward the mound of stones and picked one up, absent-mindedly rubbing his thumb over the smooth surface. "What cure would we need, Molly?" he asked. Then he turned and looked out over the view to the west. The air was still damp, though the low clouds had finally burned off, revealing the long slope of heather and gorse fields, the trails of winding, crumbling stone walls and, in the far distance, the dark bottle-green sea.

In the days when fishing fleets still sailed those waters, when the boats launched into the punch of each angry wave, decks laden with nets and holds empty and expectant, the fishermen watched for this well, straining for the sight of this small notch of gray high up in the hills, and then they made the sign of the cross. Bring us home, they beseeched. Safely back to port, alive to sail again the next day.

Now the sea was empty and at this distance appeared smooth. Thomas sighed. "Can't make your way back home when you've no home, can you, Molly?"

He looked over at the dog, who was now sitting upright, staring intently at the trickle of water running down the face of the well. If Thomas stepped to his left and stooped, the angle made Molly appear heroic against the soft gray sky over the hill. Thomas held his phone up to his face and took another photograph.

They stayed at the well for a while, Molly settling back on the smooth warm stone and Thomas pouring himself a cuppa and sitting down beside the dog. They were comfortable with one another now and as soon as he got himself situated, Molly pushed up against him and rested her chin on his leg. With his free hand, he stroked and scratched at the fur behind her ear. This was now how he usually fell off to sleep each night, with the warmth of Molly calming him and the sound of her breathing the gentle rhythm that guided him to sleep. Through dark nights and storms and howling winds, she was as much his companion as she was each day as they made their way about this corner of Donegal.

The colors of the landscape became more vivid as the day brightened and clouds continued to lift. By now, Thomas was methodically documenting the landscape on their daily walks, returning home each day with dozens if not hundreds of photos of the sites they had encountered. Most photos also included Molly, who sat patiently while Thomas moved to and fro to get the perfect angle and frame the image just right. She still didn't appear to pay much attention to any of his commands and Thomas often lamented that his mother had failed to teach the dog many words other than walk, food and pee.

Regardless of that, he considered the dog very observant and clearly bright. She usually picked up on what he wanted or was asking her to do, though there were times he could swear she was mulling over whether to comply or not. He'd also admit that the dog was doing a pretty good job of training him. There were numerous rainy days or even damp mornings when Thomas would move more slowly about the house, often pouring himself a second cup of coffee and retiring to the living room with a book. Molly would give him fifteen minutes, maybe twenty, before deciding enough was enough. Then would begin a steady parade of her toys, one after another, pulled from the basket by the fire where they were stored overnight and dropped, one by one, in Thomas's lap. Thomas would grab the toy, each tennis ball or squeaky runner bone or thick twist of rope, and toss it across the room for Molly to fetch. And this would go on, an automated, robotic process, until Thomas would look down from his book at six or seven toys sharing his chair with him and Molly, sitting at attention a foot in front of him, staring intently.

They were training each other and growing more comfortable with the results. Becoming companions.

"Well, girl, shall we get a move on?"

He rose, capped the thermos, and packed it back into his backpack. There was blue sky in the far west now, over the sea. If the winds kept coming in off the ocean, it would be a brilliant afternoon. Thomas decided to walk north, parallel to the coast, to enjoy the views from the hills, before heading back down into Dunnybegs. East of them, the hills continued in gentle undulations, riven here and there by sharp stone escarpments, the land a patchwork of fields lined by hedges and stone walls.

The sun appeared in the early afternoon and the colors, already saturated by the overnight rain and morning dew, sparkled in the light. An insistent breeze rushed in, pushing the clouds further up and over the hillsides, carrying with it the smells of the sea and leaving a salty taste on one's lips. It was a gorgeous day, a precursor of summer.

The walk back to town was quicker. Thomas had learned that the higher overhead sunlight, though dazzling, created harsh shadows and was more difficult to photograph. He was now more discerning, preferring early mornings and late afternoons, when the sun was lower in the sky and the light golden. The entire world then appeared more luminous, more magical.

32

Molly's American Admirers

It was mid-afternoon when Thomas and Molly stepped into the Shamrock. The dog made its usual way to the fire in the far back and wasted no time curling up in her tight circle and tucking her nose under her tail. Thomas struggled a moment to adapt to the low light after the bright sun outside, but soon made out Eamonn behind the bar and a few tables occupied, none by anyone he recognized. He made his way to the nearest end of the bar and sat.

"It's a grand day, innit?" Eamonn asked. "Having a glass?"

"Aye," answered Thomas.

Eamonn began pouring the stout, filled the glass about three fourths full and set the glass for the stout to settle. "Where've ye been off to today then?"

"We paid our respects to the Three Holy Women Well."

Eamonn topped up the beer and set it before Thomas. "Aye, that's a good wee hike. Used to get up there every few months, but it's a bit too much for the missus nowadays. Is it still looking well tended? I worry folks will be disrespectful."

"No, it looked just fine. I can show you some pictures here in a minute. Figured we'd stop in and do a bit of photo editing and then check my stuff online."

He reached into his pocket for his phone but immediately jerked his hand back out, grasping a smooth, dark grey stone. He held it up to the light.

"Aw, shit. Look at that. I must have dropped it into my pocket up at the well."

Eamonn's eyes grew wide. "You've got to take that back. Ye canna be stealing the wishing stones."

"Well, no, I mean I didn't intend to. But folks take them all the time, right?"

"Only if they have a specific supplication! Jaysus, if I were you, I'd take it back up as soon as I could. No good'll come of that."

Thomas set the stone on the bar, beside his glass, and ran his index finger along its smooth surface. "Don't you wonder where it's been? How many people have picked it up and brought it home with them?"

"Not just home," said Eamonn. "I know a man who mailed one to Canada, to his brother, who was sick. And a fella had one on our ship once. Carried it with him and prayed with it every day, for his mother, who was sickly. But they always returned them, eventually."

"Ach, I'll return it alright. Maybe next week. Cara is coming back for the summer. I can take her up there."

He was still staring at the stone and hadn't noticed a man and woman, who had left their stall towards the rear of the bar and walked up next to him.

"Is that all for ye, now?" asked Eamonn. "Can I get youse the bill?'"

Thomas turned to look at them. They were staring at him. Thomas guessed they were American tourists. While they weren't too common here, he had met plenty in the bookstore in Derry. Always with brand-name, brightly colored, high-tech rain jackets, rugged hiking boots better suited for the Alps, expensive camera gear that a National Geographic photographer might envy, and persistent, toothy smiles.

The man caught Thomas's eye and nodded. "I'm sorry to bother you, but we were really hoping to meet you. This is a great coincidence!"

Thomas looked at them both. A bit older than middle-aged. The man stout and slightly bent, with a bright gray goatee and salt and pepper hair. The woman was petite, with pale golden hair pulled into a ponytail. She gestured over to the dog, still sound asleep before the fire. "Is that Molly?"

Thomas was a bit confused. His first thought was that the couple may be repeat visitors who had met Molly and his mother on another trip.

"She's so pretty! Just like the photos."

"The photos?" Thomas asked.

"As our vacation grew nearer, we'd begun following a lot of accounts on PhotoLife that had photos in this area. Nancy came across yours, and, as she loves border collies..."

"I have three back home."

"Yeah, she loves 'em. So, we started following you and Molly."

Eamonn beamed. "And the Shamrock! Molly's official pub!"

"Goodness, I don't know what to say," said Thomas. He was dumbstruck. He was gaining a lot of followers, but the idea he might someday meet one had never occurred to him.

"Do you mind?" the man asked. Thomas nodded and the two took seats next to him, the woman closest. The man, who eventually introduced himself as Dan, offered to buy Thomas another pint and dealt with the payment while the woman spoke. "We just love your photos. Both the scenery and the beautiful dog. So, we decided to change our itinerary and come north to see if it was as pretty as it looked - and to see if we could meet Molly. We sent you several messages on PhotoLife, but they mustn't have gone through." She laughed. "We're not exactly tech savvy!"

This is when Thomas found that PhotoLife had a messaging function and that he actually had more than a dozen messages waiting for him. Several were clearly junk. One was from a tourist agency seeking permission to repost one of his images (receiving no answer, they went ahead and posted it anyway), another was from a mobile phone dealer inquiring about the phone he was using and offering a free upgrade, one was praise from a professional photographer and five were messages from people like Dan and Nancy, seeking travel advice or to meet Molly.

Thomas was stunned. Even more so when he checked in on his account and discovered he now had 1,680 followers! It seemed the reposting of his photo by the travel agency had garnered him more than a thousand new followers - in a day.

He had been passing the time, hiking with the dog, and satisfying his own curiosity by seeking out interesting places and photographing them. It really hadn't occurred to him that others might be interested.

But here in front of him were Dan and Nancy, from a suburb of Houston, Texas, who had abandoned plans to spend a week exploring Kerry, and instead came north to poke about Donegal, all because of a few of Thomas's photographs. And Molly, of course.

Nancy made her way over to Molly and stroked her fur, speaking to her. Molly was sitting upright and clearly enjoying the attention. "I volunteer with a border collie rescue group in Houston. I just love the breed. They're so smart"

'We're always fostering a couple," added Dan.

"Well, that's what they tell me," said Thomas. "Molly's smart enough, aye, but she only seems to know a few commands. Either that, or she's just stubborn!"

"She just has a mind of her own," said Nancy. "I mean, they have a huge vocabulary. Sounds, too. Working dogs on farms get taught to respond to different whistles. They're amazing."

Thomas had seen that, on television, collies herding sheep, zigzagging back and forth, all in response to a farmer's whistle. And Molly did appear to be smart. Certainly empathetic. But he hadn't had success with any commands beyond sit, stay and come on. He tried others, mostly when attempting to get her to pose in the right position for photographs, but she seemed pretty oblivious to his words.

"I don't know," he laughed, "maybe I should try whistling."

At that, Eamonn, who had been a few feet down the counter rinsing glasses, shouted over, "Molly speaks French, mate."

Thomas laughed again, as did the couple, but Eamonn shook his head. "Really. You didn't know that? Sure, your ma spoke French to her all the time."

"My... what?"

Eamonn now had moved closer to them. "Well, I don't know the language myself, now, so your mother, god bless her, well, she could have been putting one over on me. But she'd speak to the dog in words that weren't any English I know, and it wasn't Irish either. She told me Molly was French."

Thomas sat stunned, mouth open. In all his years, he had never heard his mother utter a word of French, or any other language but her Ulster English. He thought perhaps Eamonn was having a laugh at his expense, but the barman looked earnest.

It was one of those out-of-the-blue revelations that stop you in your tracks and set off a fireworks burst of questions. Had his mother always known French? Was Molly actually from France? How did his mother meet Molly?

And then another flash of questions lit up his mind. For he suddenly remembered that photo, taken more than 30 years ago, just down the road, along the path running to Killfish Bay – of his mother, happy, laughing, carefree, pressed up next to whom? What was she doing here, all those years ago? And then the memory hit him, of the moment he found that photo, of where it had been. He was clearing out her bookcases, tossing old Reader's Digests, Agathie Christie mysteries, crossword puzzle collections, birding books, dictionaries and other volumes in boxes to take to the charity shop. The photo had fallen from a book, a book he had thrown into the box absent-mindedly, transfixed as he was by the photo.

The book had been a French-English dictionary.

"Pal?" It was the American, jostling Thomas loose from his thoughts. "We have a proposition for you."

33

Fintan Has a Vision

It was dark by the time Fintan pushed himself back from the dinner table at the bed and breakfast and padded up to his room. He needed to pack up for the drive home to Dublin in the morning. It was a quick job – he'd only packed for the two days. He lifted his coat from the bed to set it on the chair but stopped midway and pulled it close to his face. He buried his nose in the fabric along the left shoulder and inhaled deeply. Nothing. What had he expected? It's not like she'd have been wearing perfume on her hands working at the grocer. If anything, her hands probably smelled of musty banknotes and greasy sausage rolls. He pulled the coat away from his face but hesitated again before setting it over the back of the chair. He shook it. His keys jingled in the right front pocket. He looked at his watch. It was only 8:30.

He surprised the hostess when he came charging down the stairs, awkwardly pulling the coat over his shoulders.

"Goodness," she cried. "Errything alright then?"

"Oh, yes, fine," he answered. "I just, um, just going for a wee drive."

"Well, be careful on the roads in the dark. The sheep are right wee devils."

He nodded and was out the door.

It was a long, snaking drive down the hill to the coast but

fortunately, just a single road. When Fintan reached its end, he turned right, heading north. The sea was to his left and a bright quarter moon lingered over the horizon, an hour or two from setting, its light sending a series of silver lines across the water that spread nearer the shore. The few remaining clouds had scuttled up over the hills on his right, and they glowed a pale pewter from the moonlight. There were no streetlights. None were needed.

He passed a small crossroads village cradling a snug harbor, a handful of boats swaying in the gentle waves. He had a window open slightly and a whiff of acrid grease from the fish and chips stand wafted in and pinched his nose. On he drove, passing small cottages cast about in the fields, their windows glowing amber, and hedgerows that curled through the gentle slopes leading to the inland hills. A small detached pub, alone at an unmarked intersection, was lined by three cars and a tractor.

Ahead were the lights, such as they were, of Dunnybegs. In the distance, he could make out the grocery store, now dark, and Fintan wondered if one of the cottages he'd already passed on the way was Roisin's home, and he imagined her, dotting about, worrying over a fire or settled in for the night, watching the telly. Beyond the grocer, a cluster of vehicles marked the village pub, but otherwise the street was empty.

Fintan steered off the road before entering the village proper, turning down the narrow lane leading to the small parking lot off the bay. He got out, pulling his coat closer about him, as a slight breeze was building strength and carrying in from the sea. The moon still lit the night and, though there were no lights in the small parking lot, Fintan had no trouble following the path over the slight grassy dunes to the strand.

At the edge of the grass, and spread out along the gentle curve of the bay, were several ancient wooden benches. Two were missing planks, but the one nearest him looked sturdy enough. Fintan contemplated it for a moment and then sat, looking up and out at the calm bay and the sea, stirring gently beyond the line of the natural breakwater.

She had been right, it was beautiful, perhaps even more so in this quiet silver light, with the sea a glassy dark blue and the only sounds the lullaby of soft waves shushing against the sand. He took in a slow, deep breath. Fintan was a lifelong resident of Dublin. It was itself a city on a bay, along the Irish Sea, which was but another region of the same body of water he was looking out on now. But this felt worlds away. It smelled different. These scents were conjured up from endless miles of ocean, smells from miles deep and from tropical lands. The Gulf current percolated in the Caribbean and the seas off Central America and rolled up across the western shores of Ireland in an endless parade of waves. It had been fashionable for a while for hotels, restaurants and upper middle-class homeowners in Ireland to plant palm trees. Because they could. They'd survive the winters, made mild by the river of Central American waters.

Dunnybegs had no palm trees, not that Fintan had seen. Here were dune grasses and heathers and other dwarf plants purpose-built close to the ground. And a few stooped shrubs shaped by the near-constant winds.

The evening was clear now. The moon was about eye-level, a half hour or so from the horizon. A scattering of stars blinked overhead, though the moon's brightness kept most out of sight. Fintan extended his arm, palm facing the water, blocking the moonlight, and looked up. As his eyes adjusted to the dark, more lights appeared and he scanned the skies for familiar constellations, though in truth he wasn't sure he'd recognize anything but the Big Dipper.

But, goodness, the stars! It was a vision, this sky. There wasn't an empty corner! And more kept appearing, as though they were lights of a city and him in a car driving towards them. It almost made him dizzy, so he stopped for a moment and dropped his head, looking out at the back of his hand and the bay beyond it. And then he saw it. Just a small bump in the otherwise gentle undulations of the water. If he hadn't been blocking the moonlight with his hand, he'd never have noticed it. Maybe fifty feet out? Sixty?

It was in full shadow, of course. He couldn't really make out anything but the shape. The seal could have been facing any direction, though Fintan was certain it was staring at him. In vain, he held up his right arm to block out more of the light, but the seal remained a silhouette. A phantom. He leaned forward, trying now to shield the light with his hands to his forehead, but the moon was too low, almost directly behind the small round shape holding still in the slow waves. Maybe it was a gull, or a piece of wood or even a clump of seaweed. Fintan blinked, squinted, and it was gone.

The bay was aglow now, the moon just kissing the horizon, and the surface a worn, smooth pewter. The winds had calmed. He heard a car horn in the distance. Faint music perhaps? And the low roar of the waves outside the breakwater.

Fintan had seen seals before, on the Dublin docks and at the zoo. They were an exotic part of his world, tame attractions. This one had not felt like that. This one belonged to a different world.

Though it had become still, he felt a chill, and pulled his coat closer. Time to go, get to bed. A long drive awaited him in the morning.

34

Thomas Becomes a Tour Guide

The Americans wanted a tour guide. And that is how the questions of his mother's multilingual abilities, of Molly's origins, of the book, and even of the story behind that photo of his mother and the young woman sitting at Killfish Bay decades earlier, were all put on hold for a few days, as Thomas became a host for a pair of dog-sick Texans.

The first two days both dawned with pallid and watery skies and everything damp, but brightened by early afternoon. At one point, Thomas observed that it was a soft day, which intrigued Nancy. Thomas thought to himself that they likely didn't have soft days in Texas.

The three of them, and Molly, met in front of the grocer both days and set off for long rambling walks, with Thomas relating the facts he had absorbed from his various readings and from talks with the locals. They followed routes he had hastily arranged for each day that began and ended at the store and looped through the countryside, past historic sites and stunning scenery, and passed near a pub or cafe for lunch.

On the third day, they were more ambitious. They all loaded into the Americans' rental car and ventured further north, up into the

Inishowen peninsula. They followed the Inishowen 100 – a well-known route circling the rugged peninsula. This was familiar territory for Thomas, who had grown up just across the border in Derry and whose family had made countless Sunday drives around Inishowen. Each turn, every crest, revealed another stunning view of windswept plateaus, or wide, gaping bays and endless sandy strands. Ruins littered the landscape, some hundreds of years old, others mere decades. There were hilltop forts, crumbling castles and ancient carved crosses.

The northernmost point of Ireland was also the most remote. At times, the main road contracted to little more than a car's width, hemmed by whitewashed cottages an arm's length from the road. Many still featured thatched roofs and the air was redolent with the smell of burning turf.

Thomas had been a bit hesitant to bring Molly along - he had never had her in a car before and wasn't sure how she'd handle the ride, but the Americans insisted. They laid a large blanket on the back seat next to Nancy, and Molly settled in easily. Add it to the mystery of this dog, thought Thomas.

Molly's presence gave them an excuse to stop often – not that they really needed it. Most any accessible beach was walked, every ruin explored, and every scenic view photographed. Thomas himself took dozens of photographs, nearly all featuring Molly somewhere in the frame. He was already thinking of the weeks of material he was accumulating.

They stopped for a late lunch in Ballyliffin, before driving up to Mallin Head, the northernmost tip of the country. Over strong coffee, sandwiches and soup, the Americans continued grilling Thomas about the countryside and fawning over Molly. They were surprised to hear he had only met Molly earlier in the year and shocked to learn that Thomas himself wasn't a Dunnybegs local, even if that very notion was yet foreign to Thomas.

35

The Alpha Dog

The Americans paid him. Thomas resisted, pleading that he hadn't been expecting anything and that he had enjoyed company on his outings, which was true. But they had insisted. "Best travel guide we've ever had," Dan had said. Fifty euros per day. Not quite bookstore money, but the only income he'd made in months. Of course, he had money from his mother's estate and could live on that comfortably for the year, but it still felt good – almost illicit. He wondered whether he should even tell his sister about the money before scolding himself for even thinking such thoughts as a grown man.

The weather turned after the departure of the Americans. For seven days, the place lost all color. No sapphire seas. No violet carpeted hills. No cyan sky with cotton ball clouds scudding past. No yellow gorse aflame on the roadside. No sun. Just black and gray everywhere, the sky indistinguishable from the sea. And the land as wet as them both.

The small streams that meandered through the fields became swollen rapids now, bursting their banks as they hurried to the sea. Roadside puddles became ponds. Low fields were lakes, their edges marked by vestiges of stone walls and hedges that looked in danger of going under as well.

All was wet, the damp having insinuated itself into everything, into the peat stacked in the bucket by the fireplace, the clothes hanging in the closet, the biscuits in the tin by the sofa, the towels slung on the door of the loo. It kept Thomas and Molly in, save for short dashes to the grocer and Fergal's for provisions.

It afforded time for Thomas to ponder Molly. She was so at ease and well-behaved with the Americans. Of course, they were dog folk, well familiar with how to manage a dog, but the episode made him realize he was taking the dog's intelligence for granted. She was a smart dog, he now thought to himself. Hell, she might know French!

The issue, he decided, was his lack of skills as a trainer. Well, that, and perhaps, French.

So, Thomas decided to take advantage of the week they'd spend mostly inside, together, and try some training. See if he could teach the dog new words. Molly had a half dozen or so toys - a selection of chew toys and tennis balls – that were kept in a small basket near the fireplace. Thomas began by taking one out, placing it by the door, and asking Molly to get it. He did this with each toy, giving each toy a unique name. Ball. Chewy. Fish. And so on.

It was slow going. Each time he placed a toy near the door, Molly grew excited, apparently thinking they were going to go for a walk outside, and darted back and forth between him and the door, ignoring the toy. Inevitably, Thomas would lose patience, walk back to the toy, pick it up and hold it before Molly, who would then, also inevitably, grab the toy and sprint around the house with it in her mouth, before circling back to him, her paws clattering on the wood floors and kitchen tiles, scrambling for traction or to stop, then spitting the toy at his feet.

Perhaps a week was not long enough. The lessons, however, mostly served to reignite Molly's interest in her toy collection and sparked a new routine driven by the dog. Each evening, as Thomas sat on the couch, reading or watching television, she began a parade of sorts, carrying each toy one at a time and setting it on Thomas's lap. Each delivery was followed by a hard stare from the seated dog, waiting for Thomas's response. Finally, he'd break, and pick one of the toys and toss it across the room or into the kitchen, yelling its name after it and setting Molly bounding off on a grand, exuberant chase. This she could do for hours. And so she did.

Results of this haphazard training were mixed. By week's end, Thomas couldn't be certain Molly had yet learned any of the new names for the toys. On the other hand, Thomas's training was going well - he was now throwing the first or second toy delivered to his lap, without fail.

The weekend weather was the worst of the lot, with steady rain bucketing and close skies inseparable from the sea. Thomas was restless, and eager to test a new theory about Molly. He let the morning fire die out, dressed in his rain gear, and set off for the bus to Derry by way of Letterkenny. He had 150 euros and a dire need for a decent pair of hiking shoes, a good coffee and a French-English dictionary.

The first leg of the drive, from the bus stop outside of the butcher shop to Letterkenny, was all bumps and bounces, the bus accelerating beyond what seemed reasonable and prudent, then slowing suddenly to navigate tight turns and narrow passages. On clear days, the ride was improved by the views, which would suddenly change from tight closeups of the pressing hedgerows to expansive sweeping views of the landscape, first sharp and harsh highlands carpeted by heather and then giving way to a patchwork of undulating fields, which had by now come fully to life but on this day were flat and dulled by the weather.

By Letterkenny, the rain had eased and the skies lifted somewhat and it continued like that for the drive into Derry, though the stops for passengers became much more frequent the closer they got to the big city. Every time he took this journey, Thomas was left feeling that he had moved far away from civilization. Bus rides back to Dunnybegs felt like driving forty years into the past.

He was glad to finally disembark at the bus lot by the Guildhall and to stretch his legs on the steep walk up Shipquay Street, the air full of familiar Derry accents and the diesel smells from buses and trucks straining up the road. He surprised himself with the speed at which he strode up the steep incline. Six months ago, the climb would have left him winded with sore calves.

He decided to linger in the city for a few hours, as it was surely still pouring in Dunnybegs. He dropped into the bookstore first, but was disappointed that the two clerks working were young women he didn't recognize. It was a Saturday, so the regulars were likely off, but it was a bit jarring to see no familiar faces. He found a small, paperback English to French translation book, selected a couple newspapers and headed for a cafe for lunch.

The streets were busy, teeming with families and young people enjoying the break in the weather. The first spot Thomas looked into had a crowd by the counter waiting to order, so he ducked back out and made for a smaller place off the beaten path. It, too, was bustling and noisy, but he claimed a small table and perused the menu board, happy to have something other than his own cooking.

While he ate, he leafed through the book. Outside of a very failed attempt at Irish in school, he'd avoided language classes, and now, as his gaze fell from one awkward looking combination of letters to the next, he was remembering why – and regretting the whole idea. Even if Molly did know French, he sure as hell didn't. And he had no idea how to pronounce the words before him.

He set the book aside and picked up the local paper, thinking he'd keep up with the news in his hometown, but it was mostly publicity photos and people-about-the-town shots, nothing that really caught his interest. Besides, a mother and two young children had encamped at the closest table and the toddlers sounded to be at war with one another. He sighed loudly, rattled the pages of the paper, even angled his seat away from them – the chair's feet squawking on the cement floor – but nothing pulled the mother's attention from the screaming brats.

Abandoning that tactic, Thomas hunkered down over his plate and focused on making quick work of the sausages, beans and chips before him, using the last of the chips to mop up the remaining sauce from the beans and leaving the plate spotless. Then he put the books and papers back into their bag and headed back out into the day, determined to follow the city's walls down towards the Guildhall and stroll the riverwalk.

By now, though, the Saturday crowds were out in force. The lane atop the walls was thick with families pushing prams, children with dripping ice creams, and careless teens bouncing off one another. He turned off the path at first chance and headed to the streets below, taking his chances with the traffic instead.

Here, too, the passageways were full. Cars crept along roads, moving in fits, dodging buses and lorries and swinging suddenly to the curb to disgorge passengers. It was, well, it was frankly discomforting, and Thomas had to remind himself that his last days in Derry had been back in early winter, when the days were short and wet, and him inside the store during daylight hours.

He had planned to meander, wandering along the riverwalk and taking in the sites as a visitor might, but the mobs on the path meant he couldn't be at all casual about it. The sidewalk itself was a river, a swift current that hindered dawdling. He broke off at an intersection and made a beeline back to the bus station. If he was quick enough, he'd make the earlier bus to Letterkenny and get back to Dunnybegs two hours before he'd planned. Be better for Molly, anyway, he thought.

He caught the bus as it idled in the parking lot, made his way to an empty row of seats midway back, and settled in for the ride, unfolding the Irish Times and losing himself in the news for the duration of the ride.

The wait between buses in Letterkenny was just fifteen minutes and as soon as his jerked to a stop and the door hissed open, he clambered on, making his way past the few old ladies planted in the front seats and the family spread across both sides of the aisle before finding an empty bench and plopping down, setting his bag next to him to prevent anyone from landing beside him. Behind him, there were two teenage boys at the very rear of the bus and several rows back, a folded-over figure with blue hair, apparently asleep.

By the time the bus shuddered, lurched forward and bounced out of the parking lot onto the road, he'd finished the front page and tried to open the paper, but was stymied by a crease in the broadsheet that kept the page bent over. He shook the page, trying to flatten it out, but struggled and gave up, brusquely folding and slapping it onto the seat. Sighing, he reached into the shopping bag and pulled out the French book.

He was reading the copy on the back cover, which promised he'd be speaking like a true Francophile in no time, when he realized someone was standing slightly behind his seat, peering over his shoulder.

"Are you reading French, now then?" It was Cara, who must have been sitting somewhere behind him.

"Well, hi! I, ah, hadn't recognized you," he answered. It was true. While he typically avoided eye contact with anyone on public transit, Cara was a welcome sight after a week of being mostly shut in.

She slid into the seat behind him and set her backpack close to the window. "Aye, well, it's the hair. What do you think?" She tucked a few strands behind her left ear.

"It's so different. I mean, it's very nice. Aqua, is it?"

"It was meant to be blue, but over ma blonde hair turned a bit more green. Be careful of spontaneous decisions made immediately following payday," she laughed. "Me mum will not be happy."

"Well, I think it's great," he offered. "It reminds me of the sea."

She slapped his shoulder. "There you go! The color was inspired by the water. It's a long story, but suffice to say I might have met someone at school."

"Someone who likes blue hair?"

"Ach, go on," she answered. "We might have gone on a long walk down to a park that overlooks Lough Maron - have you ever been to Cork? No? Well, there's a castle and it has a wee cafe and there's a path along the river. And we bought these, what, little pastries and lattes and had a bit of a picnic and sat and talked and, you know, it could have been forever. You know, when you meet that special person?"

She looked radiant. Thomas was struggling to show the proper amount of happiness for her, but it was all tangled up in his heart with a small helping of jealousy. The most he could manage was a nod and slight smile. "So, what is his name?"

"Her name, Thomas. Victoria. She's fourth year like me, but headed to med school. She talked about the color of the river, how luminous it was, how it was such a beautiful shade of blue. Like my eyes, she said. Well, my eyes are more bluish green, but in the bright sunlight they get bluer. Anyway, when I got paid at the end of the week, I decided on a lark to get my hair colored to match the river that day."

In the low light of the bus, her eyes looked green, though maybe that was in comparison to her hair, which appeared bright cyan. They were friendly eyes. Indeed, her face, with its soft lines and the one faint dimple on her left cheek that grew every time she smiled, was warm and unassuming. Combined with her enthusiastic manner, Thomas had felt uncommonly comfortable in her company from the start.

But he was embarrassed now that he'd forgotten Cara's sexuality. He knew, of course, but as their acquaintance grew into a friendship, the fact had lost importance and slipped away. The pangs of jealousy he was feeling had more to do with the thought of having to share Cara with anybody at all. He realized how much he had missed her company on his walks.

"Are you done with school then?"

"Naw, just home for the weekend. No classes Monday and Tuesday, so I can spend a few days at home before finals."

Thomas frowned. "I'm guessing you won't have time for a walk?"

"Sorry, no. But here we are right now on this bus! Tell me all your news! How is Molly?"

Thomas told her about the Americans, his brief spell as a tour guide and his growing following on PhotoLife - all of which she knew from following his accounts on social media.

Then he told her about the possibility Molly might understand French.

"That's why you've the book!"

"It's silly, I know. I mean, I'm no good with languages. Just looking through here, I'm not going to know how to pronounce anything. I'd just, well, I'd like to be able to communicate better with her."

"Well, I'm not an expert with dogs, yet. But I've seen you with her plenty, and you have a very good way with her."

"I do?"

"Ach yeah. Do you not see the way she watches you? I think she trusts you, Thomas, and that's the most important thing. You're her pack leader. Alpha dog."

Thomas laughed. "I don't know about that. She might be the one in charge. Hell, she's probably bilingual!"

"So, about that, you needn't have bothered with the book, you know. There are apps. I swear you are so behind the times with that phone! You have apps where you type in the word and it'll pronounce the foreign version."

"Really? Well, that might work."

They were nearing Dunnybegs by now, and Thomas's stop was first, so he began gathering up his newspapers and bags. When he stood up, Cara jumped up and put her arms around him.

"I'll be home again in a few weeks. We'll catch up then. Give that wee dog a hug for me," she said.

Thomas had stiffened at the feel of her arms around him, but he quickly relaxed into her hug, settling his chin onto her shoulder and leaning into her neck. Her hair smelt of tropical fruit.

36

A Signal of Change

Fintan had returned to work at a busy time. Fiscal end-of-year reports would be due soon and, as this was his first year compiling them, Fintan was determined to get a head start. Mostly, this involved gathering various monthly and quarterly reports and bulletins from the previous year and adding explanations and updates where needed. It was tedious but straightforward work, challenging enough to keep him occupied and helping the time pass quickly. The workdays hurried by.

The nights, though, were another matter. Fintan's routine had been supper, a quick tidy up followed by a cup of tea with the newspaper, and finally settling before the telly for a couple of hours until bed. But the regimen had somehow started to feel a bit uncomfortable, like a grown-too-small undershirt. Each day's newspaper felt indistinguishable from the previous one, the headlines differing little from day to day. On Thursday, he had devoted fifteen minutes to digesting the days' news before realizing he had been reading Monday's paper.

He flit about his flat, poking at a bookshelf, jerking out the odd book and flipping through a few pages before shoving it back in its place, only to return minutes later to repeat the exercise with a volume on another shelf. He'd flick through the channels on the television, growing more irritated by the number of adverts or reality programming. And often, he'd find himself back at the small dinner table in his kitchen and the collection of maps he had purchased in Dunnybegs. One or more would eventually end up unfolded and spread across the table, where he'd commence tracing the Donegal coastline with his index finger, reading aloud the names of the villages, rivers and bays along the way. Donegal, Dunkineely. Killybegs. Kilcar. Glencolumbkille. Ardara. Cloughwally. Dungloe. Arranmore. Bunbeg. Derrybeg. Falcarragh.

Many of them were little more than names on a map now, a clot of buildings clinging to a crossroads, a collection of ghosts.

Roads ran between them, though sometimes they were little more than lanes better suited to tractors than cars. And sometimes the roads swooped low near the coast and offered breathtaking glimpses of long, arcing golden strands and sometimes of sharp angled rock faces staring down the sea, but often the road snaked up to higher ground, revealing a patchwork of farm fields or, more typically, barren scratches of hard earth pockmarked by boulders and scoured by endless winds.

Some of the larger villages were market towns and Fintan was coming to know many of them, first the hand-painted signs a mile or so out advertising new potatoes for sale, then their main squares smaller than a Dublin block, just a scrum of businesses pressed together - butcher, grocer, hair salon, resale shop, cafe, takeaway and pub. Always a pub. And the street through the town squeezed to a lane and often blocked by a delivery truck or farmer's tractor.

Some of the towns, whether by design, chance or location, were tourist spots, their resale shops replaced by knitwear boutiques and the surrounding fields sculpted into golf courses.

Fintan was coming to know this place. The names. Even some of the people. He continued his finger up the coast, joining the familiar coast road, passing the lane running up to the B and B, and stopping at Dunnybegs, where he pressed his finger into the map. "Dunnybegs," he said softly. And he closed his eyes and imagined himself standing outside the grocer, and Roisin's hand on his shoulder, pointing him to the sea. "Killfish Bay," he whispered.

On Friday, he had made sufficient progress on the reports that the surface of his desk was mostly clear by lunchtime. He stacked the few remaining folders on the floor next to him and opened his lunch. A sausage sandwich, the last of the incredible sausages from Fergal, sliced lengthwise and planked between slices of bread, a little brown sauce covering them. He took a first bite and set the sandwich down. This was his first real free moment at work in the week. He looked at his monitor. He'd left the web browser open when he'd been searching for some statistics earlier.

He clicked through a few bookmarked sites absent-mindedly as he finished the sandwich, washing it down with a gulp of tea, until an ad for the Dublin zoo caught his attention. The small box was an advert for the zoo's sea lion cove and featured a small image of a sea lion. It stopped him cold, his left hand holding a chocolate digestive inches from his mouth. He clicked on the ad and glanced over the page for a moment, all the time revisiting that night a week earlier in Dunnybegs.

Then he maneuvered the cursor up to the search bar and typed in "what is the symbolic meaning of a seal?"

The top result looked a bit airey fairey to him, so he skipped down to the second and clicked on it.

It turned out to be a directory of spirit animal totems. "What are your animal guides telling you?" it asked across the top of the page, followed by a large photo of a seal sunning itself on a rock.

Fintan scrolled down.

"Listen to your dreams! The seal is telling you that your dreams, no matter how far-fetched or far away they may appear, are worth listening to. And following. The seal is a signal of change."

And then: "A seal also signifies trust and integrity. It serves as a reminder to use one's power carefully."

Fintan jolted back in his chair at the words, almost losing balance. He looked over at the wall to his left, where he had just this Wednesday taped up a map of County Donegal.

Follow my dreams, he thought to himself. But what are they?

37

Failing French

"Sit," Thomas said, holding his phone up to his face. "Assis," the charmless voice on the phone answered. He repeated the process several times.

He was on the couch. The dog, having already emptied her basket of toys and placing each one near Thomas's feet, was standing before him, staring expectantly, imploring him to act.

"Ah-see," Thomas said, out loud. Molly cocked her head, still staring intently at him. Her left ear was erect, the right one flopped.

"Ah-see," he said again, more forcefully.

Molly looked to be ready to step towards the couch, but instead, gathered up her rear legs, and sat.

"What?! Good girl," Thomas shouted, but the yell startled Molly, who darted off for the kitchen, where the screeching sounds of claws scraping at the tile flooring could be heard, before she rounded back out to the living room, to lay down next to her toys.

Thomas had a bag of dog treats beside himself on the couch and he held one out in his hand, offering it to the dog, who belly crept along the rug until she was able to take the morsel from his hand, her tail wagging wildly. Then, the whole process was repeated, again and again.

The treats were no larger than a coffee bean and Thomas doubted

Molly tasted anything, given how quickly she gulped each one down. Tasty small training treats, they were called. Mrs. Doherty had given them to him months ago, saying they were of no use to her, as she had no dog herself. It made Thomas wonder why in the world she even had them, but he since decided she was the sort of person who would see them in the store and pick up a bag, just in case a dog ever wandered by. No doubt she had cat treats, too, as well as a bowl of sweets, just in case.

Truth be told, of all the people he had met in this new chapter of his life, she remained the most mysterious to him. When they first met, on the day he arrived with Ginny, the two of them had pegged Mrs. Doherty as the town's busybody, the sort you'd spot whispering to other old ladies at the grocery store or getting the latest rumors from Fergal the butcher. Instead, she had turned out to be a sort of recluse. The short conversation they'd had that first day was the most they'd spoken. Nothing since then beside the occasional succinct critique of the day's weather. He'd see her now and then. On bright days, she hung her wash on the line; on Mondays and Thursdays she walked to the village for groceries and on Thursdays, stopped at the butcher's as well.

That Thomas knew all this would have startled the Thomas of a year before. In fact, it would have left gobsmacked anyone who had known that old Thomas, who had a well-deserved reputation for being mostly oblivious to the goings on about him. But Mrs. Doherty's shopping habits, like the fact Rose closed up the shop early on Wednesdays to get home in time to catch her favorite show on the telly, to the mornings (Tuesday and Thursday) Fergal kept his door locked an extra hour while he made sausages in the back room, to the exact time on Fridays (7:15 p.m.) that farmer Frankie drove his tractor to the Shamrock for a couple end-of-the-week pints – these were just a few drumbeats in the day-to-day, week-to-week rhythm of Dunnybegs.

And Thomas, though he was far from realizing it himself, was settling into the cadence of the place – right in step.

"Debout," the robot voice said. Stand. Molly tilted her head again and looked at the phone. "Dibboo," repeated Thomas. "Dibboo!"

Molly remained prone. Thomas picked up the book and flipped through to find "stand," only to discover that the French translation was not quite as direct as the app had suggested. There were different meanings of stand, some of which required lengthy phrases. Thomas, already feeling overmatched by a foreign tongue, decided to try another phrase.

He stood and walked into the kitchen, hoping the dog, who was now watching him, or more accurately, eying the bag of treats in his right hand with laser focus, would stay put. He made it to the doorway and then held the phone close to his face, whispering "come here."

"Viens ici," said the robot voice. This required another listen. Thomas repeated himself and held the phone close to his left ear. "Viens ici."

"Veeyawn he see," he said, hesitantly. Then again, louder. Again, Molly tilted her head to the side, as though Thomas's odd behavior may make more sense viewed from an angle.

Apparently it did not. Molly launched in another direction entirely, thundering off into the bedroom, where the muffled noises indicated several leaps onto and off of the bed, and then clattered back into view, with one of his slippers in her mouth.

Thomas stared at the dog, then at his phone and then back at the dog, who rather dramatically spit the slipper to the floor, with just the very white tip of her black tail showing the slightest bit of a wiggle. Whatever game they were playing, she was enjoying it. Hadn't figured out just what it was all about yet, but here the man was clearly trying to communicate with her. And he had treats. She could do this all day.

And would have, had Thomas not finally, at the end of several hours of what had devolved into a long series of his failed attempts to pronounce French commands but which instead resembled nothing so much as an old man with sinus issues, answered by the dog's frantic attempts to do whatever in the world he was asking her to do, leaving her toys scattered throughout the cottage and his shoes, slippers and loose socks left god-knows-where.

"Ah, feck it," Thomas sighed, tossing the French book onto the side table next to the sofa, which sent a photograph briefly fluttering in the air before it landed at his feet. "Let's go for a walk, eh?"

He bent down to pick up the photograph - it was the snap of his mother as a young woman, sitting on the stone wall with another young woman. "Why don't we visit the Beetle, Molly? See what we can find out about this picture."

38

A Mystery Revealed

Under a bright sky of high clouds, the sea spread out like a sheet of rippled silver, pulled back from the shore. The low tide revealed an expanse of sand pocked with gnarled and knotted kelp strands, small shells and the detritus of ocean life - dead starfish, crippled crabs and broken sand dollars – and then the shorebirds would swoop in, all spindly legs and spastic movements, seeking a meal. The breeze was light and Thomas felt no hurry, letting Molly set the pace.

The walk south ambled through fallow farm fields and open land marked by long patches of low violet heather and crippled broom shrubs, still covered in the deep yellow flowers of early summer. The geology shifted frequently along the coast, alternating between smooth, moonlike boulders dropped along the shore, house-sized shards of black shale knifing into the Atlantic, and sea cliffs several stories high. On some of their first walks, Thomas had worried about Molly edging too close to the sheer drops, but he soon realized she was far more familiar with the landscape than he was. By now, he trusted the dog enough to let her venture out of sight on her own explorations, safe in the knowledge she'd eventually trot back to his side. She was a herding dog, after all, checking to ensure he was headed in the right direction.

It was a typically quiet early afternoon at the Beetle, judging by the lack of vehicles along the road, but Thomas knew by now that the place was rarely ever devoid of a handful of locals, who'd wander in throughout the day for a pint, or pairs of hardy cyclists, seeking warmth and a decent toilet on their rambles. Indeed, as he swung the door open and his eyes adjusted to the low light, Thomas spotted a couple of cyclists parked at the bar, their shed fleece and rain gear draped on the chair to their left and nearly drained stout glasses before them. Americans, likely, identified by their pristine gear and predilection for Guinness.

Donal was behind the bar, leaning forward, a dirty dish rag draped over his shoulders, likely giving the Americans directions. His face brightened when he spotted Thomas. "Molly!" he shouted, immediately reaching for a small saucer. The cyclists pivoted as well, revealing themselves to be middle-aged women. The one nearest, tall and slender with unnaturally red hair tumbling about her shoulders in loose curls, eyed the dog. "Is this THE Molly? She asked.

Thomas was getting used to this by now. Molly was a beautiful dog, the prototypical Irish farm dog, and Thomas's photos were fast making her a celebrity.

"'Tis indeed," said Donal. 'The one and only." He carried the saucer of Guinness over by the fire and set it down by the dog, which slowly began lapping at it.

"Oh my God!" said the other woman, a shorter woman with close-cropped silver hair and a plaid scarf wrapped tightly around her neck. "It drinks Guinness! Isn't that precious?"

Thomas settled onto a bar stool a few down from the women. "This, ladies, is Thomas, Molly's manservant," chuckled Donal.

"We're such fans," said the redhead. "We even joked that we were going to ride slowly on this section, hoping we'd see Molly! Such a pretty dog!"

Molly, having finished her few drops of stout, was now curled into a circle before the fire.

"You've made her a star, mate," offered Donal, as he set a pint glass before Thomas. "Sandwich? Soup?"

"Ta, not today." Thomas kept an eye on the shorter woman, who had jumped from her stool and dropped to her knees before Molly, snapping photos.

The four chatted for a bit, Thomas answering questions about Molly and then suggesting a few short scenic detours for the cyclists. They were headed north, aiming to complete the Inishowen 100 before ending their journey in Derry. Thomas recommended several spots in Derry and then took a few photos of the two cyclists crouched on either side of Molly, who was jostled awake to pose for the pictures.

When that task had been completed, and after the two women gathered up their gear and visited the loo one last time, they departed, and a silence fell over the Beetle. Donal was humming some old ABBA tune as he stoked the fire and then resumed what appeared to Thomas to be an endless chore of drying glasses.

"So, Donal, I, uh, have a question for you."

"'Sup, mate?"

Thomas reached into his coat pocket and withdrew the photo, which he had sealed in a cellophane bag. "I have this old photo and Eamonn at the Shamrock thought you might know who this is next to my mum." He offered the photo out to Donal.

The barman grasped it tenderly in his left hand and rubbed his forehead with his right hand, running it back over his head. He let out a slow, deep breath.

"Awk, look at that. Up at Killfish."

"I recognized the place right away," said Thomas. "But I had no idea my mother had a history here before she bought the cottage."

"Aye, she did, lad. A few summers. I think she was finishing up schooling. Holidays."

"She never said..." said Thomas. "So, you knew her then?"

"I was younger, so we weren't pals or anything, but I knew her. Stayed at our house a few times."

"Go on with yourself! Do you know who that is with her?"

Donal smiled slightly. "Aw, lad, 'tis our Molly."

Thomas was confused. He glanced over at the dog and then back at Donal, who seemed surprisingly emotional. "The woman? You know her?"

"Molly. My sister."

Thomas was dumbfounded. His mother had never mentioned this part of her past, had never spoken of having been here before - outside of the few times Thomas's family had passed through on holidays.

"So, my mother and your sister were friends? I, well, she never mentioned her..."

"Oi, they were best mates," said Donal, eyes still locked onto the photo. "You know, the sort that finishes the other's sentences. Met one day at the bay and before you knew it, were inseparable. Jaysus! Look at those smiles." He sighed. "Your ma stayed with us a few times over the summer. I'd be off with my Da on the boat. Still fishing, then. So it was just your ma and Molly. Twas no one else around near Molly's age then. The two of them did everything together."

Donal finally set the photo down. He looked up at Thomas. "My own Mam called them Siamese twins."

"Did they remain friends? I just can't... My mother never mentioned her when we were growing up. We even came through Dunnybegs a few times on our holidays. You think she'd have reminisced, even."

Donal set the bar rag on the counter and leaned back. "The two of them talked about going to college together, at Queen's up in Belfast, I think."

Thomas nodded. "My mother went there, but only for a year," he said. "I think it was money."

"Well, they talked about Queen's, about going together. But our Molly earned a scholarship to a uni in Paris. It was too good to pass up, a fisherman's daughter from Dunnybegs and all. So off she went." He paused. His expression hinted that there was more to the story.

"But they kept in touch?" Thomas asked.

Donal looked over at the dog, still curled by the fire. He was searching for the words. He glanced at Thomas, to see if he was getting the picture. "You can't blame her. From Donegal? A chance to go to Paris?"

Thomas realized he was clasping the pint clasp in both hands and set it down. Had his mother been in love with another woman? His mind was reeling.

Donal took the glass and slowly poured it half full, setting it down before Thomas. He seemed to anticipate the question. "Now, I'm not saying there was anything improper or anything like that. I think the two of them were, what do they call it? Kindred spirits. Aye."

"I...Jesus. I don't know. I mean, I never heard of any of this. Wait, where is she now?"

"They were close. Like sisters, maybe. I don't know. Och, I was a wain. I knew not all about any of that. I got a postcard from her with the Eiffel Tower on it and she said she was having a grand time and told me to look after Ma." He inhaled, slowly, and let out a deep sigh. "It was the first Saturday in October when the Gardai came to our 'ouse. Two of them. They asked to speak to Da but he was on the boat. They made my Ma sit down at the kitchen table and they sent me outside, so I ran around the house and scuppered under the window and listened. You know, the streets in France are backwards? They drive on the right side of the road. A lass from wee Dunnybegs, her head all full of her studies, well, she wouldn't remember that." He took a long breath.

"Walked in front of a lorry."

"Oh Jesus."

"They said it was instant. I don't know. Sure, that's what I'd tell a mother."

Thomas looked down at the photo. Helen and Molly. Siamese twins. Wide smiles. Carefree. The whole world laid out in front of them. It was so much to think about that he forgot for a moment that Donal was describing the death of his own sister and how hard that must be. Instead, he was entertaining a disordered slideshow in his one mind - his parents arguing over a Christmas dinner, the two of them toasting an anniversary with new Waterford crystal glasses, his mother's stoic sadness after his father's death, his father jiggling his car keys impatiently whenever his mother ran late...

"Anyways," said Donal, "the dog..." he glanced over at Molly, still curled into a warm mound before the fire.

"She named the dog after your sister," finished Thomas. And she was teaching herself French.

39

No Objections

"Fintan?"

Fintan looked up from his monitor. His inquisitor was a tall, spindly redhead with a long, narrow face. He was leaning against the door, cradling a manilla folder in his arms.

"Ah, yes..."

"Jim Sheahan, though you can call me Jimmie, or Jimbo," the redhead said. "You have a minute?"

Fintan looked back at his monitor. He was in the middle of updating an employment spreadsheet. Not really. Why didn't people call first, or, better yet, email?

But Jimbo was fast, and by the time Fintan turned back to answer, had pulled a chair over and sat himself by the side of Fintan's desk.

"Ministry of the Environment. I've been assigned to review a certain fish farm proposal on the northwest coast." He set the folder on the edge of the desk and used it to push Fintan's teacup out of the way. Fintan, who was somewhat uncomfortable at his personal belongings being handled by others, grabbed the cup and set it brusquely on the opposite side of the desk, though he immediately worried his reaction was too strong.

Thankfully, Jimbo was too busy shuffling through the papers in his folder to have noticed. "Ah, here it is! Salmon Cove, International Fisheries."

Fintan looked up; he had been keeping an eye on the two digestive biscuits stacked beside his keyboard, debating whether they also needed relocating.

"Oh, yes, well, I, ah, submitted that more than a month ago. In Dunnybegs. Did I leave anything out?" In truth, it was the first such proposal document Fintan had been involved with. He'd assumed that the Ministry of the Environment would do its own investigation and send him back a recommendation.

"Well, we all move at our own pace, don't we?" answered the redhead. "No, I think everything is complete. The outline documentation in triplicate. Your notes on economic impact. Also forwarded to Licensing?"

Fintan nodded.

"Well then, I think we have everything we need."

Fintan nodded again, slightly. "So, your department will begin the research process now? How long do you anticipate this taking, before you make a recommendation?"

"Well," Jimbo answered. "Sure, you've pictures here as well. Did you take them? They're really quite nice."

"Ta. Fancied photography when I was young," responded Fintan. He swelled his chest a bit and leaned back in the chair, but nearly lost his balance and had to flail his arms to restore equilibrium. "I, ah, took several trips up there to perform a thorough economic investigation."

"Brilliant, yes," said Jimbo. "Still, should get hazard pay for dashing all about that god-forsaken place, right? Anyway, good to go, I should think." With that, he closed the folder and pushed it further toward Fintan.

"You mean, you're done? That's it? Approved?"

"Aye, I don't know, seems okeedokee to me. No objections from the Ministry of the Environment."

Fintan hadn't expected such a cavalier response. "You don't need to visit, conduct interviews?"

"Och, mate, it's Donegal. What – we're talking four hundred sheep and a couple thatched-roof cottages. International Fisheries could propose a nuclear power plant up there and no one would give a shite."

Fintan was silent for a moment as he processed Jimbo's decision, or lack of decision. This wasn't exactly due diligence on Jimbo's part, which meant it was Fintan's own report that would carry the bulk of responsibility here. His mind carried back to Roisin's words – and the view from her door. "It is a place of rare natural beauty," he finally said, in a low whisper.

"If you're a sheep!"

"You know, a lot of folk there think the bay should be left well enough alone."

"Owk, for feck sake, they'll move a few wee rocks and string some nets," said Jimbo. "The locals will be hard pressed to notice." With that, he pushed the chair back and stood up. "Mind if I have a biscuit?" he asked. Again, before Fintan could answer, the redhead snatched the top biscuit, pushed the entire thing in his mouth and turned to leave.

"All in your court now, mate," he shouted, setting loose a spray of digestive crumbs.

Fintan slumped in his chair and stared blankly at the folder, and then up at the map of Donegal on his wall. He pictured Roisin at the door of her shop, shaking a fist at him as diggers crawled toward Killfish Bay. He sighed. Then gathered up the remaining biscuit in a tissue and dropped it into his trash bin.

40

The Press Arrives

The man and dog left the pub and followed the road north as it flirted with the coast. Gulls lifted from fields as they passed by. Occasionally, the dog separated off and sprinted after them, sending birds scattering and complaining. The sea was dark teal. Smudged clouds lazed over the horizon, gathering up the next day's rains. A thin veil of high clouds stretched overhead, softening the shadows but making the daylight even more glaring.

The dog turned to its house instinctively, but the man continued along the road's shoulder, before turning down onto the lane leading to Killfish Bay. The wind was soft, but it still came in waves that carried across the top of the dune grasses, sending them swaying. The bay was calm and the tide high.

The dog quickly recovered and joined the man as he strode down the curving lane, past the stone wall captured in that long-ago photograph, through the small parking lot, and then up into the dune grasses.

At the height of the dune, the man turned and lowered himself onto one of the broken-down benches facing the bay. The dog continued on, accustomed as it was to this beach, and driven by its own need to patrol its length, which it commenced to do, sniffing at each tangled clump of sea life left behind by the tide.

Thomas wouldn't have been able to describe the walk from the Beetle, nor would he be able to put words to his emotions at that moment. But memories continued to sweep through his mind like the breeze on the dunes and he was struck by how little detail he remembered. Was that how it was for everyone? The details were gone. The sound of his father's voice. Gone. His mother's exact words THAT day. Her laughter. Her smile. Gone. He could paint his life in broad strokes, but the details, the very things that made it his life and no one else's, those were lost. Had he never been paying attention to any of it? To his own life?

For he noticed things now, this Thomas. He observed the change in Donal's voice as he spoke of his sister, the patterns the retreating waves made inside the bay, the dog's regular glances back over her shoulder for reassurance as she patrolled the shore, the smell of Rose's new perfume, the way Eamonn's eyes warmed when he spoke of his wife.

Ginny used to slag him, saying he was off with the fairies anytime he'd drift away from a conversation or lope off into a daydream. "An airy wain," as his Granny might have said, but now he wondered if he was really recalling an actual conversation. Had he ever heard her say that?

Fair to say, the day's revelations had left him winded like a hard tackle. He sat silent for a while, gathering himself, and then looked out over the strand for Molly.

"Is that THE Molly?" The voice startled him. He swung around to find a young woman standing right over his shoulder, smiling broadly.

"Sorry, didn't mean to startle yous," she said.

She was diminutive, with a deep, husky voice that seemed totally unnatural coming from her. Thin, angled face and wide eyes and, yes, a broad smile. Her frame didn't seem a match for her personality.

"Brionna Kinney, sure you can call me Brie, like the cheese." She moved around to stand before him and extended a hand. His hand dwarfed hers. Still the handshake was firm. Her thin fingers dug into his hand and vigorously shook his whole right arm.

"Molly," he answered. "I mean, yeah, that's Molly. I'm Thomas."

Even her laugh was oversized, a haha that boomed like a lambeg drum.

"I'd surmised that. Sure, yer man up the Shamrock said I might find you around Killfish. I'm with the Donegal People's Weekly. I've been following you and Molly on PhotoLife. Bang on, mate, what, how many thousand followers now?"

Thomas smiled, a bit relieved she seemed more normal than at first sight.

"Yer lass there has become a wee celebrity, hasn't she? I'd love to interview you for an article in the paper."

"You're having me on," said Thomas. "Me?"

"I've seen all the mentions. You and the dog are pretty much local ambassadors."

Thomas glanced down at the beach. Molly was on her back, writhing back and forth on the sand. She'd be a right mess.

"It's amazing," Thomas said. "Just began posting photos and now I get messages from all over the world." He shook his head.

The woman dug deep into the backpack she'd carried over one shoulder, producing a notebook. "So, yous ok with me sitting down and asking a few questions?"

Thomas nodded meekly and shifted to one end of the bench. They chatted for a good fifteen minutes, during which she asked about Molly, his photographic experience and his other experiences. She appeared to know something about his background and that he wasn't a native. She then took some photos herself and they agreed Thomas would let the paper use one of his photos of Molly, taken up at the stone circle.

Before she left, after she had packed up her notebook, Brionna turned and looked out over the bay, and remarked that she couldn't understand the fuss over the fish farm proposal. "I mean, it's not much use to anyone now, is it?"

To be honest, Thomas hadn't really given the fish farm much thought up until then. He'd heard Cara's impassioned arguments, seen the pro and con posters and knew how some other folk around the area felt, but it had remained a distant issue to him. He truly hadn't cared one way or the other.

But on this early evening, sitting on a splintering bench overlooking the tiny bay that sheltered Dunnybegs from the countless gales and waves of the Atlantic, a bench his mother likely sat at countless times, perhaps even forty years earlier, staring out at an endless horizon beyond the small rise of rocks with her Molly next to her, well, it suddenly felt to him that this small bay held important history.

"Feck 'em," he declared, with an intensity that surprised even himself. "There's life here. And beauty. And they want to turn this into a factory?"

"Aren't you only saying that because you like your view," she responded.

"Ach, I'll not be here long. None of us will. I mean, I pass by all of these empty, abandoned cottages on our walks. People come and go. Jobs come and go.

"This," he said, gesturing out at the bay, "it's always been here. It should stay that way. There are hundreds of years of memories here, in these hills, in these paths. The stubborn folk who lived here. Died here..." His voice trailed off and he turned to locate the dog.

"Moll," he shouted out. The dog lifted her head and turned to jog back toward him. He stood up.

"Anyways, smarter folks than me will figure that out."

With that, he started back over the dune towards the parking lot and the path leading back up to the road to the cottage.

41

A Buyer Appears

The weather turned that night. Strong winds churned the sea, tossing wave after wave at the ancient rock formations that formed the bay's breakwater. Rain lashed at the wee cottage's windows and rattled shingles on its roof. The gale lasted the night, and while the rain softened at the light of dawn, it left behind a pale, murky sky.

For several days, the showers kept close by, never giving more than an hour or so reprieve before washing in again. Thomas kept mostly indoors. The sky matched his mood - gloomy and unsettled. He lost himself in reading and in editing the most recent photos of Molly.

On the third morning, he awoke and picked up his phone to see the time and discovered that Ginny had called sometime overnight, leaving a voice message. He sighed. She knew the hour difference, but persisted in calling him overnight.

He toggled the phone's speaker and placed it on the closed toilet as he brushed his teeth, clicking on the play button.

"Tommy! It's your glamorous sister Ginny. You surviving, lad? Listen, great news. Your prison term is up. There's a buyer interested in the house. American, would you believe it? His assistant contacted me. Assistant! I'm sure one of those rich wankers who sees a photo and thinks it's the next beach paradise.

Really, not having you on. Anyway, this assistant is coming to look at the house at 1 o'clock Thursday. Can yous tidy up a bit? Show him around. Sure, ye may as well start packing things up - and find a place back in Derry! OK, love you... wait, did I tell you I'll be over next month? More details later, ta."

Thomas set his toothbrush in its cup and leaned both hands on either side of the sink. "Feck."

His reaction surprised him. He'd always known this was a short term situation, that he was nothing more than a temporary caretaker. That had been the deal. Sure, a deal made without his consent, to be honest, but it had been the sensible solution, and he accepted knowing it would be short term. For the first several months in Dunnybegs, he had dutifully scanned apartment listings in Derry every chance he got. But he hadn't checked in months now. At some point, he had even ceased buying the day-old Derry Journal from Rose's.

"Oh, feck, feck, feck," he whispered. Molly had wandered into the bathroom and sat on the bath mat, looking up at him. He stared at his own face in the mirror. He had several days' growth of facial hair. His hair was lighter, ever-so-slightly sun-bleached. His features were cleaner and sharper. He had lost weight - that had been obvious from his growing dependence on belts - but hadn't really noticed it in his face. He was leaner. Lighter. All the walking with Molly, the miles and miles every week, combined with a diet mostly devoid of fast food, had changed him, physically.

He stared at the face in the mirror. It wasn't the face of doughy Thomas from Culley's Booksellers in Derry. Gone were the soft, almost unformed features. He examined his newly flat cheeks, his sharpened jawline. He was undergoing a transformation and perhaps it wasn't just physical. While he had not yet figured out his life and had yet to discover his destination, all the hikes he had taken with Molly – they were steps in HIS journey. For seven months now, he had been moving towards something, and away from something else. And though the end of his journey still remained out of sight, the path most certainly did not lead backwards.

That realization, triggered by Ginny's news, left him restless and added to the sense of being unsettled he'd felt since the revelations about his mother. Seeing that the rain had lifted, he dressed and accompanied Molly to the bay. The battleship gray sky hung low over the sea, the horizon ambiguous. But to the east, the clouds were bright silver and climbing high over the hills. The rain was in retreat.

Back at the cottage, he prepared a scrambled egg breakfast for himself and Molly, then started a load of laundry in the small washer in the kitchen, guessing he'd be able to hang it out to dry. Mostly he paced, wandering from room to room, determining what might need cleaning and taking a halfhearted inventory of his own belongings. His move here had been a few boxes of books and clothes. Moving out all of his mother's furnishings would take a bit more effort.

He thought of calling Ginny back - it would be the middle of the night in Sydney. "Sis, it's me. Great news about the cottage. By the way, Ma might have been a lesbian. Cheers!"

The thought of Ginny's face made him smile, but he decided instead to send her an email. He'd need to start getting more information about the timing of a move and all of the finances, anyway. He'd no job. No idea where he'd go. Derry? Or somewhere new, like Sligo, or Dublin? He sighed. None of those felt like home.

He was too anxious to ponder why that was, his mind too scattered to settle on what otherwise might have been an obvious realization: he had indeed found his home, in Dunnybegs.

42

Donegal's Top Dog

Mid-afternoon, Molly sprung from her spot on the rug, leapt up on the chair by the window and let out a sharp bark. She was typically so quiet that each time she did this Thomas jumped. He looked up from the kitchen table just as someone knocked on the door.

He opened the door to find Cara, who greeted him with a loud, "Well, here's our local celebrities!"

She had carried the newspaper down from Rose's, and unfurled it, holding it up before him.

The top half of the page carried a photo of Molly - his photo of Molly.

"HOW DUNNYBEGS PUP BECAME DONEGAL'S TOP DOG."

"And I knew yous when," Cara laughed. "Twenty thousand followers!"

He'd forgotten about it - about the conversation with the reporter days earlier.

Cara turned the page towards herself and began reading.

"When Derry transplant Thomas McKay inherited his mother's home in Dunnybegs, he also gained a canine companion. Now, thanks to McKay's photos of the captivating collie, the pair have become internet famous. With more than 20,000 followers, they have become unofficial ambassadors for Donegal." Cara lowered the paper and looked down at Molly, "Jaysus, ye'll need an agent next!"

Thomas smiled. "I'd forgotten all about that. Ran into this writer down at the strand the other day. Said she'd been looking for us."

Cara shook her head. "Go on! Can I get your autograph, then?" She laughed. The school term was over and she was home for the summer. Thomas cycled through joy at the thought of her being around and then sadness that his remaining time in Dunnybegs was running out.

"Wait, it's even better." Cara leafed through the paper, before unfolding it and holding it up again. Another photo of Molly. Another article.

"DONEGAL'S TOP DOG TOUTS TOURISM, TAKES BITES AT FISH FARM SCHEME."

The article repeated several elements of the front-page story but added some of Thomas's negative comments about the fish farm. He'd completely blanked about that. Hell, hadn't the reporter put her notebook away by then? They were just making small talk.

"You know, I wasn't sure how you felt about the farm," Cara said. "I mean, feckin' awful and all, but I figured with you being temporary here, you mightn't be assed…"

Truth was, he hadn't really cared. He knew Cara was one of the more vocal opponents, as was Rose, but most of the other locals he had encountered appeared to be in favor of anything that might bring jobs. The headline puzzled him, though. He didn't recall having put forth tourism as an alternative that night and when Cara read out the full article - after greeting Molly and taking a seat on the couch – it was clear he hadn't. Instead, the reporter had used Thomas's own actions, highlighting the scenery with his photography and acting as an informal tour guide, to portray him as advocating that alternative.

Sitting on the chair facing her on the couch, seeing her bright smile, he didn't bother explaining to Cara that what he'd really been feeling that night was a sort of anger. It wasn't what he had learned about his mother's past that was earth-shattering, it was what it said about his relationship with her, how little he knew about her. His own mother! He'd been sitting on the broken-down bench that night stewing over his inability to forge close relationships with anyone as an adult. What he'd really been thinking that night was that Dunnybegs and everyone in it could just go feck themselves.

And then his sister sent him reeling. He was leaving. For feck knows where. And the laughing woman sitting on his couch tossing Molly's toy – well, he'd be saying goodbye to her soon, too.

"Earth to Thomas!" Cara threw a tennis ball at him. "Didja hear me? Yous up for a walk? Just a short one - need to get to the shop in a wee bit."

Thomas turned and glanced out the window. The sun was fighting through the clouds, the sea a bright silver and the broom swaying in a steady breeze. "I'd love to."

43

Bad News

Lunchtime. Fintan pulled his sandwich from the insulated lunch bag and grimaced upon realizing he hadn't cut it into halves earlier that morning. Oh well. He carefully spread an unfolded paper napkin on his desk and set the sandwich on it, then gently moved his cup of tea into its place. He tore open a bag of crisps and rummaged through the bag for a big one, which he maneuvered fully intact into his mouth.

He grabbed at another napkin, balling it slightly in his right hand to remove the grease, and then leaned over to select his lunchtime reading, the latest issue of the Donegal People's Weekly.

The front page was topped with a lovely photo of a dog on a beach at sunset, the sun a low and dark orange ball just to the left of the dog's head, as though the dog was sniffing a rubber ball on the sand. He smiled at the photo but skipped past the article beneath it, instead scanning the remaining headlines on the page for anything of interest to him.

He needed both hands to handle the sandwich - tinned salmon spread on butter on brown bread – but once finished with his first bite he again wiped his right hand on the napkin and resumed paging through the paper. A hair salon was having a charity event. A children's group was staging a play. A new priest had arrived. The usual quick read.

He placed another unfolded napkin over the sandwich and set the paper over that, reaching for his tea. He took a sip while turning the pages with his left hand until a headline stopped him cold.

"DONEGAL'S TOP DOG TOUTS TOURISM, TAKES BITES AT FISH FARM SCHEME."

Fintan set the tea down abruptly, causing a small splash that landed near his keyboard. He ignored it and read the article, then flipped back to the cover. He looked closely at the photo again. It was fairly dark, but he could just make out the low line of rocks just offshore. He had been there himself. Killfish Bay.

"Oh goodness," he whispered.

44

A Summer Walk

Thomas and Cara had started south, along the coast, but peeled inland before making it as far as the Beetle, briskly tackling the first small sloping roads leading up to the ridge of hills. The world felt swept clean after the stormy weather of the previous week and the sky was clearing with every step, as though the last few clouds were melting in the sun. Birds were busy, raucous and darting among the thick hedgerows lining the lanes.

Peak summer. Here on the west coast, with nothing on the horizon but the sea and sky, the day's light could linger past 11 p.m. Thomas had noticed his body clock adjusting - keeping him up until midnight now and leaving him groggy most mornings. Molly was always up by 7.

Cara had news. Victoria had left. Moved back to England for the summer before heading to Germany to finish her studies. It was clear, though unsaid, that the bloom of romance had faded, along with Cara's hair, which was now the shade of bleached denim.

But Cara was moving on. Her studies were going well and she had landed a great twice a week internship at a veterinary office in Sligo for the summer – a position that often led to employment upon graduation. She'd be a licensed vet this time next year.

Mostly, though, they spoke about Thomas's life. Cara was still amazed by the number of followers he had acquired and by the fact tourists were seeking him out. "You do know a lot, though. It's all those history books you're always at!"

They followed paths that ran mostly parallel to the coast below, heading north. Here sheep lulled on open fields that provided more encompassing views of the sea below. Molly ambled and jogged off frequently for more intensive exploration, though she respected fences - even single strung wires - and angled back often to see that all was okay with Thomas.

At one point, Thomas directed Cara's gaze to a field further up the hillside, where there was a boulder the size of a car, covered with carvings of swirls, circles and waves. It made you wonder, he said, what they were. Did they have any significance? Or were they just doodles?

Another field, a bit further along on their walk, held the remains of a cottage's foundation, the only sign left of the lives once lived there. "When I see these places, I can't help but think of the people who lived here," he said. "I mean, it can't have been easy. Can you imagine winters here four hundred years ago? No rubbers. No parkas. No cars." He looked over at Cara, who was smiling at him. "What?"

She shook her head. "Those tourists are telling you something, Mr. McKay. Your new calling. Your photos are bringing folk here. And you can guide them around. Thomas McKay Tours!"

Thomas smiled sheepishly and looked down at the ground. He wasn't ready yet to tell her that he wouldn't have a place to live by the end of summer, that he'd be on his way soon.

"So," he answered. "I found out more about my mother and why she came here."

"Go on."

"Well, you remember that photo I found of her? Taken at Killfish Bay when she was a young woman? Donal at the Beetle recognized it, I mean, the woman in it, next to my mother."

Molly had run up with a stick in her mouth, which she dropped at his feet. He absent-mindedly picked it up and tossed it ahead of them, sending Molly off in a burst.

"It was Donal's sister."

"Yer winding me on!"

"No, they were mates, I guess. I think they met when my mother came here with her parents one summer. Became besties. My mother even stayed with them. The two of them even talked of going to university together.."

"Wow, and where is she now, Donnie's sister? Odd I've never heard of her."

Thomas sighed. "She died. Went to France for college and was killed in an accident." Thomas stopped and turned to Cara. "I think it might have broken my mother's heart, Cara. I, um, well, I think they may have been in love." He reached down and stroked the dog's fur. "Her name was Molly. My mother was teaching herself French."

Cara let out a long, slow exhale. They had come to a crossroads on their walk. To their right, the lane narrowed and meandered up a slight incline to a cluster of old cottages and a modern home that enjoyed a commanding view of the Atlantic below. Ahead of them, Molly had already started down the broader road that veered left and led eventually to the coastal road.

"Well, that explains a lot, doesn't it?" Cara exclaimed. "I mean, Molly and her learning French, even why your mother wanted to live out here."

"Aye, it does, I guess. Though it also sort of feels like I didn't really know her at all. I mean, this is a whole part of her life I didn't know shit about." He stopped and eyed the dog, which was splashing through a muddy ditch in the fallow field beside them.

"Maybe I just don't connect. You know, back in school, I never felt I really fit in. Like I was always an outsider. I've never had close friends, not really. Growing up, it was always just my ma and da and Ginny. And then when my father died, it all changed. I dunno, I haven't felt like I belonged anywhere since then."

Cara slowed her walk and placed her hand on his left shoulder. "Awk, you can't fault yourself for being unawares of your mother's secrets. We all keep parts of ourselves hidden away. Maybe we're afraid of what folks think, or ashamed of ourselves, or maybe it hurts too much."

She moved to face him and then pulled him towards her for a hug. "Thomas, you're a good man and a good son. You've come to care for her home and her dog when she needed you. And you've learned she had memories of happy times here. Good memories. That's all you need to know. It doesn't matter what the relationship was, or that she kept those memories to herself."

Her hair smelled of ripe fruit with just a hint of the hot case at Rose's.

"And an outsider? For fecksake, you've 20,000 feckin' followers!"

Thomas smiled. "It's almost 28,000 now. But it's just social media."

Cara pushed away from him and playfully punched his shoulder. As she turned to start down the road, a cloud of starlings lifted from a tree line a field over and spun up heavenward - trailing a charcoal arc across the sky that quickly vanished.

"Gotta make tracks, Thomas. Rose will have my arse if I keep her waiting."

They fell silent then as they quickened their pace along the road. Blackberries, plumped by the recent rain, were ripening in the sunlight, and they paused several times to sample a few.

The day had continued to brighten as the last few pale, high clouds burned off in the sunlight and the sky was an uninterrupted cyan dome by the time they reached the coastal road. Thomas and Molly would continue on across two wide, empty fields to reach the walking trail that would lead home, while Cara decided to break off and follow the road up to Dunnybegs and Rose's.

"I'll see you up at the store, sure," said Cara. "And maybe we can get out for a good hike Sunday. You can give us a tour!"

Thomas laughed at that and waved, turning up a small muddy path in the field.

"Hey," shouted Cara. "Hey!" He turned. "You belong here, Mr. McKay. Here."

With that, she spun on her heels and stepped quickly up the road.

Thomas smiled back and watched after her as she grew smaller, the arms of her bright yellow rain mac tied around her waist and strands of her faded aqua hair lifted by the breeze. It was Monday. On Thursday, a potential buyer was coming to look at the cottage.

45

Oslo Might Need to Wait

Seattle's climate was well misunderstood, that's what Ove Knutson had always told friends back in Norway. All they knew of it was from episodes of Frasier on television – an endlessly gray and rainy place. And it was true that winters could be bleak in the Northwest: whole months of short, dim and damp days. But, hello, Norway?

Summers, on the other hand, well, summers were perfect for this descendant of Viking warriors – dry, sun-kissed days and cool nights.

Until the occasional heat wave crept in and then settled down in this wide valley between the Olympic and Cascade mountain ranges, covering everything with a stifling blanket of trapped muggy air. A temperature inversion, they called it, and it meant sweaty nights and days-long taupe skies that were packed full of all sorts of toxins with nowhere to go. Ove hated these spells and he had suffered nearly a week in the present inversion.

He had lived in the northwest almost all his life; his parents had moved to Seattle when he was six, following his mother's hiring as an engineer at Boeing. He had been a tall child but he topped out at 6'2". Now, in his late forties, his blonde hair was becoming white and his perpetual slump made him appear shorter. He could no longer command a room, but he was a good negotiator - a behind the scenes guy, as Clyde described him. That would soon be needed.

"What the fuck is this?" The text blinked at him from his monitor. "Come here."

Ove had forwarded an email that was waiting for him when he arrived that morning. From the Irish government. At least from the fellow they had been dealing with on the fish farm project. He hurried over to Clyde's suite.

Clyde had pushed his chair back from his desk by the time Ove arrived, his laptop already shut. This was going to be Ove's problem to solve.

Ove sat on the chair facing the desk. It was a simple, modern piece of furniture seemingly intended to torture whomever had the misfortune to sit in it. Ove figured it was Clyde's power move to keep any meetings short. "You know as much as I do," he said.

"Oh, fuck me." Clyde rubbed his temples and looked up at the ceiling. "I thought we'd this thing nailed down."

"Well, that was the last communication from Dublin. Sounded like they'd bend over backwards to get any sort of economic development in that area. But apparently, there's been some big news report about the anti-farming crowd. I dug a bit deeper. Some celebrity dog has come out against it. I think Dublin is a bit worried the press might blow up on this."

Clyde glanced out his window. The thick air obscured any mountain views. He drummed the fingers of his right hand on his desk. "A celebrity dog? For fucksake. You're headed there this week, right?"

"I leave Wednesday night. Two days in Ireland, then off to Oslo for a week's holiday."

"Yeah, well, get with the mayor and see what he's saying. If he's still good to go, that ought to quiet Dublin. But, Ove, Oslo might need to wait."

Ove nodded and slouched towards the door. His condo had no air conditioning and he had woken up the past several mornings wheezing. He had no desire to cancel Oslo.

46

The Buyer Arrives

The newspaper article only added to Molly's local notoriety. Now, any walk Thomas and the dog took was continually being interrupted by folks saying hello and taking photographs of themselves posing with Molly. Thomas's email was inundated with invitations from local businesses, asking that Molly stop by for a pint or a latte or sandwich or to view handcrafted pottery and, of course, to post a few photos accompanied by the appropriate hashtags. Americans Greg and Betsy witnessed Molly's popularity when Thomas and the dog guided them around the Donegal coast midweek. By then, Thomas's PhotoLife account had ballooned to 36,000 followers.

The weather held all week as well - soft, dewy mornings that gave way to the clearest of afternoons gifted with a golden light that appeared to emanate from every flower and every wave crest and left the Atlantic an endless sea of sapphires and diamonds until late in the evening.

It would have made for brilliant hiking, but Thomas had a house to clean. Outside of the day spent mostly beach combing with the Americans, Thomas labored indoors, overcome with a sense of gloom and an uneasy feeling of having come loose again from any mooring. He had even begun to alter his view of the house. It had been his mother's house; soon, it would be someone else's. He was removing himself from the picture.

The deep cleaning presented him with the unwanted opportunity to assess his own life by way of inventorying his physical belongings. There wasn't much, if you excluded his late mother's furnishings. But those - the couch, easy chair, bed, pots and other odds and ends – represented a step up from the possessions he had abandoned when leaving Derry. He truly hadn't accomplished much of anything. The bulk of his belongings now were things left by her.

The indoor work, combined with such humbling rumination, had left him feeling quite foul by Thursday, the day of the visit.

It was another dry day, though thin, high clouds had swept inland overnight, and their presence softened the light and made for a more subdued landscape. Would it matter to the buyer? Standing at the window, gazing down over the hillside to the bay, Thomas wondered what any American would see in this place.

Further along the narrow lane that led to the cottage, a small grey sedan motored away from Mrs. Doherty's house. It moved tentatively along the pockmarked path and slowed to a stop beside the white cottage, just moments after Thomas had stepped away from the window.

The driver emerged and, rather than making straight for the front door, wandered around to the back of the house, and began taking photos with his cell phone of the building and the surrounding land. There was no real yard to speak of, just a gradual thinning out of the heather and grasses that covered the hillside the closer one got to the house itself.

Just then, the door swung open and a dog - Molly – came bounding out, making directly for the photographer, who instinctively dropped his hands to cover his crotch and stepped back.

"She's harmless," yelled Thomas, who followed the dog around the side of the house. "Are you the buyer, then? I mean, potential buyer." Shit, he thought to himself, don't be a bloke and ruin this!

"I'm a representative of the interested party, yes. You must be Mr. McKay?"

"Call me Thomas." He reached out his right hand, which the American briefly took in his. Molly, having satisfied herself that the visitor meant no harm nor carried any food, had ambled off into the field.

"Well, it's a beautiful view, innit?" Thomas nodded towards the bay. He smiled, though internally he was already dismayed by his own attempt to make cheery small talk.

"Yes, indeed," said the visitor. "If you don't mind, I'll just take a few more photos around the property." Which he did, circling the house twice, taking numerous photographs of the building itself and of the landscape. He asked to be shown the property lines, which Thomas endeavored to answer, though he truly wasn't sure.

It took Thomas imploring him to get the American to venture inside; he almost appeared indifferent to the interior of the home. After all the photos he had taken of the exterior, Thomas was surprised that the American had pocketed his phone upon entering the home. And seemed eager to leave.

Indeed, after the briefest walk through, the American stepped back to the front door and turned to face Thomas.

"Well, I think that's all I needed to see. We will be in touch shortly. I believe a Mrs. Genevieve Browning?"

"Aye, Ginny. Ma sister. She's handling the sale."

"And she's in Australia?"

"Yes, but she'll actually be here in a few weeks."

"Ah, well, regardless, we have her contact info. Please let her know we'll be in touch?" He swung the door open, stepped back to allow Molly to barrel in, and then walked out.

"Yes, definitely," said Thomas, following him out. "Oh, I didn't catch your name?"

The American turned as he opened his car door and smiled. "Ove. Ove Knutson."

After he drove off, Thomas put on the kettle and made himself a cup of tea. It had been anticlimactic. A full week digging out and cleaning and organizing and even some more purging and the agent had been in the house less than five minutes! Almost seemed more interested in the property than the house.

With no cleaning to do, and his mood no better, Thomas spent a restless afternoon, muddling around the house. Given the potential sale of the house, his time and energy might have been best spent doing more organizing to prepare for packing up his belongings, but he was in no mood. By late afternoon, he desperately needed to get out of the house, and decided to head to Rose's with Molly, convincing himself he needed some potatoes and sausages. What he really desired was someone to talk to.

47

The Mayor Has a Plan

Closing up his shop every day was an hour-long job for Fergal. The remaining meat needed wrapping up. Counters needed sanitizing. Knives cleaned. Floors mopped. And then there was the preparation for tomorrow – ensuring that full rolls of butcher paper were in place and that the cash register had a fresh cartridge of receipt paper. It had become a habit now that he checked the temperature in all of the freezers and refrigerated cases and then checked them all again. Just to be safe.

When he was done, but before he left for home, before he walked through the door, closed it behind him and then twice tugged on the door to reassure himself it was securely locked, before that, he sank onto a chair and sighed. Shite, he whispered to himself.

As a mayor and as a businessman, he was well versed in how glacially slow governments often moved, and he was a patient man. But the latest news, delivered in person that afternoon by the representative of International Fisheries, was disheartening. The news was as unexpected as Mr. Knutson's visit itself.

The Dublin government was getting cold feet. Had he known? Was he? Thought you were on board, Fergal, thought we had an agreement of sorts here. Are we really letting a damned dog derail all these plans? He'd actually sworn, Mr. Knutson had. A first in all of their correspondence and discussions, which had all displayed a certain level of decorum.

No, of course not, Fergal had responded. He was still in favor of the project, but it was a delicate balance he had to maintain. Respect the wishes of the populace, that sort of thing. He couldn't be seen to be too eager for this, given that it would indirectly benefit him.

"Indirectly?" Knutson had howled. "No, it was pretty damned direct. A loan for your fish shop. McCart, it's balls to the walls time. Fish or cut bait, man."

Fergal lowered his head and vigorously rubbed his face with his hands. Knutson had made it clear the Americans were more than ready to cut bait.

Fergal had seen the article, of course, and had laughed at it with Bridie. He knew the Derry lad and he knew Molly. He had served Mrs. MacKay for years. Bless her soul - she came in twice weekly for ground white meat chicken, a couple of pork chops and a bone for the dog once she had taken it in. And as mayor, he was chuffed to see the dog's fame. If people came to Dunnybegs just to see the dog, well, maybe they'd like some of Donegal's best sausages to take home with them.

It hadn't occurred to him, even reading the second article, that it could make any difference what one moody hillwalker from across the border mattered. What mattered were the locals. What should count were the opinions of the people of Dunnybegs, and if Fergal knew anything, he knew how the people of Dunnybegs felt. Sure, there were a few young hippies who always howled about the environment or saving the whales or trees or whatever, but there weren't that many of them left in these parts - and the ones who were still around were just biding time until an escape route appeared. A handful of them, with the energy to draw up a few posters and post them around town. But that's it. Not much of a movement. How would any bureaucrat in Dublin know that?

And then Fergal whistled, for an idea had come to him. A grand idea that would demonstrate both his seasoned, diplomatic leadership AND get things moving again. But he would have to move fast.

He jumped up, grabbed the wrapped package of mincemeat that would be that night's dinner and stepped lightly to the door, letting it close behind him as he hurried off toward his car.

There were just a handful of posters around Dunnybegs and in several of the businesses up and down the coast. He was right about that. On paper, it didn't appear to be much of a movement. But Fergal wasn't particularly savvy about computers and he was fully in the dark about the workings of social media. So he was completely unaware that one young veterinary student had begun a hashtag and that #KeepItKillfish was currently trending, having been posted and reposted from three continents to date.

48

A Sudden Storm

"Where will you go?"

It was Thomas's good fortune that Cara had been helping in the store that day and she quickly suggested a walk, sensing Thomas's mood. They headed north through the town, oblivious to the small black sedan parked in front of the butcher shop, and turned up a small dirt lane that eventually curved to parallel the slowly rising cliffs that ran nearly a mile before giving way to a series of outcroppings and rocky beaches littered with tidal pools and seaweed. The wind had picked up during the afternoon and waves were gathering strength, sending up great spumes of foam as they battered the rocks. The spray kept Molly from wandering too close to the water's edge, but she still broke into occasional gallops, disappearing ahead of them only to fall back into view as they slowly caught up while she lingered at any interesting smell.

Thomas told Cara about the potential buyers and about his sister's impending visit. The locals had all known the cottage was for sale, but it wasn't unusual in these parts for properties to linger on the market for years.

"Back to Derry?"

Thomas looked at his feet and kicked a small stone further along the path. He shrugged. It was true - he had no idea what he should or ought to do next. Returning to Derry made the most sense. He'd have to find a new flat and there was no guarantee the bookstore would have any work for him, but he'd face those obstacles anywhere he'd go. There'd likely be money from the sale of the cottage, but he had no idea how much or when it might arrive.

They walked on. The path rose to surmount a wide spit of land that jutted out several hundred meters into the sea before giving way to vertical cliffs, as though an end had been sliced off. From the peak, if the air was clear, two small islands could be spotted in the distance, but the western sky was now darkening and a mist had cut visibility.

The path slowly descended and curved back towards the sea, leading down to a clutter of giant slate shards that emerged from the sand and stood, steeply slanted, like bulwarks against the sea, pockmarked with shells and draped with brittle husks of seaweed.

Molly scrambled along several of the wider shards, peering down into tidal pools and occasionally poking at a hurrying crab.

Thomas sighed and stepped over a discarded energy drink can. He had taken to carrying a bag along on most of his walks and collecting any trash he came across, but had left the house without one.

"Can I be honest?" he asked.

"Aye, of course."

"It's... well, I just don't really feel like I belong anywhere. I mean, my sister, she's always known what she wanted. Always been sure of herself. And you, I mean, you know what you want to do and you could probably predict pretty well where you'll be in five years. I've never, ah, I don't know. I've never felt sure of anything. Like, this is what I want to do with my life. Never.

"I mean, I was in Derry because that's where I was born. And working in the bookstore kept me busy and paid my living expenses and all, but it wasn't like I had any vision of becoming a manager or something. It's just what I did."

The mist had come in on the sea winds and the trail – a bare path cutting through a sheep pasture of short grass and heather – had grown slippery in spots. They both found themselves looking down at their steps. Cara glanced over at him. "First, it's not like everyone else has it all figured out. Be grand if we did. And, two, are you not a local celeb? Look at ye - here less than a year and you're a big star in the papers. Sure, everyone knows ye!"

Thomas smiled weakly. "Molly. Donegal's top dog. Not me."

Suddenly, his left foot slipped out from under him and he lurched to his left, grabbing Cara's shoulder to steady himself. "Shit, sorry!"

"Whoa!" Cara straightened herself and looked out at the sea. The soft day had given way to angry waves that now burst against the rocky coast with concussive slams. The leaden sky over the sea rendered the horizon indistinguishable. "Jaysus, the weather's turned!"

But as soon as she finished that, a strong rush of wind carried inland, pelting them with fat globules of rain. The drops splattered and bounced at the ground, which transformed almost immediately into a viscid muddy glop, as though it had been laying in wait to do just that.

"It's right awful," said Thomas. "We'll be soaked by the time we get back."

They turned in unison and began pecking out steps back along the trail.

"Shite, we should cross over to the road when we get a chance," shouted Cara. "Be easier..." She stopped.

"Where's Molly?"

Thomas glanced around. Visibility had dropped to next to nothing in the downpour. The dog was nowhere to be seen.

"Didn't see her pass us. She has to be back this way. Just head back, we'll come across her."

They hurried on, as best they could. The path alternated between thick, mucky puddles that grabbed at their shoes and slick stones that tested their balance.

No sign of the dog.

The trail cut down close to the shore, near the large shale formations and Thomas remembered Molly clambering along the slate. He turned and stepped towards the strand.

Looking out towards the waves was difficult. But as he stared into the wind and piercing rain, he imagined he saw a shape on the sand. Probably a small boulder, but…

"Molly?"

They both ran towards the beach. The dog was on her side, her back facing the waves, which splashed over her. She was straining to lift her head out of the water.

"Feck, the waves are going to pull her out," shouted Thomas.

He arrived at her first. Molly let out a high whine when she saw him.

"It's ok, girl, we're here."

Cara sloshed into the waves beside them and leaned over the dog, examining it. "She's lame. She can't move her back leg. We gotta' pick her up. Can you go around her back and reach under her?" The dog was soaked. Shivering.

Thomas moved between Molly and the waves, squatted down as far as he could and slid his arms under the dog. With Cara holding Molly's back hip, he lifted the dog and tilted her body tight against his, so that Molly's head rested at his right shoulder. Together, with Cara still steadying Molly's rear leg with her hand, they moved out of the waves and back to the field.

Cara looked across the pasture. "We have to get her to a vet. Do you think you can make it across this field? I think our best chance is to get to the road as quickly as we can and try to flag someone down."

"Aye, can try."

They stepped into the field. It was empty of sheep now, who clearly had better things to do than tolerate the weather in the open and who had scampered off to huddle by a line of gorse.

The ground was an uneven series of tiny hillocks, ditches, small clumps of heather and the odd football-sized stone. Thomas stepped carefully, afraid of doing more damage by falling or dropping Molly. The lashing wind and rain worked against his balance as well.

"We're good, girl," he whispered to the dog. "We've got ye."

It felt as though they were crossing the moon, slicing across this endless sweep of scrubby bog. At least he had worn hiking boots; Cara's trainers were ruined. At one point as she stepped forward, her left foot came clean of the shoe, which remained stuck in the glop. She used Thomas as balance while she retrieved it and clumsily put it back on. As she turned to step forward, she screamed.

"The road, we did it!"

Another fifteen to twenty meters and they made it onto the tarmac. They looked left and right. No traffic to be seen.

"Keep heading back," said Thomas. "Someone is bound to come along."

Perhaps the weather had soured any drivers. They walked along a good ten minutes without spotting another soul. Fortunately, the rain was lightening.

"What do you think happened?" Thomas asked.

"I don't know, maybe a rogue wave hit her? I mean, her back leg isn't right. Lord knows what else."

And then they heard it - the low purr of a combustion engine coming up behind them. They turned to look simultaneously. Slowly grinding along the road toward them was a tractor pulling along a small trailer. Cara stepped out and waved at the driver.

Farmer Frankie slowed the tractor to a stop beside them.

"Aye, what's all this?" he shouted over the rumbling engine.

"The dog's been hurt," shouted Thomas. "Can you give us a lift into Dunnybegs? We can get a car there."

"Och, sure, Frankie's uber service at your command! Can ye's get up into the trailer?"

Cara climbed up first and stacked the several scattered bags of spuds into a corner. Thomas set Molly onto the trailer bed and then jumped up. He sat down beside Molly, who rested her head on his lap. She was trembling.

"Once we get to the store, I can borrow Rose's car and we can take her to the veterinary in Letterkenny. Your man there is grand. He came to speak to my class a few times."

Thomas nodded, his hand gently stroking Molly's head. They were all soaked. The horrible day had somehow managed to get even worse. Molly whimpered and shook from a violent spasm.

Much worse.

49

The Veterinarian

"I'd say a displaced hip, at the least. But we'll need an x-ray to be certain. We need to get her dry and warm and help her with the pain before we do any real poking around."

The veterinarian, Dr. Chauncey Crockett, was a tall and lanky man with a thin, angular face and short, curly black hair. His white frock and dark, thick-rimmed glasses lent him an air of gravitas that Thomas found reassuring. He had taken his glasses off to speak and now put them back on.

Thomas and Cara were seated in the waiting area, a small room with a yellowed linoleum floor and bright fluorescent lighting, lined on three sides with gray plastic chairs, the air redolent of an ammonia and cat urine mixture. Puddles grew under their seats.

"Your Molly is settled for now," said Crockett. "The best thing mom and dad can do is go home and take care of yourselves. Get out of those wet clothes. We'll watch over her and do a complete examination as soon as we can and I will call with the news."

Cara shot a glance at Thomas. "Oh, we're not mom and dad. I mean, we're not together. He's the dad. I'm just a friend."

Thomas would have blushed had his face not already been raw red from the wind and rain and exertion of the day. He felt a bit anxious about leaving Molly, but he was also still shivering and more than ready for a fire and a good cuppa. He left his phone number with the receptionist, who made a show of handing him a brochure about financing options, and he and Cara walked back to the car.

"You've really become close to that dog," said Cara. "She means a lot to you."

Thomas looked across the roof of the car at her. Shrugged. "I guess. Took a while. I mean at first it was like she didn't really acknowledge me being there, outside of opening doors for her and filling the dinner bowl. But yeah, she's like my only friend out here."

Cara feigned an angry frown. "I'll try to ignore that remark, as you're still in shock, mister. Sure, you have plenty of friends here. And, of course Molly didn't take to you right away, she was in mourning. Ye both were."

"Still are, I think. You know, she's the only living connection to my mother here. A dog," he said, shaking his head. "A dog! And can't tell me anything about her."

"That's not true. Molly being a rescue is proof your ma was a loving person. Molly is in good care, Tommy," she said, spreading a blanket across the front seat of the car before they climbed in.

"Yeah, I know." Thomas exhaled and looked down at the flier. In a better mood, he'd have brightened at her calling him Tommy. Only his sister called him that.

But his mind was racing along the road far in front of the car, pondering the sale of his home, a move to God knows where, the need to find a job, and now this, a hefty bill.

"I've no savings," he whispered, absent-mindedly, before falling silent for the remainder of the drive.

Cara pulled up at the cottage and stopped the car. She looked over at him and shook her head. "Some day, huh?"

"Aye, some day," answered Thomas.

"Now, you'll phone me, right? Phone me, not a text, once you hear anything, right?"

Thomas nodded yes.

"She'll be ok, Tommy. So will you." With that, she turned the key and the car lurched forward. Thomas closed the door and turned to the cottage. Today, this evening, it was still where he lived.

50

A Trek to the Holy Well

Sleep had not come easy. In spite of a cup of tea and a hot bath, the day's chill had penetrated to his core. He had a difficult time getting comfortable in bed. The dog's absence was palpable. He had grown accustomed to the feel of her weight at the foot of the bed and the sound of her soft snoring. Eventually, he found an old hot water bottle and placed that near his feet. He fell asleep with the television still on.

He awoke in the morning to continued light rain and heavy, dark skies. The clinic opened at 9, but he figured it might be some time before they could perform a thorough examination and call him with details. What to do until then? He tried reading, picking and paging through various volumes in what was now a growing collection of local history books, but he couldn't settle his mind enough to concentrate on them. He turned to the television and sped through the full offerings of stations. Nothing caught his attention.

Eventually, he decided it was a good opportunity to launder the dog's bedding and blankets, so he gathered them and tossed them into the washing machine. The forecast called for a clearing by afternoon - perhaps it would be nice enough to hang them out to dry.

Next, he brought his hiking boots into the kitchen, where he first scraped off the larger dried bits of dirt into the garbage bin and then scrubbed them one at a time in the sink, carefully washing off the muck without soaking them all over again. They had dried well by the fire overnight and once he'd completed the task, he set them back before the fire.

It was 11 when his phone rang.

"Allo, Thomas here."

"Mr. McKay, it's Sharon from the Letterkenny Animal Hospital. I've got an update about your wee girl here."

"Aye, how is she?"

"Och, the wee dear's sleeping now. The doctor's given her a good look over. He initially guessed a hip dislocation and there does appear to be some trauma there but the larger issue looks to be a fractured pelvis. Rather than waiting for things to calm down a bit, he advises surgery as soon as possible. He'd like to perform that today, if you can give me an OK. Best chance to save the leg."

"Well, if that's his recommendation, yes. Will it not just heal on its own?"

"He doesn't advise that. Not where the fracture is located and not with the additional trauma to the hip. Usually, you see injuries like this in dogs hit by cars."

"We think she was knocked by a sudden wave. We found her on the ground, unable to stand."

"Oh, aye, sure your friend told me. Anyways, Dr. Crockett will call you himself after the surgery, alright love. Bye bye."

"Ta."

He placed the phone on the coffee table and sank back into the couch. Surgery was going to be expensive. He tapped his hands on his thighs and turned to look out the window. It was brightening outside. Rain had stopped. And then he swung back to look at the coffee table. There, next to his phone, was a smooth, dark gray stone, flat and oval in shape, about the size of an egg.

It was the stone he'd absent-mindedly pocketed at the holy well. What had Eamonn said – it was bad luck to take one without a good reason. He picked it up and rolled it in his hand. Well, he had a reason now. But maybe he should take this one back and do it properly. He glanced at his boots by the fire. Aye, a walk would do him good.

The rain had let up and the clouds were lifting by the time he left the house. He had the stone in his pocket along with an old collar of the dog's. He was neither very religious nor terribly superstitious, but why take chances?

In the bay, dozens of shore birds dotted the shoreline, scavenging for food stranded by the now-receding tide, all of them skipping forward and then darting back with each wave. A fresh, steady wind was making quick work of drying the road and footpaths. The day was brightening.

Thomas's mood - that was another story. The walk to the well cut through patchy fields littered with sheep and snaked up the eastern hills on lanes crowded with wild fuchsia. As the road climbed, the occasional breaks in the hedgerows revealed breathtaking views of the lowlands leading to the sea. In the far distance, the ocean sparkled silver. The sunlight would soon wash inland, chasing the clouds.

But Thomas wasn't much inclined to notice the views. His head was down, as though he were carefully picking out each subsequent footstep, but in truth his gaze was empty and his mind full. His hands were stuffed into his jacket's pockets and he rolled the small stone in his right hand.

He was no longer a young adult. He was not at the point in his life where a person like Cara found herself – on the cusp of her life's journey, the destination unknown but full of the promise of excitement and discovery.

His life had wrong-turned into a cul-de-sac. This year was supposed to have been a learning opportunity for him, a time out during which he would figure out the rest of his life. Or at least, what came next. At the moment, walking up a steep path on a fool's errand when he rightfully should have been packing, the past year felt less like sabbatical and once again like a sentence. Maybe this was grieving. Or maybe this was just him.

He hadn't experienced any revelations. Just the opposite, he thought. He had grown comfortable in the gentle routine of three meals, one or two long walks and the minor chores needed to keep house. He had, he felt, become more aware of the world around him, even if that world for the most part was a loose pattern of well-trod paths, fewer faces than he'd ever see on a single bus in Derry, the ever-changing seascape ... and a dog.

Yes, the dog. And that dog was now a further complication. Hell, he was on a fecking religious pilgrimage for an animal he hadn't even known a year prior! Figure that. Somewhere along the way, on the long walks and the daily tug of wars with her chew toys or his socks and the weight and warmth of her at the foot of the bed, she had made her way into his heart.

"You're well into a routine, lad, walking yer dog even without the dog." Thomas had arrived at the Holy Well, and upon turning off the roadway, was met by Eamonn, sitting on one end of the bench, facing out to the sea.

Thomas nodded a greeting and forced a smile. "Molly's been hurt," he answered.

"Ach, I know, sure. Have you heard any news from yer man in Letterkenny?"

Thomas sat beside the man, and looked out at the view. The air had dried out. Any boats passing would have a view of the hillside. "Surgery. Today actually."

"So you've come to the well, have ye?"

Thomas withdrew the stone from his pocket, held it up. "I'm sort of here because of you. I hadn't returned this one yet. Figured it couldn't hurt to bring it back and take one, proper-like." The dog's old collar was in his other coat pocket.

Eamonn was alone. No Izzy. No Dixie, the dachshund. Like Thomas, he'd walked up here by himself.

"Wise not to tempt fate, lad." Eamonn was well-bundled up in a waxed navy mac and tweed cap but still was a slight figure next to Thomas. He rested his arms on his thighs and held something clasped tight in his hands.

"Aye." Thomas gazed out at the vista before them. The sunlight had reached shore and the small slivers of sandy beach shone like curls of golden ribbon against a calm silver-blue sea. His mind, however, was roiling. Molly's welfare. His own future. The cost of the surgery. Where'd he go and how he'd manage finding a job, moving and looking after an injured dog. He let out a sigh. "I've an injured dog, Eamonn, and buyers are eyeing the house. I'll have no home, massive vet bills and not the slightest idea where the feck I'm going. I need any help I can get."

"You know, I'm not from these parts meself," said Eamonn, after a spell. "Felt like an outsider the first few years I was here. I mean, I had my Izzy and that helped. She loved to walk, that woman. Would walk the feet off a marching band! We wuz busy, mind ye, but when we weren't at the pub, we'd be out walking. Me, who had been at sea for ages, who got itchy legs after a week or two on shore! We walked everywhere and she'd tell me who lived in each house we'd pass and the poor souls who had once lived in the abandoned homes that were now just crumbling bricks. And one day, behind the bar – musta been a Saturday, as it was packed full of folk – well, I just remember looking around at all the faces and they weren't strangers anymore. And I realized that all those years at sea, I had never had a home, was always floating about. Until Dunnybegs."

He let drop one end of the coiled rope he'd been holding with both hands. It was a leash. It dangled like a fishing line.

Thomas looked down at the leash. "The missus and dog ok?"

"My Izzy's walks are done. She's not very steady on her feet. We can get to Rose's and back, but I'd hate to get too far out and have something happen." He jiggled the leash and smiled. "And the wee fella is an old man hisself, sure. So, I walk, and I tells them what I've seen when I get home."

Eamonn slowly eased off the bench and walked over to the well. He meticulously wound the leash around and through several branches of the thicket next to the well. Then he rummaged in his jacket's breast pocket and pulled out a women's necklace - a single strand of blue and green beads that matched the hues of the sea and the deep green fields that surrounded them. He wove it through several branches, dropped silent for a moment, and then bent over and picked up a small, gray stone.

"Think of all the fishing boats passing by over the years, all them fellas doing the sign of the cross and genuflecting, hoping for calm seas and full nets. Sure, I did it meself. But you know, son, it's not a guarantee. Many a boat has come back with empty nets. Some never come back at all. You're just asking." He let out a deep breath and looked at Thomas.

"Sure, you're just making a wish, lad. But don't count out the power of hope."

He walked past Thomas, tipped his cap, and turned on the road headed back down to Dunnybegs, to the Beetle, Izzy, Dixie and his unsettling future. To his home.

Thomas lingered on the bench. The wind settled with a few last deep sighs which carried the smell of the sea far up into the hills. Murmurations of starlings had taken flight, painting the sky with fleeting charcoal forms - all gentle undulations and abrupt, stark turns. He sat and watched and listened to the day's sounds, of robins and magpies and the bustle of the starlings whenever they settled to earth for a short respite.

He wondered, briefly, how it was Eamonn appeared to know about Molly's accident, but put it down to Dunnybegs being a small place and Eamonn, as the publican, being more in the know than most. But mostly, his thoughts rushed, formed and faded like the starlings overhead, suddenly taking the shape of anxiety about the veterinary bills or uncertainty about his own future before dissolving away and transforming into another dark worry.

After some time passed and the starlings had moved on, he arose and stepped over to the thicket, where he hung Molly's collar on a branch. The hedge was heavy with trinkets, notes, ribbons and other personal appeals. He thought of how this site was both a beacon to sailors and a holy repository of his neighbors' hopes, dreams and worries. He carefully set the stone he had been carrying back on the pile, rummaged through the mound a bit before selecting a small black stone which was bisected and circled by a thin white line. Black and white. Molly's colors. He placed it in his pocket and set off for the cottage.

51

Cara's Surprise

Thomas scuffled along the winding paths down from the well, carrying the silent weight of his own loneliness and pondering the collected lives displayed on the hedgerow at the well. All just worried prayers doomed to fail, ultimately. What endured? The low lines of old stone walls. Ancient high crosses, listing but still upright. Litter. The overgrown foundations and random walls of old cottages. Some boulders from a stone circle, all akimbo.

The debris lay scattered across Donegal, much like the trinkets bedecking the holy well's hedges. Markers. Artifacts. Of note to no one but archeologists, anthropologists and old sailors trying to stay anchored.

But the lives themselves, the flesh and blood beings who built and arranged and inhabited these spaces, they did not last. His own mother had lived a life here, had forged relationships and inhabited countless stories. And what was left of that? A house, soon to be sold? A photograph? A dog?

The day was soft and bright now, the pale sky streaked with scudding clouds the color of sheep's wool, but his own outlook stayed dark. He missed the dog. Missed the moments when she would catch up with him on their rambles and gaze up at him. He had always imagined that was for her own reassurance, but now realized it had offered at least as much comfort to himself.

It was a timely coincidence that, as he reached the coastal road, he caught sight of the bus heading north towards him. He waved it down and, once it rattled and hissed to a stop, stepped on.

It was just after noon. He would get to Letterkenny by midday and see how Molly was doing. It meant a late bus home, but it wasn't as though anyone was waiting for him.

He sat near the back, alone. The bus wound along the road. Outside, the late autumn landscape held patchworks of still-deep-green fields bordered by trees and hedges colored gold and brown and the near-black fallow farm fields.

Peat cutters labored in the higher fields. Sheep dawdled. Gulls followed the fresh-turned trail of a farm tractor, bobbing up and down on the air currents.

The town was busy. Streets filled with cars. Parents and prams meandering along the sidewalks, pausing to window shop. Children skipping and laughing, soaking up the sun.

He was feeling peckish - he hadn't anticipated being away from home this long - but ignored the small cafes and made his way to the veterinary. Inside, the small waiting room was chaotic, noisy with dogs and cats in uneasy company, restrained by anxious adults.

His surprise was audible when he turned to find Cara behind the receptionist's counter.

"What the... You working here? What's going on?'

"Sorta. Talked to the vet yesterday. Told him I'd volunteer to help out. They're busy and it's a good experience for me. You want to come back and see yer girl?" She lifted the counter and motioned for him to follow her through a door. They stepped into a large space with a high ceiling, and a long hallway off the right that was lined with small kennels.

Cara stopped at the third one and opened the door. "Here's our girl now."

Molly was curled in a semicircle, on her right side, her shaved left hip facing upward, revealing a long row of stitches. She lifted her head a bit and her tail ever-so-slowly swayed as she saw Thomas.

"She's a bit drowsy now. Sedated for her own good. Best to keep her settled. Let me go find the doctor for you."

Thomas knelt on the cold stone floor and reached out for Molly's head, cupping his left hand under her muzzle. "Hello girl, how are you, love?" She let the weight of her head settle onto his hand and let out a small whimper. The tail kept its slow swing back and forth. He whispered to her, telling her she was a good girl and that he loved her. Jesus, when had he last said those words to anyone or anything?

"Ah, Molly's dad!" The vet walked in.

"How is she?" Thomas asked.

"Resting. We're making her as comfortable as possible. The surgery went well. As well as could be expected, at least. Fractured hip. A bad crack, too. She'll be slowed for a while. She should regain use but she'll need someone devoted to her recovery. It'll take some patience and a good amount of physio. It'll be sometime before we can safely say the leg is safe. And I do have to warn you, there's a chance she'll be quite limited."

A phone sounded and Cara left to answer it.

"How soon can she come home?" The two men moved out of the kennel and the doctor carefully closed and latched the gate.

"I think she's best here for a few more days. Let us see how she begins moving. We'll start by short trips to the toilet and keep that up for a few days here. She'll not be good for much more than that for some time. We'll keep her comfortable."

Thomas turned from the doctor and looked back at the kennel. His eyes had teared up. He cleared his throat. "I know and appreciate all you're doing. I need to, ah... I need to ask about the cost."

"Aye sure. Well, with the surgery, we'd been looking at around €2,600, but the physio will probably add another grand to that by the time she's done."

Thomas nodded. Now he needed the house to sell so he could pay for the bills. Of course, then he'd have no place for either himself or the dog to live.

The vet went on. "Of course, your friend has offered to volunteer here over weekends the next month or two, and that'll take €600 or so off the bill. And then there is the amount already paid."

Two surprises, and Thomas was thoroughly confused. Cara's being here now made sense. But the amount already paid?

The doctor noticed his confusion and smiled.

"Cara also brought with her a box of money that had been collected back in Dunnybegs. I think folks there put out a few collection boxes. Another €825."

Thomas was speechless. More than half the cost had been paid already.

"Cara says the two of you are celebrities up there. Sure, we've seen yourself in the news. Donegal's top dog!"

It was a lot to process. Seeing Molly. Hearing the cautious prognosis. And now the double whammy about Cara and the donations from Dunnybegs. The next few minutes passed in a blur. He thanked the vet and looked for Cara but she was helping with an exam and left word she'd catch up with him later in the day.

The last bus headed back was an hour off. He decided to stop in at a cafe and have a bite to eat before the ride home. He passed through the waiting room, still full of the anxious energy of dogs and cats and one parakeet, and headed out the door. He was halfway down the block when he heard his name called. He turned to see Cara, leaning out the door of the clinic.

"Hey, check PhotoLife when you can!" she shouted, before disappearing back inside.

52

A Surprise from America

He found a cafe offering free wifi, ordered a ham and cheese sandwich and a bag of crisps and found a small table. He logged his phone onto the network, but before launching the PhotoLife app, he realized he had five text message notifications.

All from his sister, beginning almost a week ago. He must have turned off notifications, "Shit."

He scrolled back to the first.

"Woot! Good news! We have a buyer. You musta done a great job showing the place. Maybe a new career for you - staging homes! Anyway, I'll be there the weekend after next to sign papers. See you soon boyo!"

And then:

"We can discuss details when I'm there. We'll aim for a two-month window after the sale is signed to give you time to find a new place."

Followed by:

"Hey! Text back. What do you think? TTYL."

Then:

"Jesus, are you that busy? I'm arriving in Belfast Wednesday, will get to you Thursday late. OK if I bunk with you Thursday and Friday?"

And finally:

"FFS!!! Tommy What's up? Signing is this Friday. What's with the silence? Christ!!!"

He sighed. It was Monday. And then he typed a reply.

"Sorry sis, horrible accident with the dog. See you Thursday."

He put the phone back down on the table and fussed with the teabag in his mug, before using a spoon to squeeze it against the side of the cup and then depositing it on the saucer. His food arrived and he poked at it. He had two months, tops, left in the cottage. No plan, no destination, no grand scheme to his life. There would be a bump to his bank account from the sale of the house, but that wouldn't last forever. The momentary brightening in his mood from the news of the donation quickly passed, as though scuttled by a dark cloud overhead.

The sandwich half eaten and the crisps picked over, he took his tray to the busing station and deposited his plates there. He was almost to the door when he recalled Cara's words. PhotoLife.

He sat back down and pulled out the phone, launching the app.

New followers. Slowed a bit from previous weeks, but then he hadn't posted anything in several days.

And, wait, a few mentions. He clicked on them.

The first was by Cara, reporting the news of Molly's accident, posted to his own account. There were several hundred comments, well wishes and prayers from people around the world, all hoping for the best for Molly.

The next was a post by Don and Nancy Hogan, the Americans. They repeated Cara's news and announced a fundraising drive for Molly's surgery. Again, posted to his account and followed by hundreds of comments.

And lastly, there were two messages from the Hogans.

"Praying for you and Molly. Hope it's OK, we started a fundraiser online to help with the expenses."

And then:

"Reached our goal! $2,000 in 7 hours! Can transfer the funds to you when you are ready. And can reopen if we need more! Love from the Hogans."

He set the phone down, rested his chin on his hand and slowly ran his hand over his face, covering his eyes, which had once again teared up.

53

Everyone Likes Free Stuff

It was lashing in Seattle. An atmospheric river, they called it, a narrow funnel rushing across the Olympic Peninsula and carrying what felt like half the Pacific Ocean, an open faucet flooding rivers and collapsing hillsides. It would be good to get away, even if it were a short business trip to Ireland.

Clyde had been staring absent-mindedly at the dark grey, waterlogged world beyond his office window when the door swung open and Ove clattered in. He was in the midst of pulling a shirt over his head as he entered. Successful, he pulled at the hem to straighten the shirt and smiled at Clyde.

"Those the shirts?"

"Yep, four dozen delivered just in time!"

It was a medium brown T-shirt, perhaps a size too small, that fact emphasized by how awkwardly it fit over Ove's button-down dress shirt. SALMON COVE was written across the lower front of the shirt, in a teal-colored typeface that seemed stolen from one of those strip mall massage parlors. Above that, a yellow brush stroke spiraled up from the words, ending in a single point.

Clyde's look was quizzical.

"The agency thought it might be better not to use the company name but to highlight the new name of the bay," Ove explained, looking down at the front of the shirt.

"The color..." Clyde finally said.

"Espresso," Ove answered, brightly. "An homage to Seattle's coffee culture."

"And the yellow line?" Clyde wasn't smiling and his tone was more of an interrogation. The shirts had been Ove's idea - something they could hand out at the hearing. A freebie that would be good advertising. "It's impressionistic, I think. Like a ripple in the water, or the reflection of the moon over the bay."

Clyde scoffed. "Looks like shit. I mean, literally. Like a toilet." He leaned back in his chair. "Can we get them redone? I mean, brown and yellow?"

"Not in time to leave tomorrow." Ove looked both deflated and overstuffed, head hung, inspecting the front of the shirt.

Clyde eyed up his right-hand man and breathed deeply. "We'll just run with it, I guess. Everyone likes free stuff."

54

Ginny Arrives

The week passed slowly for Thomas. He bussed out to Letterkenny once to see Molly, her drowsy with painkillers and miserable with the plastic cone which left her clumsy and uncomfortable. The state of her distressed him. He hadn't lingered in town.

The various fundraising efforts meant her care was paid for fully, with a good bit leftover for the physiotherapy she'd require. He was still processing that. People from around the world had contributed to her care. And then the people of Dunnybegs itself, them scraping together their hard-earned euros and raiding their own savings. Jesus.

It left him uncomfortable, actually, unsure how to react around them. Was he a figure of pity now? The awkwardness led to him keeping a low profile for the first part of the week.

On Wednesday afternoon, he walked out to shop for groceries and was surprised to find ace reporter Brionna Kennedy coming down the road towards him. She started into a trot when she spotted him. "Yoohoo! Molly's dad! You have a minute?" He wondered if she had been waiting along the roadside for him to appear.

She walked alongside him to the grocer's, peppering him with rapid-fire questions about the dog's health and about the online fund that had been set up by mysterious Americans. Thomas explained how he had met them and shown them around Donegal and spoke of their love for dogs and specifically, for border collies.

"It's a real international effort to save Molly, innit?" she asked.

"I guess," he answered. "I mean, donations from around the world. The money just went straight to the clinic, and leftover funds will be used for her physiotherapy."

"And how does that make you feel?"

Thomas stopped. Looked at her. She turned to face him fully, her right arm extended and holding her phone aloft to record the conversation.

"Whew," he said. "Chuffed, you know. But almost in disbelief. And the people here, too, collecting money for her."

"It's really like they are collecting for you both," Brionna said.

The reporter, and her editor, had moved quickly. The very next day, the morning edition of the Donegal People's News had her story on page one, above the fold. The old photo of Molly from the first article ran full width across the top of the page. Underneath, in bold all-cap type, ran the headline.

INTERNATIONAL BID TO SAVE DONEGAL'S TOP DOG

The article went into breathless detail about the accident, about Molly's care, about the local funds collected for her medical bills and about the online fundraising campaign launched by a pair of Americans who had fallen in love with Molly and with Donegal. It promised to keep readers informed about Molly's recovery.

It was not an earth-shattering story. The money involved was quite small-scale in the grand scheme of things. No celebrities were mentioned - unless one counted Molly herself. But it was the sort of heart-tugging tale that newspapers and television news programs like to save space for. Human interest stories. Small, sweet stories designed to tug at one's emotions.

The article was picked up and carried by several sister papers of the Donegal People's Weekly. It ran on the front page of several smaller publications. It was even picked up on that very same day by the Belfast Telegraph, though it ran on page 19, in a small box near the bottom of the page, absent any photo.

After she claimed her suitcase and cleared customs and before heading to the car rental counter, Ginny stopped at a store in the Belfast International Airport. She was knackered. Arranging her trip at the last minute meant that her preferred route - which involved just two flights – had been unavailable. She was in Belfast, but it had taken her four planes and 23 hours of travel to get there. It was four in the afternoon. Her original plan was to drive straight to Dunnybegs but it was already getting dark. She purchased a sugared bun, an energy drink and the Telegraph, which she fully intended to read at the hotel but which instead fell unread to the floor of her hotel room once her body touched the bed.

Dunnybegs, and Tommy, would have to wait until Friday.

55

A Town Hall Meeting

The Sea Spray Inn on Dunnybegs' main road had last hosted a paying overnight guest more than a decade previous. The restaurant and upstairs hall had lingered on another year or two after the hotel shut, hosting a Sunday afternoon carvery and the very occasional wedding reception, but the building had remained mostly vacant. Various rumors floated into awareness now and then, of foreign buyers or Dublin commercial interests seeking to revive the property, but those quickly sank.

The restaurant space on the ground floor and the banquet hall upstairs were both located in the back of the building, with windows that offered up limited views of the bay, down off to the left and mostly out of sight below the long, slow slope of field between the hotel and the shore. The coastal path hugged the edge of that field, a hundred meters or so from the building, and offered guests intrepid enough to cross the hillocky pasture a shortcut to the bay.

It was, among the couple blocks long stretch of road that constituted Dunnybegs proper, the only building with space large enough to accommodate a gathering of any more than a couple dozen folk, and that, combined with its placement squarely across the road from his butcher shop so that it had been the first thing Fergal saw after his ah-ha! idea of a town hall meeting, were why the mayor had set upon the Inn as the perfect place for the event.

The building still had power. A few interior lights on the ground floor provided a constant, slight glow visible from the street and a dim flood light shone perpetually on the northern side of the building, next to a service door and the location of the rubbish bins. The Gardai station in Letterkenny had keys and the property's owners had long ago given the village permission to enter if needed. Sure, they may have been thinking more along the lines of a dire emergency such as a fire, but Fergal had decided the town hall constituted fair use.

He drafted Ramona MacIntyre to emcee the meeting. Large and loud, Ramona, or Mona as she was known, had, for a year or two in her twenties, hosted a radio show in Sligo, a Wednesday afternoon call-in show about cats. It was a short-lived career, but the notoriety had ensured that she was the first name to come to mind anytime a need was had for someone to hold a microphone and even now, at sixty-four, she still had a voice that commanded attention and an ease before a crowd.

By the time she arrived, twenty minutes or so before the 7 p.m. start of the meeting, night had long settled in and the day's last light was but a faint memory where sky met sea. A sandwich board, borrowed from Fergal's butcher shop, guided folk to the hotel's entrance. Once inside, a sheet of paper cellophaned to the wall directed them upstairs to the banquet room. Fairy lights, left over from the notorious McPhale-Doherty wedding reception – a raucous affair seven years earlier which ran so late into the night that some of the attendees broke into several guest rooms in a fruitless search for beds – remained strung across the ceiling. Plugged in, their twinkling illumination lent the otherwise bare room a slight enchantment.

Somewhat north of four dozen folding chairs had been gathered and maneuvered into several rough rows. These faced a portable speaker's pedestal set before the western wall of windows, which peered out over the lumpy field and after that the sea, now a dark green grey void. A separate row of chairs lined the wall behind the lectern. Fergal had enlisted a couple teenage boys to help set up the space and they fiddled at a folding table, dropping it twice before finally setting it proper on its legs. Fergal's wife, Bridie, was busy at another table, arranging teacups around two large kettles, ready for the guests.

After Mona, the next to arrive were two men in a large dark SUV, which anchored across the street from the Inn, next to Fergal's shop. Clyde clambered out of the passenger side first, stretched and glanced up and down the street, then made a beeline for the door to the Inn. Ove exited the vehicle, pulled an enormous suitcase from the back and rolled it across the road.

Unusually for a Friday evening in late autumn, there were other cars parked along the roadside, as well as a considerable hum of activity emanating from the Shamrock, where many of the folk headed to the town hall had first visited in search of a pint or two of sustenance. Even Farmer Frankie's rusted red tractor was parked roadside. Up at the grocers, Rose and her niece locked up, placed a sign on the door directing potential customers to the town hall down the road, and headed to the Inn.

Once he had hauled the huge trunk up into the banquet hall, Ove opened it and began setting stacks of the brown t-shirts on the empty table, next to a handful of printed brochures containing a glowing profile of International Fisheries president Clyde Van der Vaart. Clyde himself had already claimed the chair nearest to the lectern and introduced himself to Fergal, intent on learning the evening's agenda.

This flustered Fergal, who realized that he hadn't really planned an agenda, in fact, hadn't thought much at all how the evening's proceedings might go. It was quickly decided that he would introduce first himself, then Mr. Van de Vardt and then Mona, who would act as an emcee of sorts and call upon interested parties to give a short statement about the proposal, beginning with International Fisheries. Following that, those in attendance would be asked to vote on the proposal. While it was not in any sense a binding vote, the mayor told Clyde, the vote in favor of the proposal would be so overwhelming that Fergal would literally be forced to sign off on the plan.

Fergal had no sooner said this than the first group of villagers surmounted the stairs and noisily entered the room, all carrying signs, and all chanting "Keep It Killfish!" They moved around the hall in a disorganized fashion before settling into the first several rows of chairs. Cara and Rose entered next, Cara opening her jacket to reveal a white t-shirt with #KeepitKillfish scrawled across the chest in a black marker. Clyde, who had started across the room to talk to Ove, turned and glared at Fergal.

But now the parade was fully underway, as the patrons spilled out of the Shamrock, marched to the Inn and clomped up the stairs alongside others who arrived by car, bicycle, assorted tractors and even electric scooter. The crowd filled the hall, occupying every chair and then standing shoulder to shoulder around the periphery of the room, with others milling about the table with the tea kettles, chatting and laughing and helping themselves to cups.

Ove moved through the crowd, handing out shirts to anyone willing to take one. His supply quickly exhausted, he retreated to a chair next to Clyde, who appeared stunned by the number of people cramming into the space. Ove glanced overhead at the fairy lights. "Festive," he said.

"We're screwed," replied his boss.

56

Thomas Speaks

The procession had dwindled to the last few dawdlers by the time Thomas turned onto the road. It was difficult to leave the dog behind in her cone and truth be told, he had lost most of his enthusiasm for this issue. It had been Cara's issue. He had embraced in part to please her and in part because the bay was just out his front door. But the bay and likely Cara as well were about to drop into his past. He was not to be a Dunnybegs resident much longer, and his connection to Cara soon would be lost, too.

The lights in the grocery store had been dimmed and a handwritten sign on the door directed anyone interested down the street to the inn. Even Eamonn had joined the last few crossing the road, after closing the door to the bar.

There was a considerable buzz from above once one entered the hotel and began the trudge up the worn, maroon, carpeted stairs as well as a warm, sticky atmosphere that contrasted sharply with the crisp night air outside. The hall was bursting with folk, clad in wool jumpers, tweed jackets and waxed rain macs. Three men in suits were at one end of the room – one in a dark navy suit, one next to him in a light gray outfit and the mayor, in a slightly undersized brown blazer and tan pants.

Thomas located Cara and Rose up to the left of the speaker's stand and moved to join them.

"Hey," waved Cara. "How's the missus getting on?"

Thomas shrugged. "Not bad, I guess. Slow. Like, she can't adjust to the cone. Always banging it on doorways. But she let me lead her out to do her business a few times. It's just good to have her home."

"Are you using the pads we sent?"

"Aye, she sleeps on one before the fire." He glanced around the hall. "So, how long do you think this'll go?"

Rose answered. "Fergal said this morning that he wasn't expecting many people to actually want to speak, that he'd let a few folk talk and then take a vote."

"Really? We get to vote?"

"It's meaningless," answered Cara. "It's not like it's a real referendum or anything. Fergal makes the final decision."

They were called to attention then by Fergal himself. He and Mona were standing at the small lectern.

"Folks, let me start by saying tanks for coming out. I've got to admit I wasn't expecting this sort of crowd, and tanks for yous all left standing around. There are more chairs somewhere but we couldn't access all the rooms."

"Now, he continued, "the plan for tonight is for Mona here to keep us in line. She's going to let anyone with something to say about the fish farm to come up and speak. But you need to keep it short. We have guests with us tonight all the way from America and they'll need to get back to their lodging in Letterkenny before it's locked up for the night. Of course," he chuckled, "I'm sure we could find someone who'd help them break into one of the rooms here, if needed." The crowd laughed and Clyde, seated to his left, made an exaggerated show of shaking away the offer.

Fergal then gave way to Mona, who was wearing what appeared to be a series of colorful gauzy wraps and multiple chains that jangled and rattled when she moved, which was any time she spoke, given as she was to broad, animated gestures with each sentence.

Mona touched on her own history as a resident of Dunnybegs, making sure to note her time in Sligo as well as her current occupation as a crafter of all things cat related. She would, she added, be happy to show her wares and take orders from her car boot following this meeting.

Thankfully, she moved quickly to introduce the evening's special guest. "Now, I know yous all know about the plan for the bay. Sure, it's been in the papers and all and there were the mailings back in spring with the pretty drawings. Well, the president of International Fisheries himself is here to tell ye more about it. Mr. Fart."

Thomas looked at Cara, who, big-eyed, choked on the bottle of water she was drinking.

The man in the navy suit walked to the lectern. "Van der Vaart. It's Clyde Van der Vaart. But you can all call me Clyde. We're going to be seeing a lot of each other in the months ahead."

He looked out at the room. "Well, I'm happy to see so many of you in our special shirts." It was true, many of the recipients of the t-shirts had pulled them on - regardless of what they may already have been wearing. Eamonn looked like a small boy in his. Next to him was Big Eddie Curran, who had a small farm up the road. Big Eddie, as one might assume given the nickname, was a large man – a full, meaty fellow with a perpetually bright red face. Beside him was Wee Eddie Foster from the petrol station, who, in spite of the nickname, was also a full-framed, solid specimen and also, like Big Eddie, stuffed into a too-small t-shirt. Eamonn, upon seeing them both as he entered the hall, had exclaimed, "Jaysus, you look like two big piles o' muck, and I thought yous were opposed to the fish farm, Wee Eddie!"

Wee Eddie pulled at the hem of the shirt. "Och, I am, but the shirt was free!"

At the lectern, Van Der Vaart quickly ran through the plans for the fish farm, light on actual details on the endeavor and heavier on the hyperbole about how his company was changing the world. He spoke in vague terms about a shared fishing heritage and jobs coming back and then looked over at Mona, concluding his remarks by noting he'd be happy to answer any questions.

The room, however, was stone cold silent, save for the shuffling of feet and the fidgeting of hands normally occupied by work and the occasional supping of tea.

It was time for members of the crowd to voice their opinions and first up was Cara, who spoke too quickly and breathlessly but nonetheless made a strong argument in favor of preserving the natural environment and against the many untold horrors of factory farmed fish.

She was followed by a narrow man, gray of hair and general pallor, all pointy sharp features and jangly limbs, who spoke of the lives of fisherfolk and of young people too busy on their phones to do an honest day's work. It was difficult to ascertain exactly where he landed on the fish farm proposal itself, but he certainly had things to say about the softness of modern life.

It went on. Maybe fifteen or so people spoke. Some with eloquence. Some with deep emotion. With the crowd mostly silently listening and nodding along to each point made.

The speakers had formed a line in the center of the room, each one walking up to the lectern and turning to face the cord when it was their turn. Now, with no one left in the line, Cara grabbed Thomas' shoulder. "Are ye not going to talk? Ock, go on."

Thomas shook his head slightly. "No, I don't know..."

By now, the crowd was silent again, looking to Mona for guidance. And then Mona spoke up.

"Is that Molly's Da?

And at once the crowd turned its collective attention to him and there were various murmurings and pleadings that he speak. Cara herself nudged him, aiming him towards the front of the room. He shuffled through the crowd, desperately wondering what in the world he would say. He was saved by Mona.

"Now, before yous begin, I'm sure everyone here is wondering how that poor wee dote is doing, after the worldwide rescue effort," she asked.

At the front of the room, Thomas glanced out at the crowd. People completely unknown to him this time a year back, but now faces he recognized from his walks and the various businesses in the area. Flinty, hard people, grey like the sea and hardworn, like the land. Austere. And most of them dirt poor. But they'd collectively raised hundreds of Euros for Molly. For him. And he was overcome with a wave of gratitude, an emotion scarce in his life.

He started to speak, but the words hung in his throat and he was forced to take a deep breath. And as he did, he let his gaze wander slowly around the hall again. Rose. Eamonn. Frankie. Fergal. Billy. Brionna, with her notebook out. The two Eddies. The postman. And then Cara herself, smiling at him.

And it rose in him, this strange, altogether new thought, that he wasn't a stranger here. That these were his neighbors. His people. His friends.

The thought hung in his throat. He gulped.

"Aye, Molly," he began. "Well, the hope is she'll be good on her leg, eventually, that she'll be able to keep it. She sleeps mostly. And it's going to take a long time before she's able to go on longer hikes, if she ever can." He took a deep breath. The crowd was engrossed. Whisper quiet. In the pause, one could hear a cough, some shuffling of feet, and the jangling of keys in a coat pocket as someone fussed at them.

"You know, I, ah, well, we're here to talk about the bay and all, but if you'll grant me a moment, I'd like to express my gratitude for what you've all done, the help you've given me and Molly. I mean, I can't ever thank you enough..." His words trailed off as his throat narrowed again.

In the moment of silence, someone near the back of the hall shouted out "Ye'd have done the same. Sure, we've gotten used to seeing yourself and herself ambling up the road."

Just as used as he'd gotten to making those walks with Molly, Thomas thought.

"To be honest, I didn't know much about Dunnybegs a year ago. I had a wee flat in Derry, and a job. Every day, I'd go back and forth between the two. Grocery store. Library. Shopping center. And I don't think I could tell you the name of anyone there outside of a couple of my coworkers at the bookstore.

"And then, well, I felt lost coming here, like something washed up from the sea and left to dry out on the sand. And Molly!" He shook his head. "I'd never been around a dog before. I thought I'd go mad here, and wither away. That's what my mother had done, I thought, run away to be a hermit here. She never seemed happy.

"But I was wrong about her. About here. I think she was in love. Maybe with a person, maybe with the place, or maybe just with life itself. You know, you have time to do that here. To walk and to look and to think. And you just fall in love with it all. With the light in late afternoon and the gorse on the hillside on fire with the sunlight. With the seagulls flashing against the gray fall sky. With the sheep in all their colors. With the steady beat of the day to day. And the days shortening. Mornings. The waves all gold as the sun creeps over the hills." The room was silent, still, breathing in unison, all seeing the same visions.

"It's a harsh place, innit? Good luck finding a tall tree around here – all of them windbent. Waves that wrack the shore every day. The rain. Sideways rain. Sleet that slashes at your skin. Who stays here? Who puts up with this?" The words were just coming on their own now.

"Heather and lichen and gorse. They flourish here. And, jaysus if I hadn't noticed them before. The colors. Bronze and - what is it - turquoise lichen on the shore rocks. The purple heather? The gorse? The sun itself. And the sea, a different color every day.

"And then all of you. Scraping by, walking bent into the headwinds and the hail, as cheerful and strong as that gorse against the grayest of days."

He paused and looked at his feet. The words had just tumbled out one after another and he was feeling a bit self-conscious now.

"That a place can be so harsh and so splendid all at once..." He looked out at the faces, all of them focused on him.

"Well, it's beautiful, isn't it? And I know progress can't be stopped and jobs are hard to come by and all, but it's beautiful. The bay and the land and the sea. And the people." He stopped. He felt warm, not from shyness, or from speaking, but bathed in warmth, as though he was beside a full-on fire. "Well, I can't picture a better place to live.

But ... truth is I'm just a visitor here. Someone's buying the cottage. I'll be gone soon. You really shouldn't listen to me. But some people here I really care about think the fish farm is a bad idea. People who love this place and who, well, that's enough for me." He paused a moment, and then, head down, walked back to Cara and Rose, who both welcomed him with hugs.

The hall stayed whisper quiet, until Mona reached the front again and spoke. "Well, I think that's all of yous who wanted to have a say. Now, the boys here are going to give everyone two pieces of paper. One says yes and one says no. Then we'll pass this basket around and ye're to put your vote in the basket - yes or no to the proposal. As ye know, this is just an advisory vote, but the powers that be want to hear from you."

As she spoke, a pair of teenaged boys began circulating through the hall, handing out the slips of paper. Mona herself followed soon after, holding a wicker basket in front of her.

57

Ginny's Surprise

As Thomas had made for the front of the room to speak, one final guest had surmounted the staircase and entered the hall, where she remained, behind several rows of people.

Ginny had arrived in Dunnybegs fifteen minutes earlier, driving slowly through the quiet town in the dark. The large number of cars parked along the road hadn't made an impression until she pulled up to the grocers, only to find the place closed and the sign on the door announcing the town hall. Ah feck, she thought, just head straight to the cottage and have Tommie heat up a cup of tea.

But the cottage was dark, too. And when she peered into the window, it appeared quiet, save for a dog sprawled awkwardly before the fire, a bulky cone around its neck. She surmised that her brother must have headed to the town hall, so rather than enter the cottage unannounced (she had a spare key for the door), she slipped back into the car and turned onto the main road.

She parked by the grocers' and walked down the road, noticing now the vehicles fully lining both sides of the street. The hotel was obvious even without the small sandwich board outside the door announcing the town hall. She followed the lights up the stairs and entered the packed hall, where her brother's voice startled her.

Straining and standing on tiptoes, she saw him. Was this the brother she had dropped off less than a year earlier? He looked years different. Her brother had always appeared sort of undefined and soft. A bit formless, like his life. A receding energy.

But the man speaking, the man commanding the room's attention, was – handsome? He looked more angular, his features in sharper focus. Leaner, yet more formidable. His hair still wild but now streaked by the sun and sea and what looked to be the beginnings of a short beard graced his cheeks. He looked twenty pounds lighter, but more substantial at the same time.

And his manner was new, too. Upright and calm. Confident? She stood, transfixed like the rest of the crowd as he spoke, though her feelings were confounding and confused. His recent messages had all seemed lifeless and lacking emotion, but this was anything but.

When he was done, she remained still for some time, processing what she had seen and heard, which were far removed from what she was expecting.

The movement and noise of the crowd brought her back to the moment. At the front of the hall, a woman dressed like a low-rent Stevie Nicks was speaking now, telling the crowd that there would be a fifteen-minute break while the votes were counted. A number of those in attendance quickly determined it was just enough time for a run across the street for a pint, or to dart out back to the former patio of the hotel for a smoke. She moved to the side as folks began filing out.

Fergal was among the crowd to dart out the back door to the patio. While not a smoker, he considered himself to be on the clock as mayor and therefore a pint was out of the question. The patio provided a good view of the sea in the distance and by walking to the edge of the concrete surface, he could just glimpse the mouth of the bay. In the moonlight, it was unremarkable – a grasp of tumbled rocks reaching out from the north and south and the slip of a crescent of sand between them. Well protected, but never deep enough for a ship, not even for smaller fishing boats.

He had grown up on this shore, building sandcastles on that beach as a wee boy, wading into the bracing waters, feeling with his feet for shells and starfish, wearing a path back and forth across the sand, bent over, looking for treasures at low tide.

His father fished out of the built-up harbor several miles down the coastline. Fergal's grandda operated a boat and his father was a lad of twelve when he first joined him. He worked the nets for 23 years - bicycling down still-dark roads to the harbor and heading out before dawn, setting and hauling nets beside his father, moving the way generations of men in the family had moved, singing songs from centuries past.

When he reached ten, Fergal began helping at his uncle's shop, but every now and then, when the night skies were clear and the coming day held a promise of calm seas, he was allowed to accompany his father out to fish.

On those nights, Fergal pedaled along next to his father, who pointed out landmarks and constellations both. Orion, a steady evening presence in the heart of winter, would be waiting for them, high overhead. Thinking of it, Fergal looked heavenward, but the hunter would only now be climbing over the hills to the east, the view blocked by the hotel itself.

"Clear night!" It was Clyde, snuffing out a cigarette with the ball of his foot. "Takes a moment to adjust to the light, but the color of the sea is beautiful in the moonlight."

Fergal looked back out at the ocean. It's different every day, he thought. "It'll change," he said. Several hundred miles southwest, the ragged remains of hurricane Robert churned along the Gulf current on a tedious path that would stumble into the western Irish coastline in another day or two at most. "Storm's coming."

Clyde nodded. "My assistant tells me your father was a fisherman."

"Aye. And his father before him and his father before him. Up here, you either fished or you starved, or you grew thin on seaweed soup."

"But not you? You never followed into the family business?"

"Nah," replied Fergal, with a sigh. "Things changed."

"No fish left for you?"

Fergal nodded, a slight dip of his chin, eyes down. "No. Da was lost at sea.. And me grandda with him. It was just my mammy, my uncle and my granny Nicola left. You never took the sea for granted over winter. And it was a bad one, with snow piling up on the hills. Sheep stranded and frozen in place. The roads over the hills closed down. They had to fish. The waves would turn to ice in an instant on the rails, the deck, the lines." He paused. "Three boats from one harbor alone were lost that winter. If they'd have made it back, I'd have taken my place on the deck the next summer. But there was no boat."

Clyde was about to speak when the door of the hotel opened and Mona peered out. "Votes done!"

There followed a stomping and shuffling as the dozen or so folks gathered on the patio snuffed out their smokes and shuffled towards the door and then up the stairs, joining the crowd wandering back from the Shamrock, pint glasses still in hand.

58

Fintan Breaks a Tie

Before the crowd had headed over to the pub or out back for a quick smoke, Ginny had crossed the hall to her brother. He was surrounded by a small group of admirers, Cara and Rose included, all talking about the dog and about Tommy's speech.

Up close, he was even more handsome. The short beard, the chiseled features, the upright posture. "Tommy, you were great!" she said, bursting through the circle and hugging her brother. "Brilliant. And you look wonderful!"

Thomas blushed. "Jaysus, I forgot you were coming tonight! It's good to see you, sis. I'm a bit embarrassed. I don't even remember all what I said."

"It was heartfelt, lad," said Rose.

They stood and small-talked a few minutes, Ginny all the time examining this strange new man who claimed to be her brother. He bantered with strangers that stopped by to chat, easily laughing. Two young men in their twenties approached him, vowing they would have voted against the fish farm if they'd been allowed, but they were Australian tourists. They were here to see the places featured in his photography.

When they passed, Thomas asked Ginny, "Did you go to the house? Did you see Molly?"

"Drove up to it, didn't go in. But I peeked in the window. She was fast asleep."

"Grand. I was worried about leaving her for so long. Going to have to get back soon."

By then, the room around them was beginning to once again fill and Ramona spoke.

"Aright, luvs, the moment yous been waiting for. We have the final votes all counted." She held a single sheet of paper in her hands. "Now, remember, this isn't a binding vote. This was just a way to see how you folks felt about it. These lot behind me here, they're the ones making the decision, like."

Of course, Fintan had already given Dublin's approval. It was really up to Fergal, who came up with the idea for the vote in the first place, as an easy way to lend credibility to his okay.

"Well, jaysus, look at that!' Mona exclaimed. "We have 73 yes votes, in favor of the proposal." Behind her, Ove was trying to do a quick crowd estimate. Seventy three sounded good, he thought.

"Alright then, and we have 73 voting no. A tie!"

The crowd erupted, with people looking all about at the others in the hall, all incredulous at this turn of events. Behind Mona, Fintan sat wide-eyed. To his left, Ove was frozen, mouth open as if in mid-yell. Beside him, Clyde sank back in his chair and let out a deep sigh. Nothing is ever fuckin' easy, he thought to himself.

Seated next to him, Fergal had grown several shades paler. Before the night had begun, he had expected a dozen or so votes opposed to the project. His unease had grown through the evening. And now here he was. He felt naked, and he unconsciously dropped his hands in front of his groin as he stood up and walked to the podium.

Seeing him there, the crowd fell quiet again.

He looked around the room. Had anybody forgotten to vote, or placed the wrong piece of paper in the basket? Had they triple checked the counts? It really didn't matter. He knew that.

The crowd remained silent, as did Fergal, still looking about the room. As mayor, he took great pride in knowing his constituents.

Clearly not every resident of the village was here – the most recent population count had been 376. But these were the people who cared enough to come out on a cold November night to stand in a drafty old hall.

And they were his neighbors, all. The widow Murphy bundled in her big shawl. Billy. Miss McGillicuddy, who taught him how to write cursive. Big Eddie, who could always be counted on to join him in kicking a football down the road. Rose, who might be the smartest person he knew. His customers. The characters who hurried in on their regular schedules for mince, sausages, stew meat and a few minutes of good craic at the counter of his butcher shop. Ah, the shop.

He drew a deep breath. Eyes closed, and he was once again that wee lad, searching the bay's tidal pools and keeping an eye for his granddad's boat straining across the horizon.

He opened his eyes and looked out at the room. "So, I didn't cast a vote meself. A moot point, right? And maybe it's better this way, so you can know how I would have voted." He took another deep breath.

"You know, I've been thinking about what our Thomas here said. Most of us in this hall have fishermen in our families. My Da. My Granddad. His father before him, hell, as far as ye could cast a line ye'd catch a fisherman. And I know some of you tink those days are coming back, that it's just a matter of time until we're fishing those waters again and we have fleets setting out." He paused.

"That's not happening. The fish aren't coming back. They're not coming back. Overfished to the point of run, of no return.

"And then there's the sea itself. As many of you can say you had fishermen in our families can say you lost a fisherman to the sea as well. How many years ever passed, when the fishing was good, how many years passed without a man overboard, or jaysus, a ship lost? There's a hurricane bearing down on us right now, out there," he swung his left arm wide in the direction of the sea. "If the boats were out now, we'd all be in the chapel." There were nodding heads in the crowd.

"All anxious and praying, in the chapel, we'd be. And the proposal here, it's just one ship. Up and down the coast to five or six wee farms like ours, harvesting each one, processing the fish and then offloading. Never going more than a mile offshore. Safe."

He paused, leaned forward, both hands on the lectern. "Most of ye's know how I feel. But as I said, I didn't vote."

Say yes, he thought, and the farm was a go and he and Clyde would negotiate that loan and the work could start on his store by spring. Say yes, and he'd be fulfilling a long-held dream. Yet...

He looked up and around the room again, found his wife's sweet face and a slight smile pulled at the edges of his mouth. It was her dream, too, he thought, their dream. An easier life, a better living. He locked eyes with her. Yet...

There was nothing underhanded in the loan arrangement, not really. Sure, the American was likely offering it to buy influence, but it also represented a good investment. And he hadn't made any promise in return for it. But the thought of it now was bringing a bad taste to his mouth, and uncurling a slight unease deep in his body. Could he truthfully say the idea of the loan wasn't influencing his opinion? He would be using his position to personally benefit. Was that how he wanted to honor his father? Fergal had read all the colorful brochures. Properly run, the farm could be a safe and sustainable source of fish. But what would his Da think of the loan, of Fergal himself casting the deciding vote? After what seemed like an eternity, he cleared his throat.

"There's Fergal the butcher and Fergal the mayor and I'm up here tonight with me mayor's hat on. Representing the wishes of you, the people of Dunnybegs. And I think with the local opinion being so evenly divided," he continued, at last, "that it may be best to look to our national economic and environmental expertise." He looked over his shoulder to Fintan. "Let me introduce Mr. Fintan O'Dowd, from the government in Dublin, to declare his office's findings."

And just like that, the room's attention turned its focus for the first time to the wee man from Dublin in the drab grey suit, seated in the shadow of the American and already breaking into a sweat.

He struggled to stand - his legs felt ready to buckle. He wiped his brow with his left hand, coughed several times as a delaying tactic, and desperately struggled to control his thoughts, which spun in crazy loose spirals like the arms of that hurricane and darted in all directions.

The crowd waited, straining to hear him, some leaning forward in their seats, others standing with a hand cupped by an ear.

The truth was it didn't matter what he might say. If the mayor wanted to leave it up to the official findings, well, those official reports were done and closed - and all in favor of the project. But he couldn't find the words, couldn't put together a sentence while his mind raced.

He dared look up and at the crowd before him. So many faces, so many emotions ready to burst upon the room, upon him.

And then his gaze landed on Rose. Standing, watching him. Smiling. And all he could think of was the time in front of her store, her hand on his arm, her pointing him towards the bay. And the only words he could think of were the ones she had used that day - This is why people live here. Because some days, the beauty of it will sting your face and bring tears to your eyes.

He coughed again, and then spoke, looking directly at Rose. "You're right. It's beautiful. I mean, the sea, the hills, the colors. I didn't really see the colors at first. It looked so gray when I first came here. Depressed. All I saw were closed shops and empty houses. But maybe you have to look for a while before you see the colors. Maybe your eyes need time to adjust."

The crowd remained silent. What was his decision?

He gulped a breath, almost choked on the spit in his mouth. "I mean, the hills looked brown, but if you stare at them long enough, you notice the heather, like a purple fog settling across the land. And the sea? It's not gray. It's never the same. Dark blue, teal, turquoise... And the skies. The light here, like a warm, creamy brilliance..." His voice tapered off.

The hall remained whisper quiet, until a reedy, barking voice shouted out, "the feck is your decision, then. Go on, man."

It broke the spell. Fintan winced, blinked and took in a breath.

"You should not ruin that with a fish farm..."

His last few words were lost to an aural eruption from the crowd, from a mix of raucous cheers and jubilation and lamentations all at once.

Beside him, Mona was speaking now, though her closing words were lost on him in the crowd's roar. She turned and gathered her coat from the back of her chair, pivoting toward the stairs.

Behind him sat Ove and Clyde, mouths agape, Ove leaning back in his chair so that it was in real danger of pitching him ass-backwards and the CEO's body slowly folding forward, his chin coming to rest on both palms. "Goddamned Irish," Clyde muttered. Next to them was the mayor, staring at Fintan, blinking, running his hands back and forth on the top of his thighs.

Of course, any comments by Fintan could have been seen as superfluous. After all, the government position was established. And, what he did say was wholly and completely contradictory to that official position - a position reached by economic and environmental ministries, developed over months by teams of bureaucrats, including, most prominently, Fintan himself. An official position that had been tidily orchestrated by Fintan, his intended final act in what had been an inglorious and easily overlooked career in civil service.

And anyone in the crowd that night - the mayor, the CEO of the international fishing company, the reporter, anyone, could rightly have pointed that out. Fintan's words on this night were as meaningless as the whole non-binding vote had been.

Except they weren't meaningless, not on this night. To the one hundred and fifty or so souls who had gathered in the musty, drafty ballroom of the former Sea Spray Inn, his pronouncement may as well have been the voice of God. The crowd had gathered here for a decision, for feck's sake, and a decision had just been voiced. Thy will would be done.

In all the years that would follow this night, Fintan would sometimes reflect on the evening, and wonder what it was that had possessed him, after all the months of conspiring and planning, what was it that drove him to utter those words so fully at odds with all he had directed his energies towards in what were to be the final months of his career.

The answer, of course, was obvious.
It had been love.

59

At Killfish Bay

Clyde stood from his chair and brushed the front of his coat with both hands. To Ove's astonishment, his face betrayed no disappointment whatsoever. He was a good poker player.

"How many properties did you have in negotiation here?" he asked Ove.

"Six, actually," was the answer. "There was a seventh shack along the south end of the bay but I never got the old hermit to consider selling."

"Cancel them all, of course," said Clyde, locking his eyes on the doorway. The plan had been to secure all of the property fronting the bay, in case additional access roads were needed or even a future automated packaging plant. That would now go elsewhere.

Around them, the din in the hall had grown louder. A rumor circulated that Eamonn was promising half price pints, which felt both an appropriate salve for the bereaved and a way to celebrate for the others. Ove stood up, intending to follow his boss to their rental car and the hour-plus-long serpentine drive to their hotel, but before he could start off someone tapped him on the shoulder.

"Excuse me." It was Ginny, who had crossed the room as if on a mission. "My brother said you were the agent for the buyers for our cottage. I'm Genevieve Browning."

Ove looked at her quizzically. He was good at names - really good, it was one of his strengths as an administrative assistant - but the rollercoaster that had been the last ten minutes had left him a bit scrambled. "Ah, yes!" he shouted at last. Ove frowned and leaned forward. "Listen..."

But Ginny cut him off. "I'm sorry to have to tell you this, but change of plans, the cottage is not for sale. It's my brother's home. Don't even bother trying to negotiate." She stared hard at him, squaring her shoulders for a fight.

A hint of a smile spread across Ove's face. "Ah well, no choice but to respect your wishes. We'll just withdraw the offer, then. Goodnight." He wrapped his coat around him and turned for the door. Ginny watched him until he disappeared down the stairs, then turned to see Thomas and his friends next to her.

She leapt at him and again embraced him in a tight hug. "Tommy," she began. "The sale is off! I had no idea you'd settled in here so well. Why didn't you tell me? You can't move, not now! This is your home now, like, init? We'll pull it off the market and transfer it to you. It's yours. Then we can move to settle the estate, but we can deal with that later. Let's join that celebration!"

Thomas stood, mouth agape. Words were gone. He'd surprised himself with his speech, been shocked (once again) by the support of the crowd, and was by now just overwhelmed by the evening's developments. Sometimes life creeps as slowly as the sun rising over the hills. Sometimes it reshapes itself in a flash of lightning.

Their group crossed the emptying hall and shuffled down the stairs, spilling out into the clear night. The Shamrock sparkled across the street, a handful of smokers gathered in a cloud by the door. But other people were hurrying out of the pub and onto the street, streaming southward.

"Paddy," Rose shouted at a small man in a threadbare black suit coat, carefully holding his pint glass high like a torch. "Where ye all headed?"

"Some punters went down to the bay to celebrate or some shite. They called Eamonn, and said we all needed to get there right off."

Rose began another question, but he was off with the crowd, which moved along the street like a slow-moving charity run or pub hop.

Thomas, Ginny, Cara and Rose stood still for a moment, watching the spectacle before them until Thomas spoke. "Well, sure, let's go. I need to check on Molly anyway, I can look in on the way." They stepped into the road and joined the crowd.

On their right, once they cleared the last row of buildings, the moon lingered over the horizon, and it offered enough light to guide their way, though some people were using their phones as torches. Their lights bobbed in the dark like starlight reflected on a slow-moving river.

They made small talk on the way, Ginny describing her flights, Rose and Cara discussing the week ahead at the store and Thomas quiet, still processing the night's events. When they neared the path to the cottage, he hurried off ahead while Cara and Ginny waited. Rose went on ahead with the last of the crowd to the bay.

Thomas returned shortly, walking slowly with Molly on a leash, the dog stepping gingerly with her rear leg. "She needed let out for the toilet, so I'll just bring her along a bit. You don't mind going slow, do you?"

The three of them, with Molly gamely leading them, made it to the entrance to the lane running down to the small parking area. "We can sit along here," said Cara, moving towards the low brick wall that lined the lane. "Far enough for Molly."

They stepped over the wall, with Thomas lifting the dog over the wall and gently setting her down. She curled up at his feet as Cara and Ginny sat on either side of him.

That was when Cara first looked out over the sloping field down to the bay. There were dozens of folks along the strand, their lights waving and twinkling as faint camera flashes burst one after another. The people, whether huddled in small groups or standing alone, stared ahead at the long sweep of sand leading out to the sea.

Cara let out an audible gasp. "Holy fuck."

Thomas looked out at the scene before them, at the men, women and children scattered across the strand, all silhouetted by a moon slowly lowering into a solid cloud crouched on the horizon. And between the people and the moon, there was just sand. Sand, that in places, stretched nearly all the way to the rocks that embraced the bay.

Killfish Bay was almost completely devoid of water.

"Shite."

60

Left Behind

It was a once-in-a-many-lifetimes event. Historic low tides, a setting super moon, and the gravitational pull of a massive storm that was still grinding its way across the Atlantic all combined to lure the ocean itself away from land, pausing its long assault on the Irish shoreline.

The word spread quickly throughout Dunnybegs, and soon, even people who hadn't attended the town hall were streaming down the path to witness something that had been until this moment a half-believed legend.

Unlike that legend, the bay was not carpeted with marooned fish. Instead, jellyfish, crabs and enormous tangles of seaweed littered the long, gentle slope, which was busy with seagulls and terns enjoying the late-night feed.

Fergal was among a group that had ventured out some distance on the soft, wet sand. He'd first heard the legend as a young boy and had grown increasingly skeptical as he aged. Perhaps a low tide has stranded some fish on the beach once - isn't that how legends are made? A small snowball of truth rolled in a deep field of exaggerations and misremembering until it's the size of a car? But, holy jaysus, here it was. Still mostly empty, though the tide was beginning a weak struggle to reclaim the bay, with building waves pushing through the opening in the breakwater.

"Well, ain't that a son of a bitch?" It was the American, who had parked his hired car up in the small parking lot and walked down with Ove. "I wouldn't have believed this if I didn't see it with my own eyes."

Fergal looked at him and shook his head. "I'm buggered, never thought I'd see anything like this. Big storm coming tomorrow night. You wouldn't want to be out here then." He fell silent and the Americans just stood and stared ahead at the bay.

"Listen," Fergal eventually said, clearing his throat. "The loan, I, ah, well, I'm guessing that's not really in the cards anymore..."

"You know," interrupted Clyde. "I was beside myself back there when that Dublin lad made his announcement. "I mean, shit, the money we've put into this already. The plans, the surveys, the time... and you just needed to vote yes." He sighed and looked back out at the bay. Fergal looked down at his feet.

"But, holy shit! You know what you've done? Huh?" Fergal braced himself. "You've saved my ass!"

"Wha?"

"Think about it. If we'd have gone ahead and built our farm here and then had something like this happen, we'd have been destroyed. Ha, you two saved my business," he said, chuckling.

"It's true," added Ove, nodding.

"You know, Ove told me your father had been a fisherman, but I hadn't known until tonight that you lost him at sea."

Fergal looked out at the bay. The sea was slowly seeping back into the bay. "It's a hard way to make a living."

Clyde nodded in solemn agreement. "My father fished. Out of Seattle and sometimes Juneau, up in Alaska, when the fish stocks moved further north. And he'd tell me of storms that would nearly roll the boat, and waves that froze on the deck and coated everything with inches of ice. A deadly way to make a living. One November, just about now, 34 years ago, their ship was lost. The Coast Guard found two of the crew, one frozen onto a board, the other, still alive, in a lifeboat. The rest were lost. My dad too."

He turned to look at Fergal. "It's why I started this business, a safe way of fishing. The fish grow in a series of protected bays and a single service ship rotates through the bays, harvesting and processing the fish onboard. It docks to offload every few weeks during season." He looked back out at the sea. "We'll find other bays.

"And you," he turned to Fergal again, "you should expand and open the fish store. You want to honor your father and I respect that. Ove will be in touch about the details." He reached out his hand and he and Fergal shook hands. Then he turned to Ove. "Our flight gonna get us out of here before that storm hits tomorrow? Come on, let's get going." The two of them turned and began walking back to the car park.

On the way, they passed Rose. She had ventured down onto the beach, where she found the man from Dublin standing by himself, who turned and smiled at her as she stopped by his side.

"Amazing, innit?" she said.

"It's...incredible," he answered. "Quite an exciting night."

"Well, that's mostly your doing, luv," she laughed. "The man of the hour in Dunnybegs."

"I don't think that's universal."

Rose patted him on the shoulder. "You saved the bay! Tell ye what, you ever get up this way again, free sausage rolls for you."

Fintan felt the heat of his skin under his undershirt, shirt, coat and her hand. "You know, as a matter of fact, I'm due to retire at the end of the year. I've been thinking it might be nice to have a change of pace, get away from the big city. Been thinking of somewhere up here." He managed a smile at Rose.

"Well, you stop by the store when you're ready, and I'll show you around. Plenty of grand homes sitting empty, waiting for a good soul to warm them up."

61

A Home for Memories

Cara, Thomas and Ginny remained seated on the stone wall, with Cara and Thomas waving and greeting folks coming and going to the bay as they passed by.

The kaleidoscope of the day's events was beginning to settle in Thomas' mind. Molly, who continued to sleep at his feet, was also a calming presence. But Ginny was full of questions about Thomas's life. The three of them spoke about the bay, the hurricane and Thomas' unofficial tour guide business and budding photography career before they grew quiet.

Suddenly, Ginny sat up straight. "Tommy, what's this about our ma being a lezzie?"

"Ginny, shush like," said Thomas, who hurried a worried glance at Cara. "Not a good word."

His sister rolled her eyes. "You told me you found stuff about her. She had a girlfriend?"

Thomas took a deep breath. "I found a photo. Of her, as a teenager, here. Actually, sitting on this very wall, just down there a wee bit." He gestured at the stone wall, which bordered the narrow road down to the parking area.

"She was here before she got married and had us?" Ginny asked.

"Yeah. Before all that. As a teenager. Anyway, she was sitting next to another young woman and I was curious who it might be. So Cara here helped me take it around to folk. The guy who runs a pub just down the road some – turns out she was his sister. Her name was Molly. Ma and she were fast friends. The two of them planned to go to college in Paris but gran wouldn't let ma go."

"Breaking up the scandalous romance?" Ginny offered.

"No idea. Maybe it was money. Anyway, Molly went to Paris but died in a road accident that fall."

"Oh. Jesus, that's sad."

Cara had remained silent, but she looked up at them both. "Yous both seem awful worried about the sexual preference of someone more than 40 years ago." she said. "Sure, what does it matter? There's all kinds of love, just like there's all sorts of families." She smiled at Thomas.

"I know, it's just, well, it makes me feel I didn't really know her," said Thomas. Ginny nodded in agreement.

"Ach, how well do we ever know someone else?" said Cara. "And she's gone. You'll never know. You could let that eat at you forever. Or you could take comfort knowing she was happy."

Thomas smiled. "True. I don't know if they were a romantic couple or just dear friends, but ma had someone here she loved. And lost her. I think that's why she came here and I think she was planning to go to Paris before she, well, before the stroke. She was working her way through a French-English dictionary. Hell, she only spoke French to Molly here." He looked down at the dog, which had looked up at the sound of her name.

"Ah, the dog. Molly. Named after her. Shiiiit. So, mom wasn't running away when she moved here, was she?"

"I don't think so, no." He looked over at Cara. "You're right. I think she was happy here. I think it was a place of really good memories."

Ginny looked about, slowly swinging her gaze from left to right. "Memories seem important here, huh? I mean, what you said at the meeting?"

Thomas nodded. "All the empty houses. The standing stones. The old walls. The holy wells. The stories. I mean, it's like stones in the fields, older ones always pushing to the surface."

"It is an ancient place," said Cara.

"Aye, and it's my home now," said Thomas.

"We might have recruited another one!" It was Rose, who was making her way up the road, with the fellow from Dublin beside her. "Everyone, well, you already know his name, but this is Fintan, and he's thinking of retiring up here, like."

Fintan shook his head in agreement and then noticed the dog. "Is this the famous Molly?" he asked. "Can I say hello?" He bent over and held his hand out for Molly to smell, then gave her a rub on the head. "You know," he said, standing back up and addressing Thomas. "There are funds available to support tourism, thousands of euros, just waiting for the right proposals. Like a tour guide business, for example. Donegal shouldn't miss out."

"Wow" said Thomas, "I wouldn't know how to go about that, where to start."

"I can help," said Fintan. "But only for a couple more months. Rose here can put you in touch with me." With that, he and Rose turned and resumed their walk up toward the main road.

"Cara, if you want a ride home, get back to the store before 10, ok?" Rose yelled over her shoulder.

Ginny yawned. "Well, this has been quite the day. Tommy – sorry – Thomas, can I stay with you at the cottage tonight? I'm knackered. Maybe you can take me on a good walk before that storm hits tomorrow."

Thomas lifted Molly back over the wall and gently set her down.

"I'm sure we can get in a good hike before the rain," he said. "I've lots to show you."

62

Epilogue

Mid-afternoon on a glorious, open-all-the-windows day, the air crisp, the sky an electric blue, the sound of gulls laughing and waves shushing against the sand. A small white van drives south along the coastal road and into the town of Dunnybegs, such as it is, a four-block long stretch of buildings clustered together. To the right, the van passes the Sea Spray Inn, its front embraced by scaffolding and construction workers on ladders hauling new windows up. There is a new electric sign over the entrance and a pair of heavy dark wooden doors with leaded glass windows being installed.

Across the street, a fresh coat of paint brightens the exterior of the Shamrock. A curl of dark smoke snakes from the pub's chimney. Inside, the fire is hearty and a small dachshund is sprawled on the hearth as Eamonn putters behind the counter, arranging washed pint glasses and whiskey bottles. A block further along, the van passes the butcher shop. The storefront next to it is bright and airy. Window coverings have been taken down and a pair of delivery men are struggling with a large refrigerated display case, maneuvering to fit it through the door under the watchful eye of one Fergal McCart, who hopes to open Pietro's Seafood Provisions by fall.

The van continues on. The grocer is at the end of the small main street, set back from the road behind a parking lot. A few sandwich boards edge the sidewalk, advertising the day's news, a few special sale items and the "world's best" homemade sausage rolls. Between the signs, Fintan O'Dowd, wearing a name badge from the store, is sweeping the sidewalk. He pauses and waves at the van as it passes.

The van slows as it nears the entrance to Killfish Bay and turns onto the access road. A new, second parking area has been paved up near the top of the road, but the vehicle continues down to the lower lot, already occupied by a smattering of cars and a Mr. Softee truck, its diesel exhaust mingling with the fresh sea air.

The van comes to a stop against the curb. Before it is a slight mound lined with benches which overlook the bay. The van has signs affixed to each front door and the rear boot which read:

DOG GONE TOURS
SEE THE SIGHTS WITH DONEGAL'S TOP DOG

Thomas McKay exits the driver's side of the van and stretches. Cara emerges from the passenger side, then opens the door behind her and leans in. When she stands up, she has two border collie puppies in her arms. She carries them up the slight hill and sets them down before one of the benches, carefully keeping a grip on their leads.

Thomas walks around to the rear of the van and opens the hatch. "Come on, you too, old girl."

Molly appears at the hatch and he lifts her down. She immediately heads up to the bench, a slight limp, her tail erect and slowly wagging back and forth.

Thomas walks up and sits next to Cara.

"I'll take these two down to the water in a bit," Cara says. "See how they do."

Molly curls herself up with her side atop one of Thomas' feet, resting her chin on her front paws and gazes out at the beach.

"No rush, is there," Thomas answers. "Sure, it's a gorgeous day."

"So, catch me up," says Cara. "Are you still thinking of a trip to Paris?"

"Aye, not until November, though. I'm booked mostly until then. Ginny's coming with."

"Jetsetter!"

Thomas smiles. "She's moving back in a couple months. Gonna live in Belfast again. But she'll come here so we can scatter my mom's ashes out here. Then we'll take some to Paris."

"Your mother will finally get there. That's nice."

Thomas nods.

"And you, how's it feel to be done with school?"

"Ach it's grand. Letterkenny is great. Crockett has made me a full-time assistant now. Nice to get paid! And I get to play with these wee pups!"

Thomas looks at her. "With your marks, you could go anywhere. Dublin, Cork, hell, even England. Aren't you keen to see someplace else?"

Cara stands to untangle the two leads, which have knotted themselves around one of her legs and the leg of the bench as the puppies scramble about.

"No, what was it you said? There are just so many memories here. Even the ones we haven't lived yet."

The leads straightened, she starts off for the beach with the puppies alongside her.

Thomas leans over and scratches Molly behind her ear. He watches them go, then lifts his gaze to the bay – which on this early summer day is a soft, sapphire pool – and the sea beyond that, a rumpled navy sheet limned with gleaming whitecaps.

He is sure there are memories to be made here.

63

Author's note

There is no real Dunnybegs. Neither that village, nor any of the characters in this novel, are real.

County Donegal, however, is real, a glorious, windswept, achingly beautiful and desolate place on the northwest corner of the island of Ireland. It is a place of dramatic grace - of hillsides raked by constant winds and coastlines scraped by hard waves and rain. It is a land of dozens of Dunnybegs, small collections of warmth and life dotting those hills, nestled snug in valleys and strung along the coast like Christmas lights.

The coast. It is breathtaking, no matter whether you are atop a sea cliff one hundred meters above pounding surf, or chasing the tide on a mile-wide strand of fine, golden sand.

It is an intense place. Colors are more saturated, the light both softer and more fiery. The landscape is ancient, solid as the hills and mountains, but also soft and yielding, like one's footsteps in a bog or the fog which settles in the lowlands.

Perhaps it has to do with it being a liminal place. Go anywhere in Donegal and you are never more than 20-30 miles from the edge of it all, from the thin line between land and ocean. It is an in-between place, perched betwixt worlds.

It is my favorite place in the world. As a boy living for a few years with my family in Derry, Donegal was the exotic, almost foreign, world next door. And as a returning adult, I yearned for nothing more than to bundle into my uncle's car for one of his helter-skelter rambles around the Inishowen Peninsula, with stops at every scenic overlook and short scrambles on every strand.

This story is my love letter to the place and people of Donegal, inspired by Donegal itself.

And it does have a real-world inspiration. Close to a decade ago, my search for social media accounts that could feed my distant longing for all things Irish turned up a fellow in Donegal who seemed very keen on hiking around the county with his lovely border collie companion and photographing their adventures. I followed his account, and looked forward to each post. Over the years, we have become friends and I have learned more of their story and I was moved to help organize an international fundraiser when Iggy was seriously injured several years ago. James O'Donnell and his dog, Iggy, who now have tens of thousands of followers on social media, have become celebrities across Ireland. The story of a man and a dog and how they care for and help each other thrive seemed to me a good jumping off point for a story and I thank James for his inspiration and friendship.

If you are attracted to this part of the world, are a dog lover, or just love beautiful photography, look for James @james_odonnell_photography on Instagram.

As for me, I'm busy planning my next trip home. And already looking forward to my next visit to Dunnybegs.

Malcolm McDowell Woods is an editor and journalist, a communications professional and a university lecturer. Scottish by birth and Northern Irish by ancestry, he currently lives in Wisconsin with his partner, Nicki, and their dogs, Neville and Molly. He has written for a variety of periodicals in the US and Europe. He co-authored the book, "Irish Wit and Wisdom" and was co-founder and editor of the former Irish American Post magazine. He has earned national honors for editorial writing and page design and was awarded the Milwaukee County Individual Arts Fellowship for Fiction Writing. "What the Tide Leaves Behind" is his first novel.

Follow Malcolm here:
https://malcolmmcdw58.wixsite.com/writing